CHRIS B

GRAVESEND

[signature]

PLEASANT PUBLISHING

Published by Pleasant Publishing 2018

PPL-2018/0011

ISBN 978-0995459779 (paperback)
ISBN 978-0995459762 (ePub)

Copyright © Chris Bennett 2018

The right of Chris Bennett to be identified as the author of this work has been asserted by him in accordance with the Copyright, Designs and Patents Act 1988

This book is sold subject to the condition that it shall not, by way of trade or otherwise, be lent, resold, hired out, or otherwise circulated without the publisher's prior consent in any form of binding or cover other than that in which it is published and without a similar condition, including this condition, being imposed on the subsequent purchase.

First published in Great Britain in 2018
by Pleasant Publishing

Pleasant Publishing Limited
Registered in England No. 09844119

Printed and bound by
CPI Group (UK) Ltd, Croydon, CR0 4YY

www.pleasantpublishing.co.uk

With compliments

61 Churchill Avenue
Chatham ME5 0DF
United Kingdom
www.pleasantpublishing.co.uk
info@pleasantpublishing.co.uk

With compliments

61 Churchill Avenue
Chatham ME5 0DE
United Kingdom
www.pleasantpublishing.co.uk
info@pleasantpublishing.co.uk

For K, A & N — my world.

For R & J — for always guiding me in the right direction.

I would also like to thank the following for their early support: Claire Barkaway, Chris and Lindsay Bassett, Tony and Gill Bennett, Ricky Brookes, Nigel and Rachael Carrigan, Filippo Ceccaroli, Mick Cherry, Kieran Crisp, Helen Cutcliffe, Kelly Donaghy, Michael Easton, Mark Finlay, Barry Fitchett, David Gibbs, Gina Greenaway, Marjorie Hall, Matthew Marsh, David Matthes, Ian Meek, David Missen, Aimee Mitchell, Nathalie Molens, Marie Nevison, Helen Norris, Tom O'Brien, Carley Padgett, Wayne Penfold, Samantha Pollock, Rebecca Randall, James Robertson, Joey Segelman, Gary Starr, Rob Sturley, Luke Tarplett, Rupert Tinker, Tina Tinker, James Turner, Steve Watson, Becky Wood, Angie Woodford, and Julie Young.

It must be nice to see things in a colourful light.

The sky is a smudged-pencil-mark grey. So dull, so dreary, so drab and so colourless.

Lifeless and leafless trees blackened with exhaust fumes droop over graffiti-stained garden walls.

The Thames is always in full view: the brown, bland Thames. You can see it from pretty much everywhere in Gravesend.

It surrounds us like a moat.

It strangles us like a noose.

The Thames is in our veins, manky and polluted.

Gravesend is in our veins, like lead.

We are Gravesend, all pebble-dashed and full of dogshit.

CHAPTER ONE

I have his eyes. I have his scrawny wrists. I even have his pot belly. I don't have to ask his name to make sure; the tattoo on his forearm tells me who he is. Is he proud of his name? To him it's probably just a tattoo. To me it's a name that threatens mine. But I'm here now, standing before you, Kelvin Jarvis, wondering whether to reveal myself. Will you recognise me? You've been a spirit, a ghost, a myth all my life. What do I say to you? Hi Dad. Why did you put me in the front seat of a Ford Escort at the top of Whitehill Lane and let the handbrake off?

"What can I get for you buddy?" he says.

"I'll have a pint of Carling," I say.

He doesn't recognise me. Of course, he wouldn't recognise me. He just looks at me as he would any customer. How could he know that his son is standing opposite him? The last time he saw me I was still playing with action figures.

"Two pound eighty."

All the times I've pictured my father, I've never once imagined how he sounds. He's been a mute face that has haunted me. But now his voice confirms the reality of the situation. I don't like it. I want to leave. I shouldn't be here. But it's too late; the pint is poured. He holds his hand out waiting for me to put money into his palm. A tattoo of the St George's flag peeks out the bottom of his sleeve. I fumble around for the bank card in my wallet, nervous as a kid in a bar for the first time.

"No cards. Cash only," he says.

"Oh right," I say as I pull out whatever change I have in my pocket. "Here you go mate. Cheers."

He looks at the money as if I've just given him a handful of chocolate coins. "Oi! You're ten pence short."

"Shit, sorry. I think I've got it," I say. I pat my jeans even though I know there is nothing more in them.

"Don't worry about it. I'll let you off," he says as if he somehow knows that he's missed twenty-six birthdays, twenty-six Christmases, and fuck knows how many Easter eggs.

"Cheers mate, much appreciated."

But the attempted murder and lack of Easter eggs isn't.

I make my way to the back of the dingy pub and stare at my father parading behind the bar, chatting and laughing with punters as if he's a stand-up comedian. What has he got to be so cheerful about? He's spent the majority of his life in and out of prison and psycho wards, so I hear. Jesus, what am I doing here? I've been rehearsing this scene for what seems like an eternity, but now that I'm here I've got stage fright. It may be a comedy to him, but for me it's a tragedy, and I'm the fool.

I find myself mauling a cardboard beermat, and I realise that I have become the centre of attention. All eyes, including my father's, are on me. This pub is the kind of pub that doesn't like newcomers. I should have known when I first walked in, but I was too busy concentrating on the task in hand. How did I miss the personalised beer jugs, the framed photos of the darts team? How did I not scent the waxy green jackets that all regulars of unfriendly pubs possess? I begin to get claustrophobic; the same feeling I get when I'm in a crowded waiting room at the doctors. I look at the shreds of beermat scattered across the table and think this can't be doing me any favours.

"You alright up there are ya sonny?" says a balding man who looks like he has a collection of stuffed animals hanging up around his home like trophies.

"Fine, thanks," I reply.

"From Dartford are ya?" he asks. Long hairs creep out of his nostrils as if he's got a daddy-long-legs sanctuary up there.

Think of something. "I've just stopped in for a pint on my way home from work. The train stopped for repairs, so I've got an hour or so to kill."

He looks at me as if he's working out whether I'd look better next to the fox's head in the hallway, or underneath the deer in the living room.

"Work up town do ya buddy?" my father adds to the questioning.

"Yeah," I say.

They look at each other and mumble in a language that doesn't stretch further than this pub.

"Not many people come in here without us knowing their name," the hairy-nosed-hunter says.

"Oh right," I say, "it's ... Reggie." Where did that come from?

The regulars including my father start to laugh. "Reggie? Is that short for Reginald? You don't look like a Reggie. Didn't your parents like you or something?" hairy-nose says. The rest of them laugh even more.

If only you knew. "I guess not," I say, staring at my father. My cheeks start to burn and a dribble of sweat runs down my forehead. Laughing nervously, I tear another shred off the beermat.

"Oi," my father shouts out. "Like ripping up other people's property do ya?"

"Oh, I, er, I'm sorry. I'll replace it," I say, and they start to laugh.

Anger starts to get the better of my nervousness. Foolish, fucking foolish. What a fool I am. What a fool he is. Talking of ripping up people's property; maybe I get it from him. Yeah that's right. I'm your son and you ripped apart my fucking life. It wasn't yours to ruin. And my mother's life wasn't yours to ruin either. How can you laugh and point? How can you stand there so guiltless, so carefree, so fucking oblivious? I need to get out of here before I do something I regret. No — who am I trying to kid? I'm not going to do anything. I've got his cowardly pathetic genes. I run away from everything. Just like him.

I down the rest of my pint and make my way past them, hoping they'll ignore me.

"You off so soon, Reggie?" my father says as I reach the door.

"Best be getting back to the station," I say.

"Right ya are sonny. Come again soon won't ya," the hunter says.

I leave to more laughter and a drunken chorus of "Hit the road Jack, and don't you come back no more, no more, no more."

I walk through Dartford town centre as a stranger. This town is obese. On the verge of a heart attack. The streets are littered with crisp packets, cigarette butts, smashed bottles of cheap booze. The smell of mixed grills and exhaust fumes linger. At the heart of Dartford, a giant fast-food restaurant pumps processed meat and milkshakes into its arteries. I make my way to the bus stop, defeated and unable to feel the cold.

Dartford blends into Gravesend through shadows and headlights. I should have just told him who I was. I should have been strong. I should have told the hairy-nosed-hunter to shut the fuck up. I shouldn't have even gone in there. My reflection in the bus window irritates me. But the reflection is of 'Reggie'. How the hell did I come up with that? Loser.

We pass the Gravesend clocktower, Big Ben's deformed brother. It's nearing midnight and I'm still not home. But what's to go home to? An empty fridge, a girlfriend who feels like a stranger, and a cat with an attitude problem? Six-hundred pounds a month for a shoebox. I feel like jacking it all in. Maybe I should adopt a busload of children or acquire a heroin addiction. That way the council would pay my rent like they do for the majority of people in my building.

Dolly gives me the cold shoulder as I walk through the door and looks at me as if to say, "what time do you call this?" Julie doesn't look at me which kind of confirms what Dolly was thinking. "All right," I say.

"Yep," she says without taking her eyes off the TV.

"Had a good evening?" I ask.

"Look at the state of you," she says, looking at me through her spy-eyes which are in the side of her head.

I turn to look in the mirror. My shirt is as sweaty and as crinkled as a hooker's bed sheet. My eyes are screwball ice cream coloured, and the veins in my temples look like they're going to erupt. "Shitty day at work."

"Do you think I'm stupid?"

This is an easy one. "No."

Julie spreads her arms over the sofa and leans back like some kind of mafia boss about to make me an offer-I-can't-refuse. "You've probably been down to Dartford again, stood outside that bloody pub for an hour, smoked a packet of cigarettes and then come home. Give up, Pete."

Actually, I think, I saw him and spoke to him. I gave him a fake name, ripped a beermat to shreds, got laughed at by a guy with insects in his nose, and got sung out of the pub. It's even more pathetic than hanging outside for an hour. I'll play the sympathy card. "You're supposed to be supportive," I say.

She looks at me as if she's seen the card too many times. "I am supportive. I'm telling you to leave it. I've had it up to here with this crazy obsession. Tracking your father down! What's the point? If you're going to do it, then do it. If not, then leave it. It's ruining you. It's ruining us. Ever since your Granddad told you about him, it's all you've thought about."

"And what is it you think about Julie?" I say. "You're always out with your shrink wannabes, breathing this psychological bullshit. Have you thought that may be ruining us instead?"

"At least they give me a decent conversation," she says. Dolly grins. Liked that one did you, you furry little shit?

All the cards on are suddenly on the table now. "If you think that decent conversation is analysing and dismissing people, you need help," I say.

"You've got no identity," she says, as if she's just pulled an ace out of her sleeve. "You're lost."

"Psycho bollocks."

"It's true. You've got no sense of direction, you don't know what you want, you don't fit ... "

"Freudian fuckface," I interrupt. Bang. There's my ace. Not exactly a strong hand but it felt good.

She gets up off the sofa, smiles, and walks past me as if she's sympathising with a sore loser.

"Night Pete," she says calmly.

Dolly winks at me before jumping off the window sill and running into the bedroom with Julie. The door closes, and I look at the vacant sofa. By the side of it are a sleeping bag and a pillow.

It's not long before I wake from a dream in which I'm stuffed, on a mantelpiece. Julie and my father are staring up at me. "You should have finished him off," Julie says.

Mum was eating her fingernails in between sucking on a cigarette: two things she told me never to do. I was sitting by myself trying to do a jigsaw puzzle; Thomas the Tank Engine I think. I was stuck but Mum's tapping foot told me not to ask her for help. This acted as a kind of 'Do Not Disturb' sign. Giving up on the puzzle I started to make cartoon characters out of the cigarette smoke rising to the ceiling. Then Mum got up and Bugs Bunny disappeared. She went over to look at the clock on the wall, and then immediately to look out of the front window. It was the fifth time she had done this.

The doorbell rang. The dog next door barked. Why? It wasn't his house. Mum put another cigarette into the ashtray and pulled me to my feet. "Someone is here to visit you Petey," she said as she flattened my fringe with a handful of spit, "and I want you to be a good boy, OK?" I nodded and sat back down in front of my puzzle. Mum looked in the mirror as though someone was taking a photo of her. Then she went to the door.

I heard three voices; one of them was Mum's. It was grown-up language, big words and serious-toned: boring. I wondered who it was though. Who could've come to visit me? Was it another person to call Uncle or Auntie? There were enough of them always drifting in and out of the house. Besides, I had a feeling that it was someone more important because of the way Mum was tapping her foot and putting all that makeup on.

She walked back in with two men behind her. One was wearing a blue uniform and he sat on the couch, pulling a notebook and pen out of a small bag. The other man came towards me and crouched down like a giant frog. I remember his head being big — really big — with a nose big enough for me to slide down. He also had sharp hair around his chin, which I thought at the time looked like the scouring pads Mum always used to wash the dishes.

"Hello little buddy, what you doing?" he said to me. His breath smelt like the cigarette graveyard.

Why did all grown-ups used to ask me this? I ignored him, pretending I was doing my puzzle and didn't say anything back. Apart from the cigarettes, he had a strong smell of soap about him.

"Doing a puzzle are you? Maybe I can help. I like puzzles too," he said.

Somehow, he scared me. There were never many men in the house, except for those who used to sit in the corner with a bottle of something, and they would leave me alone. Oh, and of course Granddad, who usually shouted at those men with bottles. But there was something intimidating about this man in front of me. I looked over to the couch and saw the man in the blue uniform writing in his notebook. I looked to Mum and scrunched my face to try and tell her to take me away. She just continued smoking and tapping her feet.

"I've got you a present," he said.

I pretended I wasn't interested and ran my hands through the puzzle pieces.

"I hear you like Star Wars."

But then he had my attention. I looked up at him and remember thinking that I hope I don't get as ugly as this man when I grow up. "Yeah," I said.

"Here you go then," he said. He put a present in bright green wrapping paper in front of me. "Open it."

I again looked at Mum and she nodded to inform me that it was OK to open it, so I attacked the paper. Chewbacca! "Cool," I said, "I haven't got this one."

Then he made a Chewbacca noise which I found funny. The man in the blue uniform found it funny too as he continued to write in his notebook. But when I saw my mum's face, I stopped laughing. She had that same angry look on her face; the same as she did when I decided to try and write my name in chalk on the driveway. I didn't understand why she looked this way. I just got Chewbacca; she should've been happy for me, I thought.

"Who are you?" I asked the strange man.

The man in blue suddenly stopped writing and edged closer to the edge of the sofa. My mother had now eaten her fingers down to her knuckles. The soapy-frog-man in front of me looked to the man in blue. The man in blue shook his head. It was some kind of code I thought.

"I work for Santa," he said standing up. "That's why you haven't seen me before. But if it's OK with you I'd like to come a bit more often." He looked over to the man in blue.

The first thing I thought of is what it must be like to know Santa. The second thing was, why is my mum running towards this man with her fists in the air? She started pounding the man in the face and crying and screaming. The man in blue threw his notebook on the floor and pulled my mother away. Her legs kicked in the air like one of my action figures. The soapy-frog-man then kicked the plant pot and went flying towards my mother. Suddenly two more men in blue came running through the door and took Santa's helper to the floor.

My puzzle had been trampled and lay in pieces. Mum closed the door and lit yet another cigarette. "We don't need him Pete," she said. "As long as we've got each other, we don't need anybody."

Aggressive sound of hair dryer, annoying aerosol spray, squirt of scent, banging of cupboards, exaggerated rustling of cornflakes, banging of fridge door, over-exaggerated munching of cornflakes, dramatic slurping of milk: she glides through the flat like a perfumed Tasmanian devil. Time to submit: I pull myself from the sofa and mumble, "morning."

"I was trying not to wake you," she says, and bangs her spoon against the cereal bowl.

I take a seat at the kitchen table and pour myself a bowl of cereal too. She reads some nutritional advice on the back of the box and throws in a few "hmms" in between our chorus of cornflake munching. It's sad that we've got to the point where tension is silence. As I'm debating whether to apologise for calling her a Freudian fuckface last night she says, "You do know what day it is."

"What?"

She shakes her head. "Didn't think so. Anyway, it looks as though you're dressed for it already. Although it's not strictly fancy dress."

"What?"

"H-a-l-l-o-w-e-e-n. I told you weeks ago about the gathering at the university tonight."

Musical-statues-time: I freeze with the spoon in my mouth, eyes wide open. She freezes, with eyes that could curdle the milk. First thing: shit, it's Halloween. Second: I don't remember this gathering. Third: when did she start calling a party a gathering? Fourth: do I look that bad? Fifth: who is she to keep going on about the way I dress? I remember the days when she used to live in tracksuits. She's gone from Sporty Spice to Psycho Spice.

"No, course I haven't," I say. I decide against having it out with her because I will just get tangled up in a load of "I didn't means". She plays the lady so well that it even fools me.

She gets up to put the empty bowl in the sink. I think I see a tear roll down her face before she turns back to me. "You really have forgotten, haven't you? You really don't know what day it is, do you?"

"Fucking hell Ju, it's only Halloween, and I didn't forget the party," I say.

"I'm not just talking about the party tonight. I thought ... well, I thought you would have remembered ... " She breaks off and picks up her bag and keys. "Try not to call any one a fuckface tonight; it probably wouldn't go down too well."

On her way out, she rubs my back and kisses Dolly goodbye. I lap my remaining milk from the bowl. A fucking gathering.

I draw back the curtains: Halloween in Gravesend. Clouds plod through the sky like witches on brooms. In one of the flats a pumpkin that looks like Bruce Forsyth stares out the window. The Thames sends waves crashing against broken supermarket trolleys stuck in thick, grey sludge. Rain tickles the dirt-brown surface of the water. I wait for an axe-wielding nutcase to appear. But he doesn't.

I tuck the bottoms of my trousers into my socks, as always, when I walk down the gloomy stairway. The smell of piss steaming from the stairs and walls is a bit of a turn-off, but the other option is taking the lift, which is filled with cigarette ends, broken needles, and empty beer cans. On my way down the walls inform me that Tanya takes it up the arse and that Scotty P has a small cock. On the bottom floor, music blares from a flat. Two people sit outside the front door. They look terminally ill. Liver-spotted hands hold up pale fragile faces. Cold sores creep round their dry, cracked lips like red ivy up a wall. Bloodshot eyes stare into the sky as if they are in deep thought. But they're worrying where they will get their next fix. As I pass the door I get a whiff of fried chicken and vomit.

The cold air stings my eyes. Gravesend is drowsy. People stumble to their daily designated positions. The homeless move from doorways to benches, guys in suits enter shabby offices, and tradesmen in fluorescent jackets and hardhats gather on building sites. As I cut through the St George's Centre, I see a father and son playing on a roundabout in the indoor playground. Granddad used to take me here when I was younger. I would play, and he'd drink rum and smoke pipes with his friends. I think he enjoyed it almost as much as me. It hasn't changed much. Superdrug still faces the playground, kicking out cheap fragrances, and a crap jewellery shop stands the other side, gold sleeper rings and second-hand Casio watches. The playground itself has withered. Black cigarette burns and trodden-in chewing gum have defaced the wooden floor. The red monkey bars have faded; only patches of the paint remain. Monkey bars with eczema.

I've just bought a pack of cigarettes and an energy drink, when someone taps me on the shoulder. I look around and see a face that I can't quite put a name too.

"Pete Jarvis, yeah?" the stranger says.

"Yeah?" I say.

"Jesus fucking Christ. How are ya?" he says.

"Not so bad, thanks. How are you?" I say.

He's not very tall but he looks stocky and well-built in a black bomber jacket. Wild, intimidating eyes stand out next to his tanned skin. He has a pink jagged scar just above his eyebrow and his large nose looks as though it has been broken more than once.

"You don't remember me do you, pal?" he says and smiles, revealing teeth that look like mini screwdrivers. "What do ya reckon, Sid? He don't look as if he remembers me, does he?"

Sid is a small man and has curly hair pulled back into a pony tail which looks like a dust-pan brush. He has a goatee that frames his thin lips and nicotine-stained teeth. His nose is bony and pointed. It looks like a chopstick. "No Jake, I don't think he does remember you," Sid says.

Then it hits me. Jake. Jake and I used to be schoolfriends before he left in year nine.

"Shit. Sorry, Jake. I didn't recognise you mate. You look really different," I say.

"Yeah, I know. I'm no longer that little fat kid that used to get bullied," he says with a menacing kind of smile.

"St John's was hard," I say.

"If you weren't a Gypsy or a Paki then you were a nobody," he says. He puffs his chest out as if he's a somebody. "What you been doing with yourself? It's been a fucking lifetime."

"Pretty much every job under the sun. Window cleaning. Bar work. Now I'm in telesales. We try to get people to donate to UK charities. There's not that much to do round here so I had to look to London for work," I say.

He laughs. "You had brains from what I remember. Shame this ain't the town to use them in. But sounds to me as if you're doing a good thing, raising money. A lot of people tend to forget that charity should start at ho ... " Jake stops short when he sees a man walking fast with his head down on the other side of the road. Every muscle in Jake's face seems to tense. His nostrils flare, his forehead crinkles and his lips fade to white. "Is that Percy over there?" he asks.

"Looks like him," Sidney says.

Jake jolts as if he's having a kind of spasm. "I've got to have a word with that wanker," he says. Sid puts an arm on Jake's shoulder and tells him to leave it till another time.

"So anyway Pete," Jake says as he takes a deep breath and turns back to face me. "You got yourself a family and all that? Oh, this is Sidney by the way."

I shake Sid's hand. "I'm living with my girlfriend Julie at the moment."

"Julie?" Jake asks. "Not the same Julie you had at school? That little brunette with the massive ... "

"Yeah, yeah, that's the one," I say quickly, to stop him cupping an imaginary pair of tits.

"Can't believe you've been with her all this time," he smiles.

"So, what's the story with you? Married, Kids? How's the family?" I ask. Jake's mum used to take me to theirs for dinner when my mum was out getting stoned.

"No marriage, no kids. Mum's a gem. It's the rest of the family that are the fucking problem," Jake says. He scrunches his face again and bites his tongue.

"Oh," is all I can manage.

"Don't think I ever met your family, did I?"

"No, I don't think you did. Mum is fine, and I never really knew my father," I say, wondering if he knows about the situation.

"It's probably for the best, pal. Every father I've known has been trouble. Anyway, I've got some business to take care of so I've gotta shoot. Take my number."

We exchange numbers and I ask him what he does for a living. He looks a little mysterious.

"I'm a kind of events organiser. In fact, why don't you come out for a piss-up on Saturday night? One of my mates is DJ'ing at Bar 24."

"Well, I don't know, mate. I normally see my Granddad on Saturdays, but I'll see what the time is after that."

"I'll give you a bell on Saturday," Jake says as he shakes my hand. He seems to mean it. "Nice catching up with you."

CHAPTER TWO

The 46-minute train journey to London Victoria consists of dodging giant newspapers, seeing the same miserable faces, and enduring the sickening sight of fresh-out-of-school, acne-ridden young geniuses playing with their iPhones. They earn double the money I do. Graffiti-covered walls, sheep and trees zoom past. Sometimes the smell of burning wood or freshly-cut grass will seep through a window. It's easily overlooked, scenery and smells like this. People drum on about emigrating somewhere hot with a beach, but for me, I'd miss the smells and sights of England. As for the people? That's a whole different story.

And London Victoria is part of this story. Everyone is in fifth gear, heads down, walking like penguins with Tourette's through the air choked with coffee, bacon, pain-au-raisin ... The floor is a carpet of pigeons, crumbs, and buskers. Passengers with newsprint-stained fingers are stopped every few metres by someone trying to sell something. "Big Issue?" ... "No thanks." "Membership in the RAC sir?" ... "I'd need a car first" ... "Have you tried our great new organic super-duper fibre all bran muesli bar sir?" ... "I'd rather eat this pigeon." "Sir, have you tried ... " "FUCK OFF." And then the final, most almighty insult ... the tube. London Transport. The public to the slaughter. Wait behind the yellow line till all the passengers are off. There's always one smart-arse that doesn't wait. Quick, quick, shoulder to shoulder, waddle on, doors close, noses jammed against glass, armpit in face, hair in mouth and crumpled toes.

The tube smells of stale cigarettes, aftershave and sweat. I always feel dirty on the tube. It feels like jumping into someone else's bed. I stand but try to avoid holding on to the hand rails because they are coated with bacon fat and croissant flakes.

Miranda stands at the entrance of the office checking her watch. Every time I look at my boss I think of Mick Jagger. She has a mouth like a bouncy castle. She has fearsome headmistress hair and her skin has been in too many sun-beds. Maybe she sleeps in one every night. There is no "good morning" or even a "hello".

"I want you to try and get Costsless in the bag," she says.

"I'm on it," I say.

I make a few calls. I get two pleasant rejections, one "please call back later," from Costsless, and a simple "fuck off". When did people start getting so greedy? Maybe I just take it too personally.

I lean back in my chair. I hear a conversation between two temps about what their next job will be. Temps all talk about money. They moralize. Sometimes I feel like I'm drowning in a pool of middle-class in this office. It must be nice to have a life where money and pleasure are your only objectives; no worries, strong family and friends, a decent wardrobe of clothes and colour co-ordinated bed sheets.

The temps notice me and then lower their voices. Once again, I feel like the council house kid whose junkie dad tried to kill him.

"Everything OK, mate?"

Simon is the closest thing I've got to a friend in this place. He's a Star Trek geek and eats too many packs of onion rings, but he's nice enough and he isn't a temp. And we have this in common: our career prospects look fairly shit.

"How's things?" I ask him.

"You up to much tonight?"

"I've been roped into a Halloween gathering up at Julie's university," I say.

"A gathering?" he asks.

"Julie's new word for a party. I've spent the last year or so slagging off these psychology bods and now she's dragging me along to one their gatherings."

"Just tell her you don't want to go."

"It's not as easy as that."

"You seem a bit down."

I have an urge to tell Simon about my father, but I don't think he's the ideal person to talk to. His family have a holiday home on a lake. They sing karaoke together at Christmas. I decide the Julie topic is more suitable. "She's changed," I say.

He swivels his chair towards me and cups his chin with his hand like a chat show host. "In what way?"

"Take this gathering for a start. We used to go to parties. Real fucking parties. We used to get slaughtered, do some coke. Not too much. We used to smoke some spliffs and then go home and have some real drunken dirty sex. But now we're going to a gathering with people who think that drugs are the root of all evil. She's been brainwashed."

Simon nods like one of those toy dogs on car dashboards. "You've been with her since school?"

"Yeah."

"People change," he says.

"Things were just fine the way they were," I say, a little aggressively.

"But maybe not for her," he says as he kind of makes a steeple out of his hands.

"Fucking hell, what are you, Trisha?"

He looks at me as if I'm wearing a t-shirt that says LEONARD NIMOY IS AN UGLY FUCK. He spins back around and gazes at his computer screen. I feel guilty. He means no harm; he's just a fussy aunt.

"Look, I'm just a bit stressed out," I say.

Simon smiles and then holds his hand out in the Vulcan salute. I look at the clock on the wall. "Live long and prosper," I say.

The afternoon is a complete waste. I play a game in which I try and guess the time but reduce it by ten minutes so that I get a nice surprise when I look at the clock. Then I type the names 'Pete' and 'Reggie' on the computer and keep changing the fonts.

"Oi Pete," Simon says to me. "Miranda. You better close that down."

I scramble to close down the page with PETE in Britannic Bold font. It disappears just as she reaches me.

"Got a lot done today, have we, Mr Jarvis?" I feel the heat of her breath on the back of my neck.

"Quite a bit," I say.

"Costsless?"

"I got told to phone back."

"And?" she asks, standing with her hands on her hips.

"I thought it would be better to try again tomorrow."

She scratches her head as though I'm an irritant.

When I get out of the office I rub my eyes. The sky is as dreary and blurry as an old war movie. The wind propels some leaves to play ring-a-ring-a-roses. Rain starts to fall, and Simon walks past. He tells me to enjoy the gathering.

I try to get out of the way of human traffic in the middle of Victoria. People honk, people swear, people move slowly, briefcase to briefcase. Then the platform number lights up and they're off — they overtake rabidly, they honk loudly, they swear foully, no one gives a shit; this is rush hour. I go outside and light a cigarette. I have two text messages. One is from my mother. She wants to come and see me tomorrow evening. This is a bit out of the blue. She hardly ever comes over. Could she have found out that I've seen my father? The other message is from Julie: "Am going in early to uni to help prepare for tonight. C u there." No kisses. Cold.

As the bus passes through Wellington Street, the new Sikh Temple towers in the distance. It's so big you could fit everybody in Gravesend in there. It cost over 13 million to build and it was funded entirely by the Sikh community. Where the fuck do they get that kind of money from? It really is a sight. Marble and granite deck the outside. There are five elaborate domes on the roof, rows and rows of arched windows and a huge white balcony which stems out in the centre of the building; the same kind that the Pope speaks from at the Vatican. You'd expect to see a desert, men in turbans carrying curved swords and riding camels. Or you imagine a starry night, moonlight illuminating the temple, the soft sounds of a harem floating in the air, dark-haired girls sinuously waving their hands. Except you turn the corner and there's no sand, no dark-haired beauties, and no soft music. Just the desert that is Gravesend.

I can hear Bob Marley blaring out through someone's earphones. Bob says that the "sun is shining and the weather is sweet". But it sure as fuck isn't. Rain pelts the bus window and as I look around I feel like I'm in a zombie movie. It's only just gone five o'clock, but most of the dole money has been spent and all of the cider has been drunk. Guys stumble along, dribbling, asking every passer-by for a pound. Some hover until a shop has been closed before they make its doorway their bed for the night. Some are so wasted that they lie draped over roundabouts in the park. I glance at my reflection in the window and push my hair into place. Everything's going to be ok.

Dolly greets me as if she knows something I don't. She sticks her tongue out at me before walking off with a swagger.

The *gathering* is in a bar on campus and has the usual Halloween décor: spider webs hanging from the ceilings, pumpkins, rubber vampire bats. It is packed out and I can't see Julie, so I go to the bar.

I'm trying to settle my nerves by getting stuck into my beer. This guy comes over. He looks like he's picked me out as a fellow loner. Fuck.

"Hi there, enjoying the gathering?"

Fucking hell. "Yeah. You?"

"Any excuse," he says pointing to his glass.

He looks young, but he speaks like an old, embarrassing relative at a wedding. Why do people feel the need to break the ice by talking or bragging about booze?

"Nice," I reply.

I would love an uncomfortable silence, but he seems shit-keen to make small-talk.

"What is it that you study?" he says.

"I'm not a student," I say.

"Oh, cool, cool," he says as though he is trying to convince himself that he's cool. "What is that you do then?"

"I'm in telesales. I get told to fuck off at least ten times a day."

He laughs nervously. "Cool," he says again before turning around and latching onto someone else.

I down my pint, order another and walk back into the crowd. I feel like the coffee crème in a box of chocolates. I find a seat by the canapés. The room has a slight smell of hospital to it which makes me uneasy.

Just as I'm about to call Julie to see where she is, I see her with a middle-aged man in the corner. She looks fantastic. She's wearing a white dress and high heels. The man, who seems to be enjoying her company a bit too much, is in a black suit and a white shirt, which is loosely unbuttoned, revealing the top of his chest. He's trying to dress young. She's all fingers and eyelashes and touchy and giggling. He's all hands and eyebrows and feely and bellowing. I grab a cocktail off some girl walking by with a tray and make my way over. I seem to have interrupted a joke. They stop laughing and look at me.

"Oh ... Pete," Julie says, "I'd like you to meet Professor Saunders."

They start laughing again. I feel like the floppy cock at an orgy. I haven't seen her laugh like this in ages. Her constant frown has disappeared and the sharpness in her eyes has resurfaced. I can tell she's pissed because her cheeks are rosy and she's swaying a little.

This professor stands there with his hand extended waiting for me to shake it. His skin is that of a wealthy, well-travelled man. I wonder what it would be like to punch it. He looks muscular through his black suit. He has a Clark Gable moustache. I suck up all the masculinity I can and put it into my handshake. "Hello," I say.

"Pleasure to meet you Pete. Call me Jerome. Julie's told me a lot about you," he says in a deep, clear voice as if he's introducing two heavyweights into the ring.

"Has she now?" I say in an extra manly voice.

"Yep, she sure has. She tells me you work in fundraising."

"Yes, that is correct. It is a rather challenging position, but it pays the bills," I say in the manner of a man who should be wearing a tux instead of a Ben Sherman shirt. "So, what is it that you do?"

His eyes dart towards Julie. Is there something in that? "I'm surprised that she hasn't mentioned me before," he says while still looking at her. Julie laughs nervously.

"Jerome's a senior lecturer and my seminar leader," Julie says to me.

"Oh, brilliant. So, you're the one I have to thank for all her wonderful new interests," I say to him.

He opens his mouth just as another woman starts talking at him. Julie leans across and tells me to stop talking in that stupid voice. He then turns back to excuse himself and tells me to "enjoy the gathering".

A few cocktails later I'm feeling the effects. I'm sitting at a table with Julie, Professor Saunders, two other students and another lecturer who looks remarkably like Gandhi. My face aches from pulling a fake smile for too long. Academic conversation flies round the table and bounces off my nodding head. I give up on conversation and focus on Julie's mannerisms towards the professor.

"Pete?" one of the students says.

"Yes?"

Julie leans towards me as if she's about to say *now tell the nice man*. "You were just asked whether you saw the rugby match yesterday," she says.

"Oh yesterday ... no, I don't think so, I had quite a busy day yesterday," I say, and think how granddad says that rugby is for kids who never grew out of playing bundle at school.

"Hard day at the office?" Professor Saunders says.

Julie laughs. "Actually, it was a busy day because he was running around Dartford debating whether to make contact with his dysfunctional father who has spent most of his life in prison since abandoning Pete as a baby. Weren't you, sweetheart?"

Did she actually say that?

"Oh? Tell us more," the professor says.

"Well I'd rather ... "

"Come on Pete, it might do you some good to get some other opinions," Julie says, interrupting me with a smug, drunken look on her face.

What has got into her? For a second, I think about making a run for it but that would just make matters worse. "It's pretty boring really. My father left home when I was a kid and I knew nothing about him for years, until my grandfather told me of his whereabouts," I say.

The table releases what seems like a synchronised gasp. "What was he in prison for?" Gandhi says.

I look at Julie and pray she won't say anything. She just sits there with flushed cheeks and a menacing look in her eye.

"Did he ever try and get in contact with you?" one of the students asks.

"Not that I know of."

"Maybe you should forget about him if he doesn't want to know you," the other student says.

"My thoughts exactly," Julie says with a smile.

"Ahh," Gandhi says as he crosses his arms, "But do you remember reading Balcam? He suggests that the reasons for the father's absence are paramount and believes that these dictate the effects on the son. Therefore, he argues that one must resolve the mystery of their father's absence so that their current intimate relationships can succeed."

"Of course, we've read that, but I feel that this isn't always necessary," Julie says.

"So, do you not agree that when a father abandons his son, the child will often have difficulty developing and sustaining self-esteem, forming lasting emotional attachments, recognising his feelings, or have trouble being expressive with his own partners and children?" Gandhi says.

Professor Saunders clears his throat. "To some extent, I do agree with Balcam. But each case is different. The effects you mentioned will not occur if the child is raised efficiently by the mother. Now don't get me wrong — I agree that there are associations between single parenthood and social difficulties, but if the father is dysfunctional then single parenthood is the better option." He takes a sip of his Halloween cocktail before continuing. "As long as the mother can fulfil her role. She must affirm the child's unique qualities, allow the child to share his thoughts and opinions freely, tell the child that it is not his fault that his father left."

I sit as far back as I can. I'm suffocating in all these affirms and allows, expresses and emotions, positives and praises, recollections and rejections. I can no longer hear what they are saying. Mouths move, heads nod, fingers point, hands clap, and I feel like I'm under anaesthetic on an operating table. Gandhi leans towards me and mouths something.

"What?"

"You did miss a great ruggers match. You should have seen this one try," he says.

"FUCK OFF. I DON'T LIKE RUGBY," I roar.

If this was a movie, the band would stop playing and the whole hall would turn to stare at me. Everyone at the table looks at me as if I've just insulted the real Gandhi. One of the students puts her arm round him.

"Pete!" says Julie. "What in God's name has got into you?"

I look around at all the sour and pissed-off faces. "He's not even the real ... oh fuck this," I say.

As I get up, Professor Saunders stands up. "Wait a minute, Pete," he says.

"You," I say as I stick my middle finger up at him. "GATHERING."

Julie follows me outside. She tells me she's going to spend the night at her sister's house. She says she needs time to think about things and asks me what's happening to us.

"Shit like that in there is what's happening to us," I say.

Some tears start to form in her eyes. "You haven't got a clue, have you?"

"About what? That you brought me to a poxy party and made me look a prize prat?"

"You really don't know do you? What day is it?" she says.

"What? That's an easy one," I say.

"I can't believe you've totally forgotten."

"Forgot what for fuck's sake?" I say.

Julie just shakes her head and disappears inside.

I stumble through the door and the cocktails direct me straight to bed. Dolly looks gutted when she realises that she won't be spending the night in bed with Julie. I give her a cheeky wink before closing the door. My head hits the pillow and I'm too tired and drunk to start worrying about what happened tonight.

It's not long before I wake from a dream in which I'm lying on an operating table with my chest cut open. Gandhi is peering at my insides. In the corner of the room Julie is getting done doggy-style by Saunders. Suddenly my father walks into the room, looks inside me, and says, "I've found the problem, guys. He just doesn't fit in."

CHAPTER THREE

I was sitting in Science finding it difficult to concentrate on what Mr Avril was saying. The kids behind me, the cool kids, the tough kids, the kids who don't wear ties and fight a lot, well they were laughing and getting up to something. Whispers and the sound of lead scribbled on paper were flying around the long wooden table behind me. Something hit me on the head and I held my breath somehow hoping that it would freeze the moment and stop them from continuing. I was too scared to turn around. And then another one skimmed my ear and landed on my desk. It was an elastic band with chewing gum stuck to it. I raised my eyes to Mr Avril looking for some intervention or refuge. But he didn't meet my gaze. Even if he would have done he wouldn't have said anything. The kids were from tough families. No teacher wanted to get their nose broke or their car bricked just for telling a brat off. I tensed as I saw a hand reach over my shoulder. But it didn't hit me. Instead it put a folded piece of paper on my desk. "OPEN ME", it said. So I did. There was a drawing in pencil. A stick man with a beard, next to what looked like a car. The stick man had a speech bubble which said, "DIE BABY DIE". More laughter followed, more whispers and another elastic band. "How'd ya like that drawing Jarvis?" a voice said. I ignored it of course, stayed quiet and didn't turn around. I got a slap round the back of my head for doing so. It was throbbing. Mr Avril left the room pretending he had something to do. I began to panic. "Oi! I'm talking to you shithead."

I tensed again preparing for a flurry of slaps to the head. But then a voice came, a sweet voice I hadn't heard before. The laughter stopped if only for a second or so. The voice came from the new girl sitting to the right of me. "Leave him alone," she said.

"Ooooh! Someone fancies Petey. Don't know why, no one likes him, even his own dad tried to kill him," the tough kid said, and the rest of the class laughed.

The bell went. I put my books slowly away waiting for the bullies to leave the room. The new girl stayed in her seat.

"Ignore those idiots. They're lowlifes," she said.

Shell-shocked that a girl actually spoke to me, "thanks," was all I could say.

"No probs," she said as she put her books in her bag and put her coat on. "I'm Julie by the way."

When I got home, mum was stooped over a frying pan of fish fingers smoking a funny shaped cigarette. The ones that smelt different to her normal ones. She didn't seem to notice that ash was falling into the pan.

She finally realised that I was home from school. She stumbled over to me and kissed me on the cheek. The steaming alcohol from her breath made my eyes water. "Have a good day sweetie?" she said.

My throat became swollen, the hairs on my arms tingled and I wanted to cry. Mum always had that effect on me. I was trying to be brave; not just for me, but for the both of us. "Mum," I said, "the kids at school say that Dad tried to kill me."

My words seemed to affect her like a gallon of black coffee. She sobered immediately, stood straight, and her normally sleepy eyes widened. Ignoring me she turned and walked back to the frying pan, re-ignited her funny cigarette, and took a huge gulp from the red bottle on the kitchen surface.

"Mum?" I said again.

There was no answer.

"M-m-mum?"

Then she screamed throwing the frying pan against the wall, the ashtray went flying and the red bottle smashed on the floor. Red liquid seeped beneath the broken shards of glass. "Shut up," she said. "Just shut up Pete."

My feet were glued to the floor. My stomach turned, I felt sick, too sick to even cry. Then she started to wipe the mess from the floor, before putting her head in her hands and crying loudly. I put my hand on her shoulder.

"I'm so, so, sorry Petey," she said. "Don't listen to the rumours. They are just nasty rumours. They don't mean anything. You're a good, good boy who is loved very much. You're going to have a great life."

Mum turned around to cuddle me and slipped trying to avoid the broken glass on the floor.

I need to be out the door in thirty-seven minutes. Morning light creeps in like an irritating kid. Birds are singing. I try to cover my ears. I'm stuck in a mental crossword. The clues consist of what Julie said last night and the words that I failed to speak to my father. I dip my fingers in the glass of water by the side of my bed and put my hand to my forehead. A drop of water trickles down my cheek and I suddenly feel guilty for shouting at Gandhi. Fuck it; Julie shouldn't have brought up my father in front of everybody. And is she fucking that professor? Now the alarm and the birds are insisting that I get out of bed. The hangover strikes.

I open the curtains. The sky looks like a scrambled satellite TV channel. Bare trees stick up like rusty aerials and rain hits the window. I hear Dolly scratching at the door, so I let her in and she starts flirting because she's hungry. This nauseates me, the flirting.

My bowels decide to be stubborn, so I go into the living room and smoke a cigarette to loosen them. It works every time. Maybe I should call her. Maybe I should wait for her to call me.

After a shower, a bowl of soggy cereal and another cigarette I say goodbye to Dolly, who doesn't give a shit now that she has a belly full of rabbit and jelly.

There is no way I'm walking straight to the train station today. On my way to the bus I play a game in which I try to hold my breath for the duration of a gust of wind. Sometimes I lose. The wind keeps creeping into my shoes and my feet are freezing. It irritates me that I have to keep my hands in my pockets the whole way. The streets have a Halloween hangover — dried egg yolks smear windows and sweet wrappers clutter the pavement. Shrivelled pumpkins look like deflated footballs and jaded witches return from all-night house parties with faded green faces.

At the bus stop, two women are talking. "Thank God it's Friday," one of them says. "Yes, I've surely got that Friday feeling today," says the other. That Friday feeling, I think: standing in the same old freezing cold, looking at the same old faces, listening to the same old shit. And just because it's Friday, this makes it better. Because we get two days off. Numbers, I think, we are simply numbers. Branded for life as soon as we get that national insurance number. The bus pulls up and opens its doors like a giant oven. Inside, more numbers, about to be half baked.

I have to open a window. It doesn't help that the bloke sitting next to me smells of talcum powder and peach schnapps. A young couple are laughing, kissing, and sharing a joke. She's probably telling him what she wants him to do to her tonight. I think of Julie. Some other bloke is tapping his feet as if someone is barbecuing his toes. There is another man talking loudly on his phone.

A young Slim Shady wannabe in a blue tracksuit who looks like an overgrown smurf has his earphones on and is bobbing his head in between talking to a pretty woman next to him. He notices me looking at him and kind of kisses his teeth at me. "Smell the booze on him, did ya?" he says to the lady and pointing at me.

The lady just shrugs, uninterested, but Smurf Shady continues. "He should stick to shandy or somethink," he says. "He's a poof. Nothin' like me, yeah. I'm hardcore, you get me? I'll drink any fool under the table."

He carries on moving his head to the music. The woman looks out of the window. But he seems determined to carry on talking to her. "I think you're sweet innit, nice lookin' an' that. My name's Hoppo, MC Hoppo cos I'm a rapper right," he says holding his hand out. The woman shakes it half-heartedly without saying a word.

"It ain't my real name though. Real name is Neil, but I been thinking of changing it permanently. Dunno what the old girl was thinking like, calling me Neil. Sound like a gardener or somethink. The name don't match the face, you get me? But I spose it happens to the best of us. See Eminem yeah? Well his real name is Marshall yeah. So me an him right, we got a lot in common."

The woman now looks really frustrated with this conversation. "Should you not be at school?" she says to him.

Smurf looks as though his pride has been dented. "School?" he says in a high pitched, sarcastic tone. "What a load a bollocks. Do fuck all for you in this town. You only learn your shit from the streets round here. You get me?"

He doesn't need a response from the lady. He's in full flow. "Just look around at all these people," he says pointing to people on the street. "That proves that school ain't gonna get you nowhere. Ain't no way I'm gonna earn a crust by sweating my nuts off like most cunts round here. Fuck that; I'm going to the top, I'm gonna be England's answer to Eminem. Either that or I'm gonna be the main face in town. Gonna drive one of those big arsed Mercedes like that Vic bloke from Denton. You know him? Nah?! Proper gangster he is. No one fucks with him. And no one's gonna fuck with me. It ain't gonna be easy to get to the top but I got the balls. You gotta be feared, be ruthless and be ready to go toe to toe with any cunt that stands in front of you. As Eminem says, 'Success is my only motherfuckin' option, failure's not.'"

He finally gives in when she fails to acknowledge him. He puts his earphones back in and raps. The young couple are now kissing with tongues. I feel really sick now. Julie can be a right pain in the arse at times, but I'd probably miss her. I think I'm going to be sick. I stick my fingers out of the window to stop me from feeling so closed in. What if it's over for good? The talcum powder bloke's head falls on my shoulder, mobile man is talking at 100 miles per hour, Barbecue toes is now doing Riverdance. My head is spinning. I move Schnapps boy's head from my shoulder, stumble into the aisle and fall into Smurf Shady. "Oi, you fucking prick watch it," he says. I need to get off. "Stop the bus," I yell. I fall into a lamppost and throw up: canapés and Weetabix. I wipe my mouth and walk the rest of the way to the station. I don't remember eating any sausage rolls.

"So, Mr Jarvis," Miranda says, "are we going to get Costsless in the bag today?"

"Yes, Miranda, we are," I say as I fall into my seat and scroll through the database of phone numbers. Without actually looking for the number.

I twitch, I yawn, I scroll — I tap, I stretch, I scroll. Scrolling for nothing has a therapeutic feel. The flickering cursor is hypnotic, and my eyes start to close but I fight this as long as possible because Julie is imprinted on the underside of one eyelid; my father the other. I decide on playing the clock game; reducing the time by twenty minutes. This starts to bore me ... I twitch, I yawn, I scroll — I tap, I stretch, I text Julie. I don't want to ring Costsless because I don't think I could handle rejection right now.

Between the hours of nine and one I go into snooze mode. People may have spoken to me, but they wouldn't have got a response. At half one I decide that a pub lunch is in order.

After ordering a Croque Monsieur and a pint of Oranjeboom, I take a seat in the corner of the pub, away from a large group of City workers: the spritzer drinking, Caesar salad eating, olives-for-starters type wankers who talk only about themselves and their bonuses. Whatever happened to pork scratchings? In the years I've been working up here, this bar seems to have got younger, not older. The wooden floor, which used to look like the skin off a dead elephant, is now a smooth, gleaming surface that makes you feel bad for not taking your shoes off. The tatty black and white pictures of soldiers, choirboys and brides which used to hang on the wall have been replaced by colourful scribbles more likely to be found in a gallery. Or a nursery. Even the beer has changed. No Foster's, Stella, or Carling; only fancy named continental lagers which takes you ten minutes to pronounce. The slick-haired waiter brings me my Croque Monsieur. All I see is cheese on toast with a bit of ham.

As I'm getting stuck into monsieur toastie, I see one of the IT guys from the office, Rob, walk in. He purchases a pint and then starts approaching people, showing them the contents of a sports bag. Most tilt their heads backward and look at him as if he's showing them his own puke. No luck. He takes a seat next to mine. And there was me, hoping for a quiet lunch.

"All wankers, these lot," he says to me, wiping beer from his chin.

"Why?" I say.

He scratches his head, takes a big gulp of his pint and says, "No one wants to buy any t-shirts. You?"

He puts the bag on my table and I look through it. The first t-shirt I pull out is white and has the slogan, "CUNNILYRICIST: The art of reading poetry while pleasuring women."

"Good, don't you think?" he asks me.

"Great," I say.

"They're designed to help the average man get the ladies," he says.

"Sell many?"

He rolls his eyes as if I've just asked him the most stupid question ever. "Er hello? Fuck yeah." He wipes his chin again and continues. "But it's not just about the money, pal. No. It's about the crack of it. I can't go through life working in that boghole of an office with all those deadbeat turds. This t-shirt business lets me escape." He takes another large gulp of his beer and burps. "What about you? Anything to keep your mind off this shit stain called reality?"

Apart from trying to work out whether I'm included in this dead-beat-turd-category, I struggle to think of anything apart from Project Father.

After lunch I try to muster up the motivation to call Costsless. Rob is picking his nose and wiping it on the underside of his desk. Do his t-shirts really work? I start to feel slightly jealous of Rob, because he has something to look forward to. Something he enjoys doing and something he believes in. Even if it is a pile of crap.

Text vibration. I expect it to be from Julie, but it's only my mum telling me that she will be over with Bruce about eight o'clock. I totally forgot. What's the deal with this? And why hasn't Julie texted me back? I was only being polite asking if she got back to her sister's ok.

"So, you've got the Bruce-man coming over tonight?" Simon says, looking over my shoulder.

"Don't be so bloody nosy," I say.

"Sorry," he says laughing.

"It's not something to laugh about mate," I say. "Not only is he a walking oil slick that's going out with my mum, but he's a lot younger than she is."

Miranda "Ahems" us. "Time to gossip, time to call," she says. Her features look as if they're being pulled down by a magnet. "And Jarvis - here's a word: Costsless."

Right. I pick up the phone as if I'm starting a chainsaw.

"Good afternoon, Costsless, Steve speaking, how can I help?"

"Could you connect me with the manager, please?"

"I am the day manager."

"Oh, yeah, hi there, my name's Pete Jarvis. I'm calling from Share the Care. I was just wondering if you might be able to spare a moment of your time?"

The polite voice that greeted me on the phone now abruptly changes to an irritable one. "What you selling then?"

I wince. "Well I'm not selling anything actually, sir," I say.

"So why are you ringing?"

"Well perhaps if you give me a moment, I can explain what it is we do."

He groans. "Come on."

I start reading to him from the card taped to my desk. "OK. Share the Care is the UK's leading professional fundraising organisation, raising more money for charity than any other. We offer every employer a free service, promoting and raising awareness of payroll giving schemes to employees. Do you think that this is something you and your colleagues might be interested in?" I see my National Insurance number floating above my head.

He pauses. "I don't understand what you're saying."

I bite my lip. "OK sir, that's fine. Basically, with your permission I'd like to send one of our representatives down to your store to speak to you all about the possibility of donating a small amount of money each month through the payroll department."

"So, you are trying to sell something," he says.

I grit my teeth. "No sir, we are just giving employees the chance to donate a small amount each month to the charity of their choice."

"They wouldn't be interested."

"Are you sure? It would only take half an hour of their time while the representative explained everything."

"You pretty much have explained it."

"Yes, but I haven't to the other members of your staff."

"True. But we really are too busy to take time out to listen to someone talk."

I feel my cheeks burning and look down and see that I'm digging my thumb nail into my index finger. "Too busy?"

"Yep, you heard. Too busy," he says.

So, you want to play like that? "Busy doing what, may I ask?"

"What?"

"Not exactly Marks and fucking Spencer's, are you?" I find myself saying.

"Excuse me?"

"You heard me, you twat". That felt good. "All I'm trying to do is offer you and your staff the chance to perform a charitable service and you can't even be arsed to listen."

"Did you just call me a twat?" he says.

"Yes sir. I did." I believe that honesty is the best policy.

"Anything else?" he asks.

I know I should stop, but I can't. It's like having a big whitehead on your chin and you know that you'll only make it worse by squeezing it, but the temptation is just too hard to resist ... "Yes, there is. Your fucking stores look more like pet shops than food shops. And they smell like pet shops."

"Why you little shi ... " he says.

"Eat fish food, bastard." I hang up the phone. I hear the silence of untapped keyboards. Shit. I look up and see that Simon is looking at me with his mouth wide open. Rob has a great big smile on his face. He's sticking his thumbs up. All eyes in the office are on me. Miranda is green, her arms and neck extended. She looks like a pissed off iguana. It's five o'clock, but I'm not going to be saved by the bell.

"I'll see the rest of you on Monday," Miranda says quietly. "Jarvis. My desk."

I feel as though I'm back in school.

"What the hell was that?" she says.

"I don't know where that came from."

"You told him to eat fish food."

She's got a point. "It could have been worse."

"Worse? Do you realise he's probably calling his head office as we speak?"

I don't say anything for a moment and she looks at me with her hands on her hips waiting for a response.

"Miranda, I complimented Marks and Spencer's. Maybe we should let them know of our loyalty. Would you like me to call them?" Shit, did I really just say that?

"Christ, Peter, we have over two hundred accounts with that company."

She looks as sour as un-sugared coffee and the tone of her voice starts to sound like a satnav. This is not a good sign. The rest of the staff walks past; some daring to nod at me, others scared shitless to communicate with the enemy.

"I'm sorry," I say folding my arms.

She looks at me and sighs. I half expect her to tell me to perform a U-turn where I can. "Look Pete, I just don't know where your head is at lately. For weeks now, you haven't been yourself. You look like you've got a million and one things on your mind and work isn't one of them. And..."

She folds her arms, I unfold mine. Now is the part where she will tell me to continue on the road ahead or exit at the next junction.

"I like you Pete, I really do," she says. "But I can't allow outbursts like that to go unpunished. Which is why I'm suspending you for a week. Unpaid."

Shit. "Just give me one more chance. Losing a week's wage packet will cripple me," I say.

"You should think yourself lucky that you've got away with just a suspension. That was a sackable offence."

"I know, but it was a one-off. It won't happen again," I say.

"I'm sorry. But you can't do stuff like that and expect to get away with it."

I remain silent. She leans against the desk behind her. "Just take some time for yourself." she says.

When I get outside the building I light a cigarette as though it might spark some ideas as to what I'm going to do. How will I afford to pay the rent without a week's wages?

Walking and smoking often clears my head. But lately it hasn't. I walk and smoke and walk and smoke and walk and smoke: absorbing all the London mayhem. Sirens whiz past my ear every couple of minutes. Homeless people are scattered everywhere. Some stumble past asking for loose change. Some lie unconscious clutching a bottle of cheap cider. Some sit on street corners with a half-dead dog draped over their legs. Some sit with their heads in their laps holding their hands out, too ashamed to reveal their faces. London is a thousand faces per minute: blacks, whites, Chinese, Indians, Eastern Europeans. Lip piercings, eyebrow piercings, bushy eyebrows, eyebrows that join in the middle, big foreheads, creased foreheads, big noses, wonky noses, fat cheeks, red cheeks; no smiles. Not one single fucking smile amongst these fancy mirrored buildings and designer suits. It's just a cover up; a fancy dress. London is like putting clean clothes over an unwashed body. Sure, it conceals the dirt for a little while; but soon the stink will become horrific. When I get to Victoria, GRAVESEND flashing up on the departures board just seems to take the piss.

A pair of my trainers sits alone in a shoe rack. As I walk through into the living room I get a hollow feeling. Julie is sitting on the corner of the sofa looking at the floor. A black suitcase lies by her side.

"You're leaving, aren't you?" I say.

She finally lifts her head and her eyes, puffed up and watery, meet mine. She nods. "Things are bad, Pete."

Shit. "Look, last night was ... "

"Terrible," she says to interrupt me. "And I'm so ashamed of myself for how I acted. I should never have brought your father into the conversation. It wasn't fair."

"Is that all? Don't worry about that ... you're forgiven. Now unpack your bag and I'll put the kettle on," I say as I walk towards her.

She holds her hands up and winces, a tear running down her cheek. "No, Pete. It's not as simple as that. Do you know why I acted like that last night?" She clasps her hands together and holds them to her lips. I know she's willing me to give the right answer and this serious look of hers signals this.

Think... Think ... Don't screw this up... You don't want her to leave... Come on... Think...

"Those bloody cocktails were killers. Knocked the bollocks off me. We both say things we don't mean when we're drunk."

My words seem to float in the air for a while before hitting her. She sighs, stands up and picks up the suitcase.

"No ... wait ... I know why you're upset ... "

She stops and stares at me. I'm getting warm I can tell. I put my hands on her shoulders and study her face for clues.

"It's because of me ... and ... my obsession with my father?"

Must be right ... No. She heads for the door.

"Wait ... and it's because ... I'm dithering about and I'm not being assertive ... and I don't know what I want, and you want me to be more assertive ... and fit in more with your uni friends and apologise to the Gandhi geezer and tell the professor bloke that I shouldn't have called him a gathering."

I pause for breath and yet she still puts her hand on the door knob. Now I feel a prat.

"Well fucking hell ... what do you want from me? You want me to be one of your tarty little clever clog friends who you can talk brains with? Well I'm just not like that. So, go on then, piss off if you want to."

The door closes, and I hear her footsteps echo down the stairway. Riddles: always fucking riddles with her. Why couldn't she just tell me what it was I've done? Let her go then. If it was the old Julie, I'd be devastated; but with this new Julie? I'm not so sure. Seeing her laugh yesterday brought back some old feelings. But it wasn't me that made her laugh. I'm not even sure if I'm capable of doing that anymore. I look at the clock and it tells me I've got an hour and a half before my mum and Bruce arrive. So, I do what I do best and think some more.

CHAPTER FOUR

I open the door and odours of cigarettes, herbal bath salts and diesel greet me.

"Hello Mum."

My mother takes off her rainbow woolly hat and pulls some knots out of her red hair. She kisses me on the cheek and Bruce and I half-heartedly shake hands. He gives me the I-really-can't-be-arsed-to talk-to-you-nod. I give him the I-really-can't be arsed-either-nod. Me and Bruce have never got on. To me, Bruce is the bad guy who took my mum away from me. To him, I am an inconvenience, a punctured tyre.

"Cup of tea anyone?" I ask.

"Here darling, I've brought my own." She passes me a box of green tea.

"Bruce?"

"Nah, don't drink none of that poddington pea piss. Got any beers?"

In the kitchen, the sound of the kettle drowns out flirty giggles coming from the living room. Dolly perches by the window. She looks suicidal. The basil plant next to the sink looks depressed. "Couldn't have loved you that much, could she?" I say to them. On my way out, I give the basil plant a nod of encouragement. I give the tea to my mum and a beer to Bruce. He burps after his first gulp. My mum glances between me and Bruce and smiles. She has this habit of trying to make the two of us talk; as though she's a marriage counsellor.

"Bruce's business is doing really well at the moment. Isn't it, love? Go on, tell him how well it's doing." My mum nods at Bruce.

Bruce kind of growls. "Yeah. Doing well."

"Must be a lot of dirty cars at the moment," I say.

"Well, it is a top-class valeting establishment," my mum says.

"Don't just clean cars though," Bruce says.

"No?" I say.

"No," he says. He runs his hand through his jet-black hair which might be held in place by car wax. "More of a business man really. Do the figures and plan on how to expand. Take it to new levels. I'm in the office. Me workers get grimy."

But his hands are really dirty. They look as if he's got a couple of recently picked potatoes attached to his wrists. Bruce notices me looking at them. He takes a large swig of his beer and burps again. "Bit of engine work ain't I. Extra dough on the side like. Leave the cleaning and scrubbing to me monkeys."

"Bruce has lots of staff working for him now," my mum says as she pats his knee.

"Really? How many monkeys have you got?" I say.

"Five. Well four and a half, cos the Polish one has arthritis. But he's on less money than the others," he says.

"None of them are on particularly good money anyway, are they?" I say.

"Course they ain't. Cheap as fucking chips these foreigners ain't they. And they work just as hard. It means more money in my pocket don't it."

I nod and take a swig of my beer. Mum sips her drink and says "mmm". Bruce gulps his beer and says "ahhhh".

"How is your job going Pete?" my mum says.

Before I can answer, Bruce jumps in to have his say. "Managing to save the world from that computer?"

My mum winces. She knows it's a touchy subject. I feel myself redden. I know that I'm doing a job that I never planned on doing. But then I had no idea what I wanted to do. I didn't fucking strive. Maybe that's half the problem in this town.

"Well it's a job isn't it? It helps pay the bills. Which puts me in a better position than most at the moment don't it?" I say deciding to leave out the part of being suspended.

"Of course it does love," my mum says. "Have many people been donating?"

"Not really mum. It's rejection after rejection. Most of the managers don't give a shit. They're happy with their bulging wallets; they don't even allow us to ask their staff if they want the chance to donate," I say.

"Lot of hassle though, ain't it?" Bruce says. "All that payroll business. Makes a lot of extra work. People should just pop their pennies in a pot or something. I wouldn't have one of your lot come down and speak to my staff."

Bruce is every ignorant fuckhead I have ever spoken to down the phone. One of these typical fuckheads who are quite happy swanning around in their brand-new Volkswagen motors with their nice three-bedroom-semi, leather settees and gas fires. A fuckhead so oblivious to the people struggling around them. "That's probably because all your workers aren't English, Bruce. Probably not even legal. So why the fuck would they want to donate to UK charities?" I say.

Bruce tightens his grip on his beer can and dents it. "Why you swearing, Pete?" he says as he looks to my mother in a kind of "I'm-telling" way.

37

"No Julie tonight, love?" my mum says to change the subject.

I pause for a moment to decide what to say. My mother edges closer and raises her eyebrows. They're drawn on.

"She's staying with her sister tonight. She's not very well," I say.

"Who? Julie or her sister?" my mum says.

"Julie. No, I mean her sister."

My mother leans forward and squints as if she's having an eye test. "Is everything ok love?" she says.

"Yeah why?"

"You can be open with me and Bruce," she says.

Bruce puts his hand on her hand and winks at me. "That's right Petey. We are both here for you mate."

I grit my teeth. We sit amongst the sounds of sipping, gulping, ahh'ing and hmm'ing; I begin to wander if this really is just a social call. She hasn't said anything about me going to meet my father yet. But something isn't right. She's as twitchy as she was when she kicked the drugs; keeps scratching her ears, biting her lip, and tapping her foot. The skag, crack and whiz have a lingering presence over the user; it never really goes. It clings to the brain cells like a recurring illness, lets them know that it's still living inside them, makes the user fragile. You see it in every park, shop doorway and bench in town.

"Bruce is competing in a judo tournament tomorrow down Margate way. I thought it would be nice if the three of us could go down there. We could watch the tournament then have a walk along the beach and get some fish and chips. Would be nice wouldn't it?"

Ok this is getting weird. Is she on the whiz again? "I'm seeing Granddad tomorrow," I say.

Bruce looks relieved and then, whether to spite me or not, he puts his arms round my mother and pulls her into him. She looks tiny with Bruce's bulky arms wrapped round her; it reminds me of a scene in King Kong. "Oh," he says, "shame that. Might do you good to learn a few moves."

I look at the two of them on the sofa and think of the notion 'opposites attract'. I've always thought that Bruce and my mum wouldn't last. To her I guess she saw Bruce as a long-term thing: the younger man with a stable income, a mortgage, a business, and a few extra bob to have a couple of holidays a year. To him though, I thought it would just be one of the phases blokes go through when they want an older lady to show them a thing or two. Every man goes through the MILF stage. I've always been worried that the phase will end, and she'll be heart-broken.

"So," my mother says looking around the room, "how is Julie?"

"Not bad," I say.

"She must really feel it this time of year. Must be really sad for her."

"What do you mean?" I ask.

"Wasn't it around Halloween a few years ago that she lost her brother? Horrific that. God rest his soul."

I almost choke on a mouthful of beer. Shit. So that's what Julie meant. How could I have forgotten?

"Look," I say, "I've been feeling pretty rough today and I'm gonna hit the sack in a moment. So, shall we catch up again soon?"

"Oh," my mother says and then looks at Bruce. "Ok love. Why don't you pop round on Sunday for a nice roast?"

"Sure," I say.

On the way out, Bruce shakes my hand as if he's now King Kong squashing a helicopter. My mother kisses me. She lingers for a moment as though she wants to say something. "See you Sunday love."

When I close the door, I call Julie. There is no answer, so I leave a message. I go into the kitchen to grab a glass of water and see that Dolly hasn't moved. I start to feel sorry for her, so I stroke her back. She swivels her head round and glares at me like the girl in The Exorcist.

I open the window in the bedroom and lie down. The Asda car park has become a playground for teenagers in baggy clothes and modified Ford Fiestas. Clouds of smoke roll out of car windows and sound systems rattle with an overload of bass. A police car drives slowly by and when it's out of sight, one of the teenagers pulls a moony. I lay my head on the pillow and close my eyes while Gravesend comes alive.

A giant gorilla gets me in a head lock while my mother lies naked on top of the Empire State Building. When I look closely I see that the gorilla is my father. "Put me down," I say. "Why?" he asks. "You're only another number." I wake up in a sweat.

Anxiety kicks in in my morning shower. How am I going to afford the rent if Julie has decided to leave for good? Shall I return to see my father? Am I going to lose my job for good? Is she fucking the professor? The thought of her lying naked with another man delivers an uppercut to my pride. I start to think of her naked. I start to think of the tiny little bumps around her nipples, the scar on her left arm from the TB jab, the delicate little mole just above her belly button, her cracked heels from wearing uncomfortable shoes. Professor Saunders's hair was grey, but a good grey; like an intellectual grey who looks-for-lost-treasure-on-his-day-off-grey. He's got to have had a couple of books published too. They probably go for espressos and talk about sociological experiments as a pre-fuck warm-up. Maybe they go back to his house. No, he's probably married but is too worried to leave his wife and son because he knows what specific psychochemical effects a single parent family has on an adolescent teenager. So, they probably get a hotel. Julie has shaved her bikini line into a tidy little patch. She decides that this is the best idea because if she shaves it completely off then he will think she is slutty, if she leaves it be then he will think that she is unadventurous and boring. He on the other hand has probably trimmed his chest hair; just enough to show that he likes to take care of himself. Quite possibly he works out and he's so cool that he will never suffer from a midlife crisis. Fuck. Fuck. Fuck.

With only beans and Weetabix in the cupboard, I decide that a trip to Ella's Café is a good idea before going to see Granddad. Dolly is still sulking; even more so after realising that she's not getting breakfast either. I leave her on the window sill licking her lips at pigeons.

I take a shortcut into town by walking through Asda. The car park bears the ruins of last night. Stubbed-out spliffs, empty bottles of Smirnoff Ice and Mars bar wrappers loiter in the disabled bays. A sweet smell of freshly-made bread wafts through the air for a moment before a delivery truck comes along and drowns the smell in diesel fumes.

Asda brings me out at the top of the high street. It looks like a human pick-and-mix, hundreds of different heads bobbing along. Bald heads, hairy heads, turban-covered heads, dreadlocked heads, afro heads. Such a small town, so many different heads.

A Sikh religious emblem hangs in gold above a newsagent's. Some Indian rap and a scent of herbs and spices leak through the open door. Next door some agitated punters gather outside the betting shop, chewing on their fingernails, puffing on their roll-ups. A commentator's voice covering a greyhound race hurtles round the shop. On the corner, a shop decorated in red and green looks more like Santa's grotto than a Chinese grocery store. The staff inside always look so happy. My Grandfather says this is because the Chinese are always celebrating something.

As I cross at the traffic lights, Gravesend's signature building, the Job Centre, stands like a mountain. A queue is already forming and stretches as far as the Pound Shop. Elderly people, victims of the recession, look wide-eyed, scared and even ashamed that they have to ask for money after working hard all their life. Others stand there who don't even know about the recession. This is regular protocol. If they look nervous it's because they're worried that the local speed dealer will run out of stock before they receive their money.

The rain ceases and thick dark smoke rising from the chimneys from the industrial estate hovers above the town. I head past the ghostly Woolworths. Through the window I can see empty shelves, deserted cash tills and un-opened letters lying on a faded carpet. A simple sign plastered to the window reads: NO LONGER OPEN FOR BUSINESS. It looks like a gravestone. Next to Ella's Café, the landlord of the Buffalo's Head is sweeping up broken glass. Somewhere nearby someone is probably picking pieces of the same glass out of his head.

"Double bacon, egg and chips please, Tony. Oh, and some bubble, mate."

"Coming right up squire," Tony says with a spatula in his hand.

Tony eats, breathes, and lives Ella's Café. He was born upstairs and has lived above it all his life. His mum Ella was bought the café as a present by her father. Whenever Tony hears something he doesn't like, he always looks to the ceiling, sighs, and says, "If only my dear mum were still alive. She's probably turning in her urn."

His arms are bulky, really pink, and look as if he's got two piglets hanging off his shoulders. Creases and scars are indented in his forehead and rolls of excess skin just above his neck look as if his skin has been pulled backward over his skull. Never seen in anything else other than an apron and some England football shorts, he is always quick to greet his customers with a big smile revealing a mouth full of gold teeth and bacon rind.

"Where's that bird of yours?" Tony says as he drowns some chips in the deep fat fryer. "You haven't brought her in for ages."

"She's moved out Tone," I say while pretending I'm reading the plastic menu sellotaped to the counter.

"Shit. Sorry mate. But if you ask me," he says as he flips a rasher of bacon over, "I did think she was a bit snooty."

"Yeah, you're probably right," I reply.

"I am most of the time mate," he continues. "She may have been blessed in one department," he puts his spatula down, turns to me and gesticulates having a pair of tits. He winks at me. "But she was one snobby old cow. Always looked as if she was sitting on something she shouldn't be."

Before I can tell him that she may not be moving out for good, Tony serves me up my breakfast. "Get your gnashers around that matey."

Ella's is a working-class House of Commons. Irate postmen rant about the state of society with egg yolk dribbling down their chins. Men in fluorescent jackets speak of ludicrous taxes in between talking about the perfectly formed nipples of Daily Sport girls. Delivery drivers moan about the dire condition of the M25 and argue that the government should spend our taxes on something useful, like improving it. Or blowing it up. And others — well they just enjoy Tony's bubble and squeak.

Some taxi drivers are discussing the lack of work. One of them has salt and pepper hair with sun-dried tomato skin. Smoker and drinker. "It's hard enough to get fares, let alone them fucking foreigners doing fares on the cheap," he says as he pours some sugar into his cup.

The other driver has a small head. He looks like an upside-down plug socket. "Well what can we do about it?"

Tomato looks into the bottom of his tea cup as if it's some kind of crystal ball. "Fuck knows mate. But I know what I'd bloody well like to do about it."

Tony joins them at the table. "I know how you feel lads. How many English cafés in this town do you see serving the traditional nowadays?" Tony says.

"Not many Tone," is the answer from Dried Tomato.

"They come over here, sell some two-bob foreign meat for cheaper than what I do and make more money."

"It's a fucking liberty Tone."

"Exactly. You wouldn't find me opening up a kebab shop and playing the Turks at their own game. Stick to what you know. That's what I say," Tony says as he tightens the strings on his apron.

"They take the English out of the breakfast mate," Plug Socket says.

"If my dear old mum were still alive," Tony says, as he looks to the ceiling, "Jesus ... she'd be turning in her urn."

After buying my granddad some tobacco I make my way to his sheltered accommodation in Blenheim Grove. He lets me in with a grunt and goes back to reading the local newspaper, *The Gravesend Reporter*. Getting conversation out of Granddad is like starting an old car on a winter's day. You have to warm him up first.

"Hello, Gramps", I say.

He sighs.

"How's things?"
He groans.
"Anything interesting in the paper?"
He murmurs.
"Been keeping yourself busy?"
"Yes."
"What you been doing then?"
"Not a lot".
"Mum been to visit you lately?"

He turns the page of the newspaper and pulls his chair closer to the table. He starts tapping his fingers on the arm of the chair. His arms are muscular for a man of his age. The boxing gloves tattooed on his wrist prove he was once platoon boxing champion in his army days. Now they just look like little grapes. I root around in my pocket for his tobacco. He senses I've brought something for him. He looks at me out of the corner of his eye like a kid enticed by sweets. I think I begin to see a smile forming but he covers it up by pretending that he has just found something amusing in the newspaper.

"I've brought something over for you, Gramps," I say.

"Oh yeah," is all he says. This is the part where I'm determined for him to turn around and face me. It's also the part where he pretends that he doesn't give a shit about what I've got for him. I take the tobacco out of my pocket and start rustling the plastic pouch in my hand. His fingers tap the chair at a faster pace, his foot follows suit and he's blinking frantically.

"Oh, what you got for me then you little bugger?" The shield drops, and the engine starts running.

He grabs the bag of Golden Virginia then turns his chair around so he's facing me. As he opens the tobacco pouch and inhales, he closes his eyes and raises his white bushy eyebrows. He takes a deep breath and looks content. When he exhales, his whiskey riddled cheeks puff out. The tiny purple veins seem to multiply. "I love the smell of fresh tobacco," he says as he pushes his fringe into place.

My granddad has been fortunate to keep a full set of hair all his life. He always has a comb in his inside pocket and a pot of Brylcream is never far away. He is a proud man. I think it knocked him for six when Nan died but he's a strong character. Presentation is always important to Granddad. He is always clean-shaven; his shoes must always be polished, and his ironed shirts must always be tucked into dark-coloured cords or trousers. Every Sunday he wears a tie.

"So, you been ok then son?" he finally says.

"Well, I've got a bit of a jumbled head really, Gramps."

He squints and raises one eyebrow. "I bet I know what that's about," he says. "Been to see him?"

"Yep."

"And?"

"It didn't go well at all," I say. Then I tell him how it went.

"So, are you going to leave it now?" he says.

"Isn't there anything else you can tell me about him, Gramps?" I ask.

He averts his gaze back to the newspaper. "I've told you all I know. When I found out he was working in that bar I felt you had a right to know. But what good was going to come from telling you I don't know. It's your decision whether you want to pursue it."

We sit in silence for a while until Granddad prepares himself a bowl of cornflakes.

Over his breakfast Granddad continues to flick through the local newspaper, when all of a sudden, he drops his spoon into his bowl.

"Stabbings, stabbings, death — is this all they write about? Bloody hell, nothing like a bit of death to kick start your day."

"It's just the way it is nowadays, Granddad. Someone has to write about it."

"Let me tell you about nowadays. It's a bloody joke. The streets are like no man's land. I put myself on the line to save our country, and for what? Look at the fucking state of it now: all those bloody gangs in sportswear, running around and causing trouble. And all those bloody immigrants coming in and causing mayhem, wielding knives. Whatever happened to fair fist fights? What happened to honesty and respect? I would have preferred the bloody Germans."

Granddad's face starts to shrivel; his eyes, nose and mouth seem to join together, his breathing becomes heavy and the white hairs which peep out of his nostrils do the polka.

"People have stopped caring," he continues. "This bloody country is like an old lady with Alzheimer's: expects everything to be done for her and has forgotten that she was once beautiful and proud. It's a bloody shambles," he says.

Granddad looks out of the window and snarls, then pushes his cereal to one side, gets up and says, "Come on then son, let's get out of here. I'll buy ya an ice cream if you're well behaved."

Granddad always insists on walking past the bakery he used to work in. Being just a stone's throw from the Thames, he made most of his money making and selling bread for the boatmen and dockside workers. Now it's a Subway sandwich store. He'll always take a few moments to look at the front of the shop. Staring at the giant poster of the sub-of-the-day, he'll always shake his head. "A real job that was son, back in the day," he says, "something I took pride in. I'd work all bloody night to prepare the dough. Big old vats of flour and water there were. Ah, you'd have to get the ingredients right and I was a bit of a dab hand at it if I do say myself. Stirring, stirring, stirring, kneading, kneading, kneading. It used to take the skin off my fingers that job did, right down to the bones. Being barechested with the sweat dripping off me in front of those roaring flames. Ah, I felt alive. It was well worth it son. When my bread was taken out of the oven the smell travelled all the way down the Thames right into the nostrils of Greenwich. The good ol' dockside workers — you should've seen their faces at the sight of my hot bread after a twelve-hour shift."

He lights a roll-up as we walk past the clocktower and Nuxley Toys. Nuxley's was a like a dream world to me when I was a kid and Granddad knows to look at my face every time we pass because he knows that he'll see me smile. If he had a successful week at the bakery then he would take me to Nuxley's on a Friday and treat me to a wrestling figure. Granddad straightens his back and stares at the shop as if he's saluting an army officer. "It's nice to see a good old traditional shop still standing strong," he says, "unlike that bloody waste of space there." He nods his head towards the Bollywood cinema which is now an empty building. Faded posters of old Indian films hang on cracked tiles around the entrance. I feel a shiver run through me as I peer through one of the cracked windows; there's something eerie about a deserted cinema. But I feel sad too. It wasn't always a Bollywood cinema. It was the first cinema I ever went to. I even took Julie there to watch Titanic on one of our first dates. I have no idea why it changed to a Bollywood cinema. Granddad says he thinks it has something to do with the mayor of Gravesend being Indian.

As we walk down the cobbled street just before the indoor market, Granddad almost loses his footing for a second. I offer my hand to help him and he growls at me. The town court is just by the entrance to the market. Various people stand outside awaiting their fate for petty crimes — driving offences, possession of cannabis. Granddad comes to a standstill, so he can finish his roll-up. "Will you look at them standing there," says Granddad. "Bring back National-bloody-Service, that's what I say."

CHAPTER FIVE

A strong wind sweeps over the Thames as we enter the promenade. It blows my granddad's fringe out of place and he reaches for his comb. I just zip my jacket up as far as it will go. Although the rain has stopped, the cold forces my hands into my pockets. Granddad still buys us both an ice cream with chocolate flakes dunked in the top. "You can't visit the promenade without an ice cream son. It just wouldn't be right."

We take a seat and look upon the choppy waves of the Thames. Small boats bob on the surface, bullied by the waves. The ferry that takes passengers across to Tilbury is trying to brave the wind. A large container ship simply brushes the waves aside as it sails smoothly through the current. My granddad points out the Princess Pocahontas boat coming in to dock to the left of us. The boat is named after the famous Indian princess, who is rumoured to have taken her final resting place in Gravesend. But it's just a booze cruise where people do a copious amount of drugs for a couple of hours without being hassled by the police.

"So how is Julie?" Granddad asks as he licks some vanilla ice cream from the corner of his mouth.

"Not too good to be honest Gramps. It feels like we are growing apart. She's moved out for the time being. I was thinking that it was her that was changing and didn't give a shit, but then last night I was reminded that it was around this time that her brother was killed a few years back. I'm thinking that I should have, I don't know, maybe said something," I say.

"Well it was a terrible thing son, and yeah, you're right, maybe you should have said something. But don't go beating yourself up over it. You've been occupied with other things lately," he says.

"That's the thing Gramps, I don't feel she's been supportive in any kind of way over all this business with my father. So why then should I feel bad for not supporting her? I've tried calling her, but she hasn't answered. I don't know. I'm just not sure what I want anymore. My head is all over the place. Everywhere I look there is something that depresses me. And at the moment I just feel ... I don't know ... insignificant or something."

Granddad points his finger at me and his cheeks redden. "Don't ever say you are insignificant son," he says. "Don't talk so bloody weak. You're a strong man Pete, so pull your bloody socks up and grab life by the bloody balls."

I laugh. "Mum and Bruce came to see me last night."

"Bloody hell," he says, "surprising, that."

I'm trying to eat my ice cream as quickly as possible, so I can put my hands back in my pockets. "But I have no idea why they came to see me."

"How did it go?" he asks.

"Not great. You know how things are with me and mum."

He dents his ice cream cone with his finger. "She does love ya though."

"Well it hasn't seemed that way for a number of years. I just don't know why she came around with him. It was like she had something to say to me, but couldn't quite bring herself to do so. I thought that she may have found out that I've been to see my father," I say.

He looks at me out of the corner of his eye and then massacres a flake in one bite. He stares out over the Thames. "The thing with your mother is that she never really opens up. She never has. Never to me, never to you, and never to her own mum; God bless her. I don't think she's able to. Whether it has something to do with that father of yours ... But since he left, she's a different woman. But the real Lilly is in there somewhere."

I seem to be staring into nothing, thinking about how my mum has been over the past few years. And it's hard for me because the truth is ... I don't really know.

"What you going to do then son? Are you going to see him again?" he says without making eye-contact.

"I don't know Gramps. I don't even know what I'll achieve by making contact with him. It just feels like this is something I need to do," I say.

Granddad looks me in the eyes. "Well, make sure that it is the right thing to do. And like I said son, grab life by the balls. Don't take any shit."

And on that note, we continue to look out over the river, watching evening arrive. The Thames gets darker and the wind gets sharper.

We decide to get a bus back to Blenheim Grove because Granddad is getting tired. On the short journey home, he falls asleep with his face pressed against the window. He stirs slightly at the next stop and a group of five or six kids, no older than twelve years old, get on and bowl towards the back seat like some kind of rap group. It's not long before they start harassing an elderly Asian man sitting in front of them in the opposite row to us. They dare each other to tap the man on the shoulder and then on the head. The man, whether out of maturity or fear, ignores it all; perhaps he is used to it. At first, I think that it's only kids being kids and messing around, but then out of the corner of my eye I see one of the little shits spit on the man. The Asian guy still doesn't move, even though a puddle of white spittle sits on his shoulder. Why the fuck is he not saying anything? When I see another wad of phlegm hurtle towards him, I turn around to face them. My words freeze somewhere between my Adam's apple and my tonsils. Jesus, they're only kids, but they look fucking scary. One of them catches me, and he stares at me like he wants to rip my intestines out. "Yeah?" he says, "Gotta fucking problem?" He looks like a 40-year-old psychopath trapped in a twelve-year-old's body.

I quickly turn around and in doing so I make eye contact with the Asian man for just a moment. He rolls his eyes as if to signal that nothing will stop these little shits. Cowardice pumps heat into my cheeks while anger clenches my fists. I hear one of them say "fucking pussy". But now I too am looking straight ahead, and know why he doesn't say anything. I look to see that Granddad is still snoozing, which is probably a good thing; he would definitely say something, which could end in things getting nasty.

I wake him up just before we come to our stop. He struggles to open his eyes and his tiredness makes him look vulnerable. He rubs his eyes and wipes some dribble from his chin. "Right, let's get off this mobile chicken farm, hey son," he says as he pulls himself out of his seat. As the bus drives away, the kids at the back of the bus stick their fingers up and show me the 'wanker' sign. The Asian guy also nods at me in some kind of recognition.

After seeing Granddad back to his accommodation, I make my way home through town. Last year's Christmas lights drape the street, unlit. They look like barbed wire. Above the lights, a few stars linger in the black sky like confused homeless people wondering whether to spend the last of their money on some crack or a bed for the night. Chippie workers fire up their deep fat fryers and kebab shops prepare meat for the Saturday night pissheads. An extravagant flashing sign displaying doner meat on a skewer causes me to squint. The smell of cooking oil and spiced lamb fills the high street. Corrugated iron shutters are pulled over shop windows like armour, bouncers who look like walking biceps in woolly hats take their position outside pubs and clubs, and taxis begin to clutter the kerbs like hookers. A group of people walk past and laugh loudly, which irritates me. I start to walk at a faster pace, my breath in the cold dark air like fumes from an exhaust pipe. I pass a church and a First World War memorial plaque attached to a small stone is slightly illuminated by a dim light. Engraved names of great British soldiers who laid down their lives for their country are barely visible by the low wattage bulb. The soldiers' names rest above half a dozen cigarette ends, a used condom, and an empty can of Stella. My heart starts pounding and I feel as though I'm strapped to a roundabout as I continue walking. Different styles of music blare through open windows. There is a different sound in every direction. Accents, laughter, car horns, car stereos, modified engines, coughing, sneezing, hiccupping, footsteps; slow, fast, extremely fucking fast. They blend together like tinnitus. Short of breath, I stop for a second outside Tesco and try to compose myself. I catch my reflection in the window. I look like a meerkat on cocaine.

I fierce my eyes and lips like Clint Eastwood but I just look constipated. I hum the Eye of the Tiger theme; it always works, doesn't it? Yeah, yeah; just like Rocky. But why are you doing this? It's not as if you're tough. You shit your pants today, didn't you? I stop humming and look at my reflection. "You're the motherfucking man, you're the motherfucking man, you're the motherfucking man ... " But why are you saying this? It's not as if you're fucking anyone's mother. Your self-motivational skills aren't working too well, are they? I put my hands on my head and then there is a bang on the window. A couple of staff members from Tesco have been watching me the whole time.

Embarrassment hits me. The most sensible thing to do is get back to my flat as soon as possible. I run past the bookies and past the drunks counting shrapnel outside the off-licence. I cut through Asda until I get to my block of flats. When I open my door, I see Dolly looking at me like some kind of pissed-off school teacher. Shit, I forgot to get cat food.

When I make my way back down the stairs, the two junkies that live on the bottom floor are perched on the last step. One of the men is sitting with his head hung between his knees moaning and mumbling. The other rubs his back encouraging him to puke telling him that the buzz will mellow out once he's thrown his guts up. Both of them are dressed in food stained t-shirts that are too small for them, and holey jeans.

"Excuse me fellas," I say.

The one giving the puking-pep-talk turns his head slowly, rolling his eyes, fluttering his eyelids. A nose, shiny with thick grease, sticks out between two golf-ball-like cheekbones. He looks to the hand railings and seems to contemplate just how much effort it will be to stand up and move out of the way. "Aww man, this is heavy shit," he groans.

He takes a deep breath, manages to raise himself slightly but then falls back on his arse. "Told you it was heavy man. Can you just jump over us? And you ain't got a ciggie have you?"

Ignoring him I just jump between the two of them. As I turn my back on them I hear a loud retching, more demonic than human, a splatter on the floor, and cries of celebration.

After picking Dolly up her food, I return to find the two of them still there, both of them on their knees, laughing wildly and pointing to the floor. As I go to walk round them one of them tugs on my jeans. "Look man, look," he says all excited. "He's puked up a map of the United Kingdom!"

Barely able to believe what I'm seeing, the two of them run their fingers through the pile of puke trying to work out where Gravesend is on the map.

"I'm telling ya man, it's about here, right by this kidney bean!"

"No, no, it's more up this way ... wait a minute, when did you eat a fucking kidney bean?"

At the point of puking myself I leave the two arguing about the missing tin of chilli con carne in the cupboard.

I settle down on the sofa. Saturday used to be curry night but now that Julie has gone, it just wouldn't seem right ordering chicken madras. Plus, after seeing what I just did I wouldn't be able to stomach mushy food. I hear my phone ringing, erasing all thoughts of a puke shaped map of Asia. It's Jake. He's going to hassle me about going out tonight. Do I answer? I've got about 20 seconds to make my mind up. No, I can't go out. I haven't seen Jake in years and this means that I'll have to get my sociable head on. No, no, definitely not; I've not got much money anyway. But on the other hand, I have had a shitty couple of days. Ten seconds. Maybe a night out is what I need. What have I got to lose? I may enjoy myself. I hear the theme tune to Holby City coming from the television.

"Hello Jake."

"So, let me get this right: you've been dumped, you think that she's now banging someone else, you've been suspended, and you live alone with a cat named after Dolly Parton?" Jake says.

"That's pretty much it," I say.

Jake scrunches his face to try not to laugh and in doing so his nostrils and mouth look like the finger holes of a bowling ball. But then his nose starts to twitch, and his mouth expands into a canoe sized smile. "Fucking hell," he says with a chesty laugh, "Things sure are shit for you ain't they pal."

Sid then looks at Jake and laughs like a Jack Russell. I try to hide my embarrassment by basically squeezing my face into the pint glass.

Jake's laugh transforms into a bellowing cough. After he extinguishes it with a mouthful of lager he looks at me. "Shit," he says, "well if you thought you had it bad, just think of poor little Sidney here."

Sid starts to laugh in little nervous spurts. "Dunno what ya mean mate," he says.

"Well," Jake says as he leans towards me and I smell the steak and kidney pie he had for dinner, "young Sidney boy here has been banging a lazy-eyed prozzie down Denton way. He fucking loves her. And that's not all." He bangs his chest as if to knock some tar off his lungs. "The one serious bird he did have who wasn't a prozzie dumped him cos he gave her a dose of genital warts. His cock looked like a leper's arm!"

Jake is now curled over the table in laughter while Sid is whimpering like a Jack Russell left on his lead outside a shop for too long. "Yeah, well what about your one and only bird, Jake?"

The laughter stops, and Jake rises from his seat, towering above a red-faced Sid. "I swear Sid that if you carry on I'm gonna put that pint glass through your fucking teeth."

"Come mate, it's only a bit of banter," Sid pleads.

"That's not something to joke about. Now shut your fucking mouth or I'll shut it for you," Jake says.

Sid apologises. Silence for a moment or so before Jake sits down. "I'll tell you what though," Sid says as though he's trying to diffuse the situation. "That lazy-eyed prozzie licks my balls like they're strawberry flavoured gobstoppers. Now who wants a pint?"

The conversation turns to my job. I'm surprised to see Jake looking serious. It's as though he is absorbing my every word as I tell him exactly what it is that the company does. As I finish, he puts his arms over the side of the chair and looks like Henry the Eighth about to pass judgement.

"Your company have got it damn fucking right," he says. "Charity should start at home. I can't understand these people who wanna give their dosh to help people in other countries. Pete," he says, "we have homeless without shelter, children going to bed without grub, elderly going without needed meds, mentally ill without treatment, and servicemen and women fighting without the best kit. So, tell me, why would any English person in their right fucking mind want to help another country when all this is happening on their very own doorstep?"

I just nod and try to take cover in my glass again. Jake leans back and inspects his right hand as though it is a gun he is getting ready to use. I see that he has the St George flag tattooed on his wrist with the initials, 'D.O.R' inscribed above it. Before I can ask him what it means, he bangs his chest again to signal that he is about to speak.

"The fucking state of it," he says as he looks genuinely upset.

"Yeah, the fucking state of it," Sid says and nods his head as if the two are a ventriloquist act.

"It's as if people don't wanna be English no more," Jake says as he turns one of the chunky gold rings on his fingers.

People don't wanna be English anymore? I think of the pub I was in yesterday where I had the Croque Monsieur. Jake stares at the table, deep in thought; perhaps massacring a few of these people who have forgotten how to be English. I can see that he is in a world of his own, or at least he'd like to be.

"Where the fuck are we?" he says, gazing at the table. "Bombay? Poland? Kosovo? Albania? It's hard to tell walking through this fucking high street. And the thing is, these people manage to get jobs even in a recession, and if they don't, they get benefits." Jake then looks up at me. His eyes seem to demand an answer.

Sid nods his head again and says, "the fucking state of it."

"See what you mean mate," I reply.

"Do you know what?" he says. He leans forward as if he is about to tell a knock-knock joke.

"What?" I say.

"A business rival of mine is starting to steal my customers. And what really fucks me off about it is that he ... " Jake pauses and takes a deep breath. "Oh, fuck it; it doesn't matter. The fucking state of it."

"The fucking state of it," says Sid.

Silence forms a barrier around our table. The other punters' conversations hum like a distant pylon. Jake frowns and miniature trenches form in his forehead. He slouches in his chair like a bear that's just been shot with a tranquiliser. I remember how Jake said he was an events organiser. This one could do with a bit of organising. Before I can ask him what kind of events he organises and what customers he has lost, he stands.

"Let's get SMASHED," he roars.

Five pints, two Sambucas and three vodka Red Bulls later, we are walking down the high street towards Bar 24. Sid is singing

'Three Lions on a Shirt', while leapfrogging bollards. Jake is also trying to sing, although I don't think he knows the words. He just joins in at the chorus. The wind sweeps empty cans and cigarette ends down the street, which tells me that it's cold. But I don't feel it; I'm pissed. A few hours ago, I was intimidated walking through the town. Gravesend is like getting into a cold sea; once you get your shoulders under you're fine. Sid falls over a bollard, picks himself up then says, "Rack 'em up then Jake."

"Shut your mouth Sid," Jake says and looks towards me.

"Oh, come on mate, he's fine," Sid says.

"Are you fine?" Jake asks me.

"I'm fine thanks mate," I reply.

"But are you really fine? You know", Jake says as he taps his left nostril. "A bit of the old toot."

"Toot?" I ask.

"The old marching powder," Sid says as he over-exaggerates sniffing through his nose.

"Oh," I say. "Yeah."

"Come on then, let's have ourselves a little livener before the club," Jake says.

We walk down a side street. Jake hits the central locking and the three of us jump into an X-reg, silver BMW. Sitting in the back on cream coloured leather, I see a small red boxing glove hanging over the rear-view mirror. The smell of a crowded ashtray blends with the vanilla air freshener shaped like a tree. Sid pulls an empty CD cover out of the glove box and hands it to Jake.

"You ever done this before?" Jake asks as he pulls out a little plastic bag and tips some white powder onto the CD case.

"I used to do some. But that was years ago. I can't really remember what it was like now," I say.

"Must have been shit," Sid says as he dabs a bit on his finger and rubs it into his gums. "Now this stuff — this stuff here will blow you away."

"Why? What does it do?" I ask.

"It makes you untouchable, mate. You'll be on fire." He creates three lines with a bank card.

I know that I shouldn't, but I want to be untouchable, I want to be on fire, so fuck it. I take the rolled up twenty-pound note, put it to my nose and look down at the small line of cocaine. In one swift movement I sniff the coke.

"That's my boy," Jake says.

I don't feel much different as we walk back up the high street. If anything, I feel more sober.

"Oi Pete, how you feeling pal?" Jake says.

"Not bad actua ... " I stumble on my words and heave as I feel like a big bit of phlegm has lodged itself in my throat. Everything becomes louder, brighter, faster. My drunk brain is joined by a tense, exhilarating feeling; almost like a firework blowing my brain cells with a million dancing illuminations. My stomach sizzles, my joints are jumping, my fingertips tingle.

Jake and Sid both laugh. "It's just dropped now. Enjoy it bruvva," Jake says. We reach Bar 24. Jake whispers something in the ear of one of the bouncers. We walk straight to the bar. I get a head rush and I want to smoke and talk and drink and smoke and talk and drink and smoke and talk and drink.

I'm introduced to more people. Great people. Loads in common, I think. Loads of conversation. Words flying from my mouth like miniature Concordes. Drink? Yes please. Employment. Football. Tits. Arse. I'm now an expert on every subject. Cigarette? Yes please. On the dance floor, voddy and red in one hand, other in air moving to the music. LOVE IT, FUCKING LOVE IT Jake says, I think. LOVE IT, FUCKING LOVE IT, I say. I'm moving like John ... Drink? Yes please ... Travolta. Loads of girls. Bare legs, stilettos, bright colours, perfumes, swinging hair, swinging handbags. They looking at me? Must be. I'm pulling all the moves out. Grab one. Jake bear hugs a brunette. I follow suit. Grind hips, bend knees, mimic her moves, two become one. Turn her round. Kiss? Yes. Tongues? Yes. Sweet. Jake in ear. Line? Yes please. Toilets. Now. Ok. Jake whispers in bouncer's ear. Cubicle. Shit stained pan, piss on floor, bogeys on walls, wanna fuck? Call 07292 something written on door. Don't care. Talking about women and how fucking great this place is. Brilliant. Big sniff. Ouch. Mmm. Nice. Another one for the road? Yes please. Big sniff. Ouch. Mmm. Nice. Talk more. Back to dancefloor. Drink? Yes please. Cigarette? Sure. Find same girl. Kiss. Tongues. Hand on my arse. Hand on her arse. French knickers? No, thong. Nice. Whispers in my ear. Got any coke? YEAH! Er ... find Jake. Tell her to come back to mine for after party. Loadsa people. Loadsa coke. Loadsa sex. He roars. I roar. Tell girl. Bring your friends. Stop dancing. Talk more. Drink? Yes please. Employment. Football. Tits. Arse. Sex. I'm qualified. I just felt a thong on the dance floor. Sambuca for the road. Dance more. Grab girls. One more Sambuca for the road. Leave. Jake whispers in bouncer's ear. Parade through town centre. Girls. Me, Jake, Sid. Invincible. Own the street. Let's take a photo. We are a team. Pop that on Facebook. Girls laugh. Sid pisses up clocktower. Girls laugh. Chants of D-O-R, D-O-R, D-O-R. I chant too. D-O-R. D-O-R. D-O-R. Get to Jake's. Big. Plasma TV on wall. Boxing trophies. Film posters on wall. Music loud. More vodka. Beer chaser. Line? Yes please. Talk. More talk. Kiss girl. Going to get lucky. Doorbell rings. Jake looks on edge. Door opens. Familiar face. It's ok. Tony from Ella's Café. Still in shorts. Small world. Greet him like long lost brother. Kiss girl. Drink more. Cigarette. Fuckin love you Pete. Fucking love you too. Kitchen talk. Concorde words. The problem with this country. Islamic hatred. So fucking right. If my dear old mum were still alive ... Get a pen let's write this down. Line? Yes please. We have the right. We are English. Our countrymen are so few. Stop the hatred. Ignore our screams. In the shadows we lie. Keep writing Pete. This makes sense. Intellectual. Fucking poetic. Could be politician. All in agreement. Brilliant Pete. I'm on fire. Never been so passionate. Drink? Please. Talk to girl. Write some more Pete; on to a winner here. Ok. Be a patriot. Be real. Be English. Our traditions are dying. Extremists are rising. We will fight. Take back our land. Words on paper. Must print this up. Put it in the newsletter. Sure. By Pete Jarvis. No, no. By Reggie. Who? Never mind. Just write Reggie. Plain old Reggie. Kiss girl. Hand on my balls. Wanna take me home? YEAH! Dial taxi. Shit. Borrow tenner from Jake for fare. Goodbyes with my new best friends. Hugs. Love. Home. Bed. Underwear. Skin. But not Julie's skin. Fumbles. Not Julie's smell. Not Julie's touch. Just not her. What's wrong? Don't fancy me? Or you just too off your head? You're not ... you're not ... you're not her ... sleepy ... you're not her...

CHAPTER SIX

I was sitting in my bedroom sneaking a cigarette out of the window. I should've been revising for the GCSEs, but mum had her friends around and the music kept distracting me. I decided to call Julie. We usually spent a couple of hours on the phone each night. We'd play a game called 'Would You Rather'.

"Would you rather be invisible, or have the ability to fly?" Julie said.

"Oooh, that's a tough one. I think I'd rather be invisible," I said.

"Why?"

"Cos then I could sneak round to your house and see you in the bath."

"You cheeky git. Ok, here's another one. Would you rather be psychic, or the cleverest person in the world?"

"Easy. I'd be psychic because then I'd know what the questions are going to be in this exam," I said.

"But if you were the cleverest person in the world, then you would know what the answers were anyway," she replied.

"Oh yeah. Didn't think of that."

"Plus," she continues, "if you were psychic then you would know everything that was ever going to happen to you. Do you think you would like that?"

"I dunno."

"Ok, what about this. Would you rather be the fastest animal in the world like a cheetah, or the most feared like a lion?"

At that moment the doorbell rang, and the music went off. "Hang on a minute Julie," I said. I walked out of my room and stood at the top of the stairs.

Granddad barged his way in. "Get out all of you, you junkie bastards," he shouted.

Mum's friends stumbled out of the dim, smoke-filled living room. I crouched down.

"Leave off Dad," my mum said, clutching at a bottle, and swaying like a jack-in-the-box. "I'm not a kid."

Granddad looked towards the coffee table. "I've got a bloody right to say something when you're down here shoving all that powder up your nose and my grandson is up there revising for his exams." He kicked the table.

Mum didn't say anything. Granddad combed his fringe over and took a deep breath. "Sit down," he said. "I've heard that Kelvin's getting out soon."

"Oh, I don't give a shit about that tosser," she said, slurring her words, and refusing to sit down. She took another swig from the bottle.

Granddad poured the contents of a glass into the ashtray to extinguish a cigarette. He took the bottle from my mother.

Mum sits down and looks to the floor. She puts her hands to her head probably to try and stop it from spinning.

"I think we need to talk to Pete. What if he comes around looking for him?" Granddad said.

"We'll move," my mum said.

Granddad looked at the ceiling as if to help himself think more clearly. "That may help, but Pete's becoming a man now. I think he deserves to know what happened."

Mum started to cry. "But Dad, I've been shielding him from it all his life. All the rumours, the nasty things he got called at school. I've always told him not to listen. How can I now tell him they were true?"

I needed to hold onto something to stop me from falling. My father really did try to kill me? And they lied about it? To protect me? No. Fuck sympathy. I deserved the truth. Didn't I? Why did they lie?

"I think it's about time," my Granddad says.

"I'm scared," my mum says.

"We can't afford to be scared," he says.

I stumbled back into the room and remembered that Julie was on the phone. "Julie?" I said.

"Pete?"

"I'd rather be the most feared animal in the world ... like a lion."

The land line wakes me up. I feel terrible. Mum. Talking about roasted meat. I feel sick. And why is my mother being so motherly? I struggle to talk. I feel as if I've eaten a sandpit. Music and cocaine-fuelled conversations ring in my ears. I put the phone down and it sounds like a cannon. As I roll over I see a flurry of brown hair creep out of the covers. Blurry nakedness flashes before me. She stirs, pops her head out of the covers and looks at me. Is she as startled as me? I pull the covers over myself.

"Good morning," she says and pulls her hair into a pony tail, appearing not to care that her tits are exposed. I don't know where to look. I don't want her to think I'm pervy. Last night we were lovers, passionate lovers. Shakespeare would have put us in a play. Until I couldn't get it up. This morning we lie in bed, two naked strangers. But it wasn't right. It's mine and Julie's bed.

"So, you want a cuppa tea or something?" I say being careful to look her in the eyes.

"I gotta be off. The other half will be doing his nut having to get the kids up and dressed. Ta anyway," she says.

"No problem," is all I can say.

She doesn't get up. Is she expecting a quickie before she goes back to her family? She pulls at a loose thread on the quilt. Ripping and pulling things apart is a sign of sexual frustration isn't it? Not surprised after last night. On the other hand, I am feeling quite horny.

"Look," she suddenly says, grabbing me by the balls. "Are you going to give me one before I go or not?"

Fucking hell. She squeezes them tight. It feels as though my balls have moved into my stomach. "I can understand you having a flop on last night; it's just the coke and the booze innit. Happens a lot," she says pulling the sheet completely off her now, revealing a heart tattoo with JIMMY written inside of it, just below her belly button. "So, let's just forget about it yeah, and you can give me a fuck before I go,"

This just isn't happening. Not only am I thinking of Julie but I'm also picturing JIMMY as a big bastard, no teeth, and knuckles the size of snooker balls. With her hand on my balls she soon realises that it isn't happening either.

I feel about as small as my manhood now and sweat is rolling off me.

"You a homo or something?" she says, pulling at it like a dairymaid.

"What? No. Of course I'm not."

"Rahhhhh," she roars pulling the covers off her and getting on all fours mimicking a tiger. Then with her claws she pushes me in the chest. "Is this what you like huh? Rahhhhh, I'll fuck you like a wild animal, Rahhhhh, I'll fuck you like you've never been fucked before, Rahhhhh, yeah ... you want it ... yeah? Come on you pussy, fuck the tiger, fuck the tiger hard!"

She's pulling away at it like it's the only udder left in the world and I'm thinking some horrible shit. I'll never be able to watch an Attenborough programme again.

Then she grabs hold of my hair and yanks my head towards hers. "You don't want to fuck the tiger?"

"Shit! No, I don't want to fuck the tiger."

"Fuck. The tiger thing always works," she says letting go of my hair and looking as though her pride has seriously been dented.

"Look," I say rubbing my scalp, "I've got a girlfriend. Well I had one, anyway, it's kind of an interesting — "

"You're boring me now limp dick," she says. She gets out of bed and I see more tattoos of blokes' names on her arse. STU. TERRY. JOE. NEWTON. Newton? Lovers? Kids?

"I'm sorry, it just wouldn't be right," I say, my balls now throbbing.

She puts her clothes on and picks up her handbag. "Yeah, could you like not mention this to anyone? Cos I don't want people thinking I'm shit in bed. I mean if someone like you can't get it up with me, what are people gonna think? I'd never get laid again."

"Right ... "

"I'll see myself out. Sweetie."

I get up and strip the bed. Dolly looks at me like a disapproving parent as I walk to the kitchen. She actually shakes her head at me.

I place the sheets in the washing machine and then sit on the floor watching them go round and round in the water. My first failed one-night-stand puts my hangover on hold for a moment but then it comes racing back. Dolly strolls in and reminds me of Julie. My nose is bunged up and throbs. How much coke did I do? A pillowcase whacks against the glass as though it's desperately trying to escape.

I call Granddad to see if he wants to come to Mum's with me. He says he can't because he's got some very important Marmite pots to clean out before they go in the recycling bin.

The industrial air starts to clear as we move further away from Gravesend and the greys and browns blend into greens and reds. As we pull into Istead Rise, the village looks immaculate, as if someone has carefully constructed it with Lego. Lawns are mowed to football pitch perfection, roads shine like bowling alleys, and tree trunks looks like Kit-Kat Chunkies. I'm half expecting to see Postman Pat walk around the corner but instead I see Bruce sitting in front of the house with his shirt off and his eyes closed. What is he doing? All eyes on the bus turn towards him, so when I get off I pause before walking up the drive until the bus has disappeared.

Bruce sits on the lawn in front of his three-bedroom-semi with his silver Volkswagen parked on the drive behind his work van.

"Alright Bruce," I say.

No reply. "Bruce?"

The front door opens and my mother "sshhhs's" me. "He's doing his tai chi love, don't disturb him," she says.

In the porch I am greeted by the odours of joss-sticks and leather. I take my shoes off. Greasy work boots tower above flimsy sandals. A torn flight jacket hangs next to a jacket which looks like a skinned goat.

"Tai chi?" I ask, "I thought he was more of a judo man?"

"Oh," my mother says as she re-positions my shoes so they are symmetrical, "he likes to do both: judo for the physical and tai chi for the mental."

Couldn't have put it better myself. "So, why's he got his top off?" I ask.

"I don't know love. You'll have to ask him when he comes in."

The kitchen is a cross between one of those Chinese herbal remedy shops and a butcher's. A wildflower calendar hangs on the fridge. Underneath the calendar, magnets spell out 'Bruce Luvs Lilly'. By the kettle a bulky A-Team mug sticks out between petite china cups.

"Something smells good," Bruce says as he walks through the door and tenses his pectorals. "Bloody starving."

"Quick give him some rusks," I say.

He looks at me and bites his lip. "Oh Petey, scared the shit out of me you did. When did you get here?" he says as if he really didn't see me walk down the drive.

"You were doing your tai chi," I say.

"Sure," he says and sighs, "nothing distracts me during meditation. Focused. Another world. Peace and tranquillity."

"Sounds good," I say sarcastically.

"Vital to meditate. Vital to combine peace with hardness," he says as he tenses up.

Peace with hardness? Is he for real?

"I'm off to wash these beauties," he says as he kisses his biceps and then my mother's cheek.

When Bruce vanishes upstairs I want to ask her what the hell she sees in this big kid, but she looks like she's got into a warm bath after the attention she received from him. She sees that I disapprove and says, "He makes me smile Pete," before putting the Yorkshires in the oven.

"Can't beat a good roast," Bruce says as he smells his plate of food.

The coke and booze still in me aren't having any of this eating business. The food looks good, but my stomach feels like a deflated balloon. My jaw hurts just chewing on a Brussels sprout.

"Isn't this nice love," my mother says to me. "Just like an ordinary family."

Bruce rolls his eyes as he chomps away at a slice of rare beef smothered in horseradish sauce. "Traditional thing for families to do on a Sunday, ain't it? Have a roast like," he says with a sarcastic smile aimed towards me.

His words hit me like tinfoil on a filling. "First of all, Bruce, we are not a fucking family, and secondly, I'm fed up of this traditional thing to do. There are always traditional fucking things to do. But why do them? Because it's traditional to have a roast on Sunday? Because it's traditional to have fish on a Friday? Traditional to listen to Cliff fucking Richard at Christmas? Traditional to leave school after A-Levels, go to university, get a degree, get a job, get a wife, get a house, have kids, pay your mortgage, pay your tax, retire and die?"

"Whoa, mate," Bruce says. "Slow down. It's Sunday."

And is it traditional, I think, for one's mum to get involved with a muddleheaded, meditating, musclebound dickhead? I become dizzy, I feel as though I'm on the giant conveyor belt of life.

I begin to wonder what it would be like to turn it the other way around. Start life from the day of your funeral, get put into a residential home and have your pension to spend. Then instead of things getting worse, they get better. Your hair starts to grow again, you get your own teeth back and you ditch the Zimmer frame. Next you leave the home and start employment on an excellent wage. Although your wages decrease you won't really care because the only money you need to spend is on alcohol and clothes. After employment you shag your way through university and the work gets easier as you pass from secondary school to junior to infant school. You believe in Santa again. What a fucking treat that would be. Christmas once again becomes great and magical, and by now you are even getting spoon-fed and having your arse wiped for you. Finally, when death comes, it comes easily, and it isn't painful at all. After all, you will be zero years old and you won't feel a thing because all you will be is a tiny cell, happily swimming around each day and shrinking into nothing; an ice lolly melting in the sun.

"Pete?" my mum says.

"Yeah?"

"I just said that it's a shame Julie can't join us today," she says.

I know I should tell her the situation, but I really can't be arsed. I don't want to be drawn into a serious conversation when I'm feeling like shit, plus I don't want Bruce knowing my business. I just want to get this roast over and done with. "Yeah, it's a shame," I mumble.

The three of us munch, sip, and murmur. My mother keeps looking at me as though something is still on her mind. Her head bobs up and down like a turd that won't flush. If she knows that I've been to see my father, then I'd rather she just came out with it.

"Look mum, I don't mean to be rude, but can you just say whatever it is that you want to say?"

She looks to Bruce and then back at me. "What do you mean love?" she stutters.

"No disrespect mum, but how many times have you been to visit me in my flat? How many times have you invited me over for a roast? And why were you asking me to go to a judo tournament? I know when you've got something on your mind. So just come on out and tell me," I say.

"What, love?" she says.

"I think we should just tell him Lilly baby," Bruce says.

Tell me what? Oh, wait a minute. Fuck no. This can't be happening. They link hands over the table. The 'we've-got-some-good-news' look. Except it really fucking isn't.

"Well love, Bruce and I have decided to ... "

"Just don't say it for fuck's sake," I interrupt.

Mum looks at me with eyes like a timid guinea pig and Bruce looks at me with the eyes of a tyrannosaurus rex. "I thought you might be happy for us," she says.

"Did you really?" I say.

"Of course I did, love, I always think about you," she replies.

"No, you don't mum. That's the problem. You never think about me, only yourself," I say as I stand up from my seat. "You can't marry him mum. He's younger than you. He'll probably get bored of you soon. And look what else he does. He employs foreign labourers for cheap wages when there are so many English people out there looking for work. That's not the kind of man you want to marry mum."

Bruce stands up to face me, sticking his chest out and clenching his fists. His cheeks flood with rage. "Fuck does that have to do with you?" he says. "You standing for Parliament?"

I find myself pointing my finger at Bruce. "You don't give a shit about anything other than yourself and lining your own pockets. So how could you give a shit about my mum?"

"You cocky little ... " he says inching closer to my face. The red in his cheeks turns a bruise-like-purple. He reveals his gums like an angry Rottweiler. A stringy piece of saliva hangs from his front two teeth. "You talk a load of crap you know that?"

"Yeah," I say before thinking of something else to say. "What about kids? Bruce hasn't got any kids, and what if he wants some? You're too old for that mum. You can't have kids at your age."

"That's none of your fucking business," Bruce says and then looks to my mother. "Just be happy for your mum. Just because she married a fuckup before doesn't mean she's going to marry another one."

I feel Bruce has overstepped the mark, commenting on someone he has never even met, that someone being my father. "He might be a fuckup, but he is my fuckup." Bruce stares at me; for the first time in my life I'm defending my father. "From where I'm standing, you look the biggest fuckup ever. You might do alright for yourself; but you sure as fuck don't deserve it. Are you happy knowing that some local workers with families are living on the dole just because you would rather employ a cheap foreigner with no experience?"

"You little fucking bastard," he says with a face that now looks like it's going to melt. Even his ears are throbbing. "I don't give a shit what you think."

My mother bangs her fists on the table. "Will you two just shut up?"

Bruce takes hold of my mother's hand. As for me, I'm on a roll. "Stop the tears mum. You're just selfish; you always have been. And I've got some news myself," I add. Both of them look up at me. Part of me knows that I shouldn't, but I want to get even. "I've been to see my father."

"What?" my mum asks.

"You heard me. I found out where he works, and I've been to see him. Got a problem with that?" I say.

My mum pushes her plate away and rests her head on the table. Bruce stands up and tells me to get out as he leans over and covers my mother. A human shield.

"Thanks for the roast," I say on my way out.

Darkness starts to seep into the village. The perfect white front doors seem luminous. The village is an X-ray. This village needs an X-ray. A sharp wind chills my bones but I don't care. I boycott the bus stop. I just need to walk; walk as far as my skeleton will take me. Hills, fields, pavements; they're all irrelevant. I just need to walk.

CHAPTER SEVEN

Jake has sent me a message telling me that he wants to pop around tonight. So, I text him back with my address and tell him to come over in a couple of hours.

Dolly looks in the mood for an argument, but I haven't got the energy. Instead I fill her bowl with some dinner and she looks shocked. She looks at the food as if it's some kind of sick joke, but when she sees me walk into the hallway she soon realises that it's not. I go to put the heating on to warm this frozen shoebox up. Back in the living room, I jump onto the sofa, pull the sleeping bag over me, and shut my eyes for a moment or so.

Bruce and my mum's planned marriage is doing its best to stop me from sleeping. But my thoughts on this start to flicker and then there is a knock at the door.

I roll off the sofa and stumble to the door. When I open it, Jake looks hazy.

"You alright pal? You look like shit," he says.

"Err yeah, I'm just knackered, that's all," I say.

"So, nothing to do with the fact you got wasted last night then?" he says as he makes his way into the living room.

"Probably something to do with that too," I say.

"Got a bit of a fuzzy head myself after last night," he says as he bangs his head as though it's a crackling radio. "Great night though. So, did you end up banging that bird?"

"Er, no," I say, "I don't know how all that happened; I don't even know her name."

"Don't give me that pal. You don't have to be shy. Cyndi's her name. She never lets the lads down. Mind you pal, I hope you put something on the end of it. She's a baby-making machine; must have at least six little chavvies running about. Suits her fine though. Good career if you think about it. Pop a few babies out, look after 'em, get a free house, get the bills paid for ya plus a bit of extra dosh for yourself, and then drop the kids off with their fathers at the weekends so you can go out and get pissed. I bet she gave you the old tiger routine too. Fuck the tiger, right?"

Just as I start thinking about ambition, careers, and how I'm glad that I didn't fuck the tiger, Jake says, "You know you had a good night though, hey pal? Sometimes it's good to let a little steam off. And after talking to you I feel that you need to let a shitload of steam off."

"I sure do mate. I just feel so wound up at the moment," I say.

"Yeah, I bet you do, after what you told me last night I'd be wound up too," he says.

"It's just so fucking frustrating."

"Don't you worry about it. Uncle Jake's here now and all the lads last night thought you were a diamond. Last night was your baptism," he says.

I laugh. "Yeah, they were all a great bunch."

"Oh, and you were on form with that thing you wrote. In fact, it was so good I've handed it in to the D.O.R newsletter. I had to make a few changes, but I got it in just on time. It should be going to print tomorrow," he says as he slides his shoes off and rests his feet on the table. "And I like your pen name; Reggie. It's got a ring to it."

Memories of last night flash by like scenery from a moving train: the tattoo on his hand, the chants of D.O.R, the pen in my hand, Islamic hatred, words, words, and more words. "What was D.O.R again?" I say feeling quite embarrassed.

"Shit, you must have been wasted. Quite simply, it's the way forward," he says.

Jake springs up as though he has just been resuscitated and I can tell this is something he is passionate about. "What do you think of this country pal?" he says as he stretches his arms in the air. Before I can answer he says, "It's broke; completely fucking broken."

I sit back and watch Jake as he paces up and down speaking as though he is preparing a speech.

"I know you agree with me Pete. I know how fucked off you are playing by the rules and getting a raw deal. This country is unrecognisable now; a fucking disgrace. The glory days have gone. But the Defenders of the Realm are changing things; trying to get them back. We are really starting to make a difference. We're being heard, Pete, and we are trying to wipe out all the shit that is ruining England. Our country has become a laughing stock."

Jake pauses for breath, puts his hands on his hips and looks at me. I feel the anger radiating from him. "The D.O.R gives a voice to those who aren't supposed to be heard. People like us Pete." He wipes some sweat from his forehead and bangs his chest. "Just as I said yesterday, people don't wanna be English anymore. But I fucking well do. Don't you? Don't you want you see a better future, a brighter one?"

It would be nice to see things in a colourful light ...

I find myself standing up to join him. "So, what do we do about this then?" I say.

Jake looks at me with a slight smile. He kind of inflates and looks as though he's in his own personal spotlight. "We fight back pal. We go on demonstrations and rallies. We urge people to be patriotic, be true and be English. We want everyone to wake the fuck up, and anyone who seeks to fuck our country up even more is going down too."

"Going down?" I ask.

He turns to look at me; he raises his eyebrows and the jagged scar above his eyebrow sharpens. "We are not a violent group but sometimes you have to be harsh to be kind."

Suddenly I feel proud. I feel brave. I feel alive; almost as if the coke from last night has reignited and exploded into every cell in my body. Right now, I feel I could take on an entire army. Jake's smile indicates some sort of brotherly emotion, as though we are in this together; as though we are now comrades. He sits back down next to me and seals this new relationship with a pat on my shoulder. "We are rallying in London. Trafalgar Square, next weekend. Fancy it?"

I nod. "For sure."

He puts his chunky arm around me and squeezes. "I fucking knew it. I knew you had it in you. You fucking beauty," he says.

We take a seat and Jake pulls out his phone. "I'm just sorting the rally out now."

"You texting other members then?" I ask.

"Nah, we've got a group on Facebook and we also spread the word by this BlackBerry Messenger thing. It's quite handy really. No one can trace the messages apparently."

"Fucking hell. That Facebook thing is everywhere, isn't it? All you ever see on TV is social networks this and social networks that," I say.

Jake doesn't seem to be listening as he continues to tap the buttons on his phone. I start to think more about social networks. It's a scary thought how much influence these things have and how quickly rumours can travel through them. I mean some people could really fuck things up. Imagine a World War 3 started through Facebook. I begin to picture a future where Facebook is like Big Brother. Not the stupid brain-draining, arse-numbing reality show, but Orwell's Big Brother. I remember reading *1984* in school. I see it clearly. Facebook basically orchestrate a massive civil war. The government is squashed, the royals are dethroned, and the army and police end up switching sides because their wives or mothers have a profile on Facebook. And then here comes the clever part. Facebook release a rumour that a nuclear gas has been released.

The country is advised to stay indoors. It soon spreads and before you know it we find ourselves living in a world in which everyone is confined to their houses and the only way of communicating is through networking. The social networking site now rules the country. Any thoughts of rebellion are impossible to materialise because the Facebook police regulate everything that appears on the screen. Then we live out the rest of our days, learning how a girl you used to go to school with paints her toenails a different colour every fortnight.

When Jake leaves, I run a bath. I check my phone: still nothing from Julie. She and the professor are probably fucking in a library somewhere after getting turned on by reading Freud. Sick fuck. Thinking of mothers reminds me of my own. Not about banging her of course. Maybe I was a bit out of order telling her that I'd been to see my father. But fuck it — she's moved on, she'll be ok. She's got Bruce anyway. Besides, what's she done for me lately? But I don't want to think about it. I feel almost like a new man as I ease my balls in to the bath. I leave my hands out of the water for a few minutes just so that I get a nice feeling when I put them under. It works every time. The Trafalgar Square rally and the D.O.R run through my mind. A strange feeling hits me. I feel excited. I feel big things are about to happen. For the first time in ages I've got something to look forward to.

That night I dream Jake is cradling me in his arms. Then I'm in a church. It's the wedding of Bruce and my mother. Jake kicks the doors open and walks down the aisle. "Get the fuck out," he says to the couple waiting to seal the deal, "we've got more important things to do here." As my mother and Bruce make their way out, Jake holds me over the holy water font. When I look up, my father, the priest, dabs holy water on my forehead. "We are gathered here for the baptism of Peter Jarvis," he says.

I wake to the sound of shouting and barking. As I drag myself out of bed, I look down to see three men with two bullmastiffs arguing about money. The balding grass with decapitated dandelions is their arena. Above them, dreary grey clouds gather like people at a wake. The one shouting the loudest is wearing fake Adidas trousers, no top, and a No Fear baseball cap. His whole torso is covered in tattoos but it's hard to distinguish any of them. From up here it just looks as though he has been attacked by a school kid with a fountain pen. Holding his breakfast in his hands, a can of Super Tennant's extra strong lager and a roll-up, he seems sure that one of the other men owes him twenty quid. The defendant, who has a head full of stubble and scars, swears on his baby's life that it is only a tenner that he owes him. His skinny arms look like twiglets as they dangle out of his nicotine-stained vest. The last of the trio wears glasses, an all-in-one purple shell suit and looks like a crackhead version of Timmy Mallet. I'm half expecting him to pull out a pink foam mallet and hit the other two idiots over the head. Crackhead Timmy is holding on to the two hyperactive bullmastiffs, trying to get a word in, in his quest to borrow two quid to buy some tobacco. The whole thing sounds like a broken record: "Twenty quid you prick". "Tenner; swear on my baby's life", "woof, woof", "lend me two quid". One of the bullmastiffs cocks his leg, and just as I see that the clouds have followed suit, I close the window and decide to start the day. Broken, I think.

I start the most hated day of the week by feeding Dolly. I wonder if she knows it is Monday. Is every day the same for her? Sometimes I envy the furry little fucker.

It feels weird not having work on a Monday, so I decide to go for a walk into town. Not for the exercise so much; mainly because I need some smokes.

I'm walking out of Asda and someone shouts, "Oi! Fuckhead!"

I turn to see the Smurf Shady kid I fell into on the bus the other morning. He walks towards me and puts his hood up as if he's putting on a helmet to prepare for battle. Two others draped in sportswear follow him. One dressed in red and one dressed in green, an evil Little Red Riding Hood and a bad-ass Robin Hood.

"You know what blood?" he says in a half-American, half-English accent. "You fucked me up during my lyric the other day blood." He mimics a gun with his hand and points it at my head. "Falling into me and shit. You a fuckin faggot or sometin?"

"W-what?" I say.

"Shut your mouth you stuttering fuck," Smurf Shady says while still pointing this imaginary gun at my head. "What you gonna give me to say sorry?"

"Look, sorry about that. I was having a bad day. I'm sorry mate," I say.

He pushes his imaginary gun into my forehead. "Sorry ain't good enough. You get me?"

Red Riding Hood steps forward and says; "You heard him bruv. Sorry ain't good enough. You distracted his music innit. Now you have to pay."

"What are you on about?" I say.

"Don't get lippy blood," Smurf Shady says.

"How much money you got on ya?" Robin Hood says.

"I've got nothing on me," I say as I pat my pockets somehow hoping that this will make them believe me.

"I'll be the motherfuckin' judge of that," Smurf Shady says as he comes towards me. He winks at me as he goes to put his hands into the inside pocket of my jacket.

With as much force as I can, I push him away and just run. I run as fast as I can, dodging people and cars. I glance back and see them chasing me. It's times like these when I wish I didn't smoke. My lungs are giving way, my heart is working overtime, and I'm short of breath. Then my legs are kicked. I totally give way and end up flat on my face outside the doorway to a shop. I manage to crawl in hoping that I'll be able to take refuge. No such luck. The Merry Men stand over me.

"Look mate, I'm really sorry. I don't want any trouble," I manage to say.

"Too late for that punk," he says. Punch to the side of my face. Muffled noises. Echoed shouts. Blurred floor tiles. Flying feet. Hand to nose. Hand to ribs. Instinct says cover head. More flying feet. Pain? Not too bad. Adrenaline?

"Get out, you bloody hooligans," a man's voice says.

I peer through my hands and see an Asian guy that I recognise.

"Shut the fuck up you Paki wanker," Smurf Shady says. "You fucking want some as well do ya?"

The feet stop flying towards me. "Get the fucking till while we're here," Red Riding Hood says.

Smurf Shady jumps the counter and the Asian man puts his hands in the air to signal he doesn't want any trouble. Smurf Shady then pulls the till out and runs towards the door following the other two. He tries to get over me lying in the doorway, but I stick my leg out and sweep his legs from under him. He falls. The till drops. Money falls everywhere. Smurf Shady jumps up, leaves the money and kicks me once more. "You'll regret this blood, I'm gonna fuckin gut you," he says to me as he runs out the door.

The Asian man comes over and offers me his hand to help me up. "Are you ok?" he says.

I wince as I feel a pain in my ribs. "I think I'm ok."

He looks at me and turns my head from side to side. "Everything seems to be in the right place. I would call the police, but they never bother," he says.

"People have robbed you before then?" I say.

"Oh yes, on many occasions. But the police have more important things," he says and laughs. "Can I get you a drink or anything?"

"No, I'm fine. Thank you."

"It's me that should be thanking you. You stopped them from getting away with my till. That's twice you have stuck up for me now. It is something that I won't forget," he says.

I try to think back. I do recognise him. "Of course," I say, "you were the man on the bus with them little shits spitting on you."

"That's right," he says.

"Didn't that bother you?" I say.

"Of course it bothers me. But this is just the way it is. Gravesend is full of horrible bastards and it's never going to change."

I dust myself off and stretch my arms out. "I just really wanted to hurt that arsehole," I say. "I've got to be honest I didn't even think about him robbing your shop at the time. I just wanted to get even."

"Don't we all," he says. "The name is Hasan. Pleased to meet you."

"Pete Jarvis," I say as I shake his hand.

"Can I offer you anything from my store Pete? I'd like to give you a bottle of something to say thank you," he says.

"No, honestly it's fine. I'd just like to get home now," I say.

"Well anytime you want a bottle of booze or a pack of cigarettes or anything else, please don't hesitate to drop by. It would be a gift from me."

As I make my way out the door he starts to pick the money up. "I hope that one day I can stick up for you," he says.

Walking back to my flat, I feel like an accidental hero. But a hero on edge. I keep looking over my shoulder to make sure I'm not being followed. When I get indoors Dolly lingers around the living room looking smug as though she somehow knows that life is pretty wank at the moment. I don't fancy sitting in by myself tonight, so I ring Jake to see what he's up to.

"Fucking hell pal, that's a bit of a nasty bruise," Jake says as he opens the door. "Come on in and tell me how you got that."

Everything about Jake's front room typifies him. The two armchairs are made of tough brown leather with stocky armrests. They sit in the middle of the room like two bulldogs on guard. In front of the armchairs is a solid pine table with numerous copies of Auto-Trader resting on top of a sheet of cocaine-smudged glass. A light, which looks more like a punchbag, rests in the corner of the room. On the wall a chunky round clock with bold numbers rests between a black and white print of Rocky Balboa and a Moonraker film poster with Roger Moore aiming his pistol. A cabinet displays a few boxing trophies and a framed photograph.

"They make me fucking sick," Jake says after I tell him about the incident. "Most of them scumbags bowl around with their pants hanging out of their jeans. I mean what the fuck is all that about it? A few years ago, a fella who walked around with his pants out, would have been called a nonce. Now people think they are tough."

"Yeah," I say, "on the bus the other day, some of these bastards were bullying an old fella. He was shit-scared too."

Jake strains as though he is constipated. "These two-bob wankers don't even talk English. Anyone would think they're from the Bronx the way they carry on. It's as if they have invented their own language too. 'Yeah blood, innit, you getting me blood.' What is all that about?"

I laugh. "That's exactly the way they were talking today."

Jake leans forward. "But it ain't a laughing matter Pete. These wannabe-gangsters are yet another skid mark on the pants of English society. These people are just the type of scum that the D.O.R are trying to stamp out too."

"So, is it a big group?" I ask.

"Gets bigger and bigger by the day. Our unit is at least a hundred strong. We've got members from Gravesend, Dartford, Bexleyheath, and some of the Medway towns like Chatham and Rochester. We've got a meeting tomorrow night to sort out the rally in London. You're coming, right?"

"I'll be there," I say.

Jake sits back satisfied with my answer. "SIDNEY," he shouts, "put the kettle on pal, dying of thirst here."

"I didn't know Sid was here," I say.

"Fraid to say he is pal. The little shit is staying in the spare room up there till he manages to sort a place of his own out," he says.

Sid comes running down the stairs in just a pair of boxer shorts; he's all hair and bones and looks like an anorexic caveman. "Alright Pete," he says as he runs into the kitchen to put the kettle on. "Er, Jake mate, can I borrow your beard trimmer?"

"No, you can't," Jake says.

"Why not mate?"

"Because I know what you do with it you little gobshite."

"That pube was not mine," Sidney says.

"Well who's was it then? You and me are the only ones living in this house you fucking doughnut."

Sidney looks down as though he has just discovered something on his nipple, perhaps to bide some time to think of an answer. "It wasn't mine," is the best he can do.

Jake shakes his head. "I don't know why he even bothers to shave his balls," he says to me. "The only person who sees them is himself. How many sugars do you have Pete?"

"Two please, mate," I say.

"Pete has two sugars Sid," he says, "and I'll have half a one today. Nice one pal."

When Sid walks in with the tea and some biscuits, he notices the bruise above my eye. "Bloody hell Pete, you been fighting?" he says.

"Oh, well done clever fucking clogs," Jake says. "Put some clothes on, you're putting me off me Hobnobs."

"Yeah Sid," I say, "I've had a pretty shitty day today."

"Looks like it," Sid says as he runs off to put some clothes on.

"Yep I'm broke as a joke and with Julie gone, I haven't got a clue how I'm going to pay the rent," I say.

Jake suddenly disappears upstairs for a while. He emerges again holding a bundle of cash. "How much is a week's wages pal?" he says.

I feel myself turning red. "Oh no, I couldn't mate," I say.

"Pete," he says, "what are mates for? Now stop mugging me off and tell me how much a week's wages are for fuck's sake."

"Well about two-hundred-and-seventy quid, something like that," I say.

Jake licks his finger the way a bank clerk would do. "Here's three-fifty. A little extra so you can buy me a pint tonight," he says.

"I feel really bad about this, but thanks a lot mate. I swear I'll pay you back as soon as I can," I say.

"I know you will, otherwise I'll force feed you Sidney's arse hair from my beard trimmer," he says followed by a chesty laugh.

I go over and look at a framed picture on the cabinet: a photo of a young Jake with his mother.

"Wanna know why I started boxing?" Jake says. "I started boxing for that wonderful woman right in front of you," he says pointing at the photo.

"Did she want you to box?"

Jake shakes his head. "Far from it. She would never want me to get hurt. I started to do it so that one of us could hit back."

"Hit back at who?" I ask.

"You can choose your friends, but you can't choose your fucking family." Jake stares into the photograph. "She's a fantastic woman she is. Everyone should love their mum. But they don't. How can you bring children into this world only for them to mug you off?"

"What do you mean?"

"I got so many brothers and sisters floating about, I don't even know all of them. But the ones I do know are scum. I mean how can you fuck your own family over? Your very own flesh and blood?"

His voice sounds shaky and I go to put my hand on his shoulder. The hairs on my arms stand up. I feel an affinity towards him. Suddenly I don't feel so alone. "I know how you feel," I say.

I feel compelled to tell Jake everything about my father. But Sidney comes running down the stairs. "Fucking hell you two, you want me to fetch the Lionel Ritchie CD, some candles and bottle of wine?" he says.

I laugh as I remove my hand from his shoulder. Jake puts the photograph down and clears his throat. "You'd love that, you little fucking perv. Just cos you ain't had no pussy for years. Little shit," he says. "Now come on you bum bandits, let's go and meet Tone and then get down the boozer."

CHAPTER EIGHT

Jake pulls up outside Wallis Park. This housing estate has loads of little houses all built the same and overlapping each other. It looks a bit like a Butlin's. In Afghanistan. A feeble cat strolls along a garden wall searching for food but doesn't appear to have the energy to catch any birds or mice. Some school-kids are kicking a Coke can around in the middle of the street, using a burnt-out Ford Sierra as a goalpost. Jake pulls open the BMW logo in the centre of the steering wheel and picks out a small bag. He tells us that he won't be long and when he returns he pats the pockets of his jeans and says "ka-ching."

We meet Tone at the café. We head towards the pub. Big Tone leads the way wearing his brand-new West Ham football shorts and seems to be taking great pride in every step he takes. The wind is an aggressive fucker tonight so keeping him at least partly warm is a beige-coloured Stone Island fleece. On the other side of the road, Bruce's car valeting place looks as though it's closing up. I lower my head as some of the Kosovan workers emerge wearing out-of-date football shirts, Gola tracksuit trousers, and moccasins. A bit further up the street Tony gives a Big Issue seller a fiver without taking a copy of the magazine. "You know," he says to us, "old matey standing there probably wouldn't have to stand out here freezing his nuts off selling that shit if people like them," he points back to the Kosovans, "weren't taking all the local jobs working for lower wages. If my dear old mum were still alive ... "

The King's Head: Henry the Eighth on a sign above the doorway. Inside, the floor is sticky, the tables are sticky, the toilet floor is soaked, and the chairs are wobbly.

"So then matey, Jake tells me you're gonna be joining us?" Tony says to me and gives me a playful jab to the ribs.

I wince because my ribs are still sore from the kicking I got earlier. "Er, yeah, Defenders of the Realm, right?"

"Hell fucking yeah, the D.O.R," he says and raises his glass. Jake and Sid raise theirs followed by a quick chant of "D-D-D.O.R, D-D-D.O.R."

"I think you'll fit right in," Tony says. "It's a real good cause. It's something you can be proud..." Tony suddenly pauses and looks at Sid, "What the fuck you drinking Sid?"

"Beck's. Why?" he asks.

Tony laughs and looks at me. "We forgot to tell you that Sidney's a Kraut, didn't we?"

"Ya, ya. Ich bin Sidney," Jake says as he holds two fingers under his nose and salutes with his other hand.

Soon the drinks are flowing, and a few snorts of cocaine are being passed around on a two pence piece. Tony is doing most of the talking. He's been ejected and banned from most of the football stadiums in England. He says that he has grown out of football hooliganism and has found something sincere, something for the greater good, something which makes him feel alive. He claims that he wakes up each morning with a smile knowing that his mum in the urn would be proud of him for being a part of the D.O.R. Sidney's mouth has gone into light-speed and he is speaking of how he wants to start a business around town called 'Princess Pocahontas Tours'. But as Jake points out, no one ever visits Gravesend — why would they? Plus, she was dead before she even got off the boat, "so where the fuck will you take people on the tour?" Jake notices a tall, gangly fella, with sideburns the size of lamb-chops walking into the pub. I recognise him to be the same man that Jake saw when I first met him and Sid in the St George's Centre. Jake's eyes fierce and he starts to bite his nails. He tries to keep engaged in the current conversation, but his gaze keeps averting to the tall man standing at the bar. "Oi Percy," he calls out to the man. Percy sees Jake and swallows as if he has no saliva. "Oh Jake, hiya mate, ain't seen you for a long time," he says looking as nervous as a guy in a line up.

"I know you ain't. Wonder why that is?" Jake says. "Well don't just stand there Percy, bring them big old sideburns over here and say hello."

Percy looks worryingly towards the barman. The barman just lowers his head and Percy scuffles towards our table as if he's walking the plank. Jake gets up out of his chair and ruffles Percy's hair. "Where the fuck you been all my life Percy?"

"I, er, I've been around mate," he says.

Jake looks at Percy as though the man has just had offered to buy him a shandy. "I know exactly where you've been," he says.

Percy's face turns the shade of a strawberry bonbon. "Look mate, I hope I haven't offended you in some kind of way."

"Oh," Jake says and leans his head to one side, "and why would you have offended me Percy, apart from waving those big old sideburns in front of my face?"

Tony and Sid both start to laugh. Percy starts to laugh as well, nervously, as if he has just been told a terrible joke. "Oh no reason Jake, just thought you seemed a bit off with me, that's all," he says.

Jake laughs and ruffles Percy's hair again. "Would I be off with my old pal Percy?"

"Guess I'm just being stupid," Percy says.

"You said it Percy. I guess you just are pretty stupid," Jake says. "You like fruit machines Percy? Bit of a gambler?"

"Not really mate, no."

"Great," Jake says, "me too. Let's have a quick go on the machine just there and see if lady luck is on our side."

"But..."

"Come on Percy, don't be stupid now," Jake says.

He puts his arm around Percy's neck and leads him to the fruit machine just to the right of our table. "Gotta quid then?" Jake asks. Percy reaches into his pocket and puts a coin into the fruit machine.

The machine fails to light up and makes a 'nir nir' noise, signalling that they haven't won.

"Ahh, fuck it. We didn't win Percy. Guess it's not your lucky day," Jake says.

Percy laughs nervously again. "I guess not," he says.

Jake looks around the pub and then lowers his voice, it still being loud enough for us to hear. "So why don't you come to see me anymore Percy?" he says.

"Er, money's just been tight lately."

"I see," Jake says clamping his tongue between his teeth again. "But you've still got enough dosh to go and see them though, haven't ya pal?"

"Look mate, I don't want any trouble ... "

"I know you don't Percy, cos you're not stupid, are ya pal?"

"N-n-no. It's just their prices are cheaper Jake," Percy says.

"Ahh," Jake says and pulls Percy's cheek like he's a grandmother doting on a cute baby. "So, you'd rather line their pockets for just a few quid less than line the pockets of one of your own?"

"It's not like that Jake, I swear," Percy says.

"Well from where I'm standing it seems exactly like that. In fact, Percy, I think you're a fucking disgrace," Jake says and tugs on Percy's cheek harder.

"N-n-no, it's just if something is cheaper then I'm going to go elsewhere. It's as simple as that. Sorry mate. I didn't mean to piss you off."

Jake lays his other hand on Percy's left shoulder. "Percy, Percy, Per-fucking-cy. It seems to me that you don't know the meaning of loyalty. If everyone thought the way that you do, then there would be no trust, friendship, or honour left in the world, would there?"

Percy's jaw drops in line with his Adam's apple. "What? Sorry mate. I don't understand."

"Exactly. And you never will Percy. If I were you, I'd grab your passport, get to Gatwick, and catch the first plane to a country that wants you. Try India; you seem to love those people so fucking much more than your own countrymen," Jake says.

"Oh, come off it Jake, it's not tha... " Percy goes to say.

"Percy, Percy, Percy," Jake says and gives him a slap on the cheek. "You really are one stupid wanker. If I hear just one more tiny little word out of that stupid, stupid mouth of yours, I'm going to put that stupid, stupid head of yours through that fruit machine. Now take your stupid fucking sideburns and fuck off."

Percy scrambles out of the door and Jake returns to a round of applause. He sits down and raises his glass. "To honour," he says.

To honour, I think, as I sit back in my chair and feel the alcohol and coke starting to seep into my bloodstream.

Drink? Please. D-D-D.O.R. D-D-D.O.R. Fucking love England. Fucking love it. I'd cheat on my wife with England. If you had one, you ugly bastard. We are the greatest. Why are we the greatest country in the world? Line? Please. I'll tell you why. Sniff. Cos we invented time. What? Line? Please. Greenwich Mean Time. GMT. Not Edinburgh Mean Time. Not Dublin Mean Time. No. Laughs. GMT. GMT. GMT. We tell the rest of the world when it's time for bed and time to wake up. Drink? Please. Who needs the pissy little Ireland and Scotland anyway? Wales? Ha, what the fuck is all that about? Fly the cross of St George, not the Union Jack, Let the world know we want our England back. En-ger-land. En-ger-land. En-ger-land. Need a piss. Jake pisses too. Bog chat. Know why I do what I do? No, why? Line? Please. Because there is nothing else to do. Ahh. Piss feels good. People like us don't get many chances. We get a false start. Understand? Yeah. Course I do. Knew it. Fucking love you. No, no, fucking love you pal. Line? Please. Don't have many options. All the jobs are taken. Even my trade is being threatened. Traitors like Percy the prick don't help. Ha. Percy the fucking pig. Stinking sideburns. Stupid bastard. D-D-D.O.R. D-D-D.O.R. You see this girl. What girl? Line? Sniff. My girl. No my ex. Fuck knows. Drink? Please. Julie. Says I don't fit in. Fuck her. Forget about her. You're part of the brotherhood. Like ... Like ... Like a fucking crusader or some shit. Yeah. Fly the cross of St George, not the Union Jack, Let the world know we want our England back. En-ger-land. En-ger-land. En-ger-land. Yeah, a knight of the round fucking table. Cigarette? Yeah. Sniff. I'd be

Arthur. No, I would be. I'd be Lancelot then. The good-looking fucker. Ha. No way. You couldn't fuck Guinevere. Well you couldn't fuck yourself. I'll fuck you up the Merlin in a minute. Up the Merlin? Ha. Up the fucking Merlin. Great bloke. True patriot. We love you Merlin we do, we love you Merlin we do, oh Merlin we love you. Drink? Yeah. Sniff. Great piece you wrote Pete. Sorry Reggie. Ha. Haven't read it yet. A few changes but most of it was by Reggie. It's ok to be secretive. Many of the leaders remain unnamed. Funded by powerful people. Who? Secret. Line? Yeah. Drink? Nice. Powerful people? Yeah. Powerful. We are powerful. Changing the world. To secrecy. To honour. To power. To Reggie. Ha. Sniff. D-D-D.O.R. D-D.D.O.R. One for the road. Walk through streets. Nothing matters. We are brothers. We are family. Hug brothers. Powerful brothers. Goodnight brother Tony. Back to Jake's. Kip on sofa tonight. Power. Powerful. Have the power to change. Need to. Power does change. I lie down powerfully. Sleepy but powerful. Sleepy. Powerful.

A draft hurls through the open window and slaps me round the face, left, right, right, left, as if someone is challenging me to a duel at dawn. I open my eyes and see Sid sitting on a cushion two inches away from the television eating a bowl of cereal. The unfamiliar surroundings give me butterflies in my stomach. But that may be because I'm starving. I don't remember eating yesterday.

"Morning Sid," I go to say, but my throat took a battering from the coke, fags, and lager last night. I clear it. "Morning Sid."

He doesn't take his eyes off the screen. "Morning," he says.

"What are you watching?" I say.

"Trisha."

I sit up and catch a smell of myself. Jesus, I stink. I'm still dressed in the same clothes as yesterday. Round sticky patches of alcohol cover the elbows of my shirt. The bottoms of my jeans are wet and dirty, which is probably a mixture of piss, mud, and rain. Stale fags simmer from my shirt and hair, and my armpits smell like I've been smuggling onions in between them. Thank the Lord I haven't got work today.

"Are you working today?" I ask Sid.

"Nah, I only do three or four days a week. Gives me a bit of pocket money," he says. "A dawdle."

"Really? I thought that working in a bakery would have been hard work? My granddad used to work in one and he says that it was tough graft," I say.

Still engrossed in the TV, he doesn't move. "Far from it, mate. Guess it's not like the old days. Everything comes in frozen. I just simply take it out of the freezer, pop it into the oven and then straight on the shelf. Easiest job ever. Only bad thing is what I have to wear. Health and Safety gone mental. Protective fucking headwear, goggles, and pissy little rubber gloves which look I've got condoms on the end of my wrists. Fucking embarrassing it is."

Just as I start thinking how my granddad would react to being told he had to wear rubber gloves and goggles back in his bakery days, Sid says, "Fuck me, will you look at the state of that." On the television there's a bloke dressed in high heels and a skirt. "Too much," says Sid.

"Too much?" I look round to see Jake standing at the bottom of the stairs. He looks groggy as he stands in just a pair of boxer shorts. His chest and arms are covered in curly black hairs, jagged scars, and above his right nipple he has a tattoo of an English bulldog resting his foot on the globe.

"Don't you think so?" Sid says.

"No Sidney, I fucking don't," Jake says as he wipes some crusty sleep from the corner of his eye. "Some messed up geezer decides he wants a fanny and some tits instead of a cock? And it makes national fucking television?" Jake shakes his head, lights a cigarette, and points at the window to the street outside. "That my friend is more than too much, that is fucked up. Like one day a fella goes to the dole office, cos he's claiming right? Well the fat spotty kid behind the counter tells him that the only job he can find suitable is a job cleaning the toilets and mopping the changing rooms at the local swimming pool. Now if the fella refuses to do this shitty, degrading job, then the fat spotty kid will make sure he loses his dole money. So, this fella leaves the dole offices to go home and think about things. y'know, maybe look through the job pages of the local rag. Well anyway, the fella goes home and finds his mum slouched over a bottle of Smirnoff with two fat black eyes staring between a razor blade and her wrists. There's not much the fella can do about it cos the culprit, one of his brothers, is as hard to find as a fart in the wind. All he can do is put his arm round his good old mum and comfort her, give her some loving words and then remove the razor blade. He hasn't forgotten about the job situation, so he eventually reads the local rag looking for jobs. In the paper he sees a picture of an old granny lying in a hospital bed beaten to a pulp. It turns out some lowlife crack-head followed her home and mugged her after she went to collect her weekly pension. This ain't a good day for the fella. It's all a bit fucked up right? So, this fella decides to unwind a little and he goes down the boozer with a couple of pals to have a few lagers and a game of pool. Well there's a lot of banter flying around, and people start to place wagers over games of pool. One of the fella's pals wins a game and the loser decides to smash a claw-hammer over his pal's head. So, this fella ends up trying to stop his pal's head from bleeding with tracing-paper-like bog roll, waiting for an ambulance to come. Except an ambulance doesn't come, cos no one wants to come to a boozer in Denton and no wanker wants to ring one. The landlord just wants you to get the fuck out cos his floors are getting ruined with blood. So, in the end the fella's pal turns into a vegetable. Fucking brain damaged over a game of pool." Jake pauses, looks out the window and takes a drag on his cigarette. "Now that doesn't make national TV. No one bats a fucking eyelid cos it ain't out of the norm round here. It's just an ordinary day around here. See?"

There isn't much you can say back to that. "Oh, fuck it," Jake says. "I'm off to get changed. I'll see you both tonight for the meeting."

Sid returns his gaze to the television. "Well, someone is in a bad mood this morning," he says.

I watch Sidney as he sits engrossed in the Trisha show. He seems content.

I feel hollow.

As I cut through the St George's Centre, I see a young boy sitting on a bench next to his father. They're getting stuck into an ice cream each until the young lad drops his to the floor and starts crying. The crying stops when his father gives his own ice cream to his son to replace it. I feel as though my insides have just been ripped out as I watch the kid look at his loving dad, and think just how lucky he is. Going home seems pointless. I know what I've got to do.

CHAPTER NINE

Unwashed, unshaven, empty, and running on the amphetamine left over from last night's binge, I glide through Dartford town centre. The busy high street goes about its daily business. Existence thrives while I question my own. I walk but don't feel like I'm doing so. My head is heavy, as though it's fighting to keep insanity at bay. No one recognises me, no one understands me. I'm a ghost. My heart works overtime as I near the pub. I see the door. I'm just going to come straight out with it. I'm your son. I'm your son. I'm your son. Give me some answers. I open the door. Give me some answers. I see him and walk towards him. His presence is an assault; a GBH to my nervous system.

"I'm sorry," he says.

I freeze. "What?" I say.

"I really am sorry, Reggie."

"Reggie? Sorry for what?"

"The way I figure it, is that there can't be too many people with that name living round here can there now? Plus, I saw a picture of you on the D.O.R Facebook page with some of the Gravesend members. When I saw it I thought I recognised you. You are him, right?"

"Who?" Fucking Facebook ...

"I was bang out of order last time you came in here. Was only having a laugh like. I didn't realise you were one of us," he says and pulls the sleeve of his shirt up to reveal "D.O.R" tattooed above the St George flag.

I watch him as he points to the tattoo with a proud smile beaming from his face. "And what you wrote was simply stunning. A real statement, written by a true patriot," he says.

Maybe I'm still asleep. But it feels too real. I feel my heart beating in my throat, in my chest and in my eardrums. I can feel the sweat running down my back and my forehead. I feel it in between my toes and in the palms of my hands. This is far too real.

"Oh, I see," he says, "you've still got the hump, haven't you?"

Wide-eyed, insensible, and numb, I'm unable to speak or nod or do anything. He laughs. "You look as though you want to kill me or something," he says. "Now sit down, accept my apology and let me get you a pint. The D.O.R look after their own."

He pours the pint and puts it in front of me. "It's like a family to me," he says as he leans over the bar and rests his elbows on a beermat. "The Defenders of the Realm saved me. They took me in when no one else really wanted me. Before that I was a bit of a lost cause. I never had any direction in life and nothing to look forward to. I was a dead-beat, a bit of a fuckup, and had done things I regretted in life. But the D.O.R taught me to look to the future."

I look at this man in front of me. My father. The famous Kelvin Jarvis. He stares into nothing. His eyes are heavy, tired, and regretful looking. The dark patches underneath them appear to be pulling on his eyelids in an attempt to close the shutters on reality.

"What kind of things do you regret?" I find myself saying.

"Too many things," he says.

The head on my pint has deflated to a tiny white puddle.

"I let society get the better of me. I had a fire inside me and I used it in the wrong way. I turned to drugs and violence because it seemed to be the right thing, no, the only thing to do. You see, people who are born with nothing, those of us who are born with sod all and are raised on the grotty seabed of society with no chance of swimming upwards, yet we're born with a fire inside of us, a certain fucking yearning, a passion, a hunger which the people above us just can't understand. Now, without guidance, this fire inside of us spreads beyond control. You see it happening everywhere. But this is what those above us want to happen, you see? They want to see all of us no-hopers running around causing chaos because it keeps the social ladder stable, it keeps things in the right order. But the D.O.R taught me to use this fire in the right way. A way which is sure to improve things. Can you imagine a thousand of us, all with the same yearning? Imagine the impact — imagine the recognition we will get. 'Who would've thought it?' the people will say. 'Who would've thought that those lowlifes at the arse-end of society could have fixed our country?' And you, and I, and all the D.O.R will be proud to say we've been a part of this." He pauses for breath and looks to me, his eyes now wide, ignited with pride and excited with passion. "Know what I mean?"

I do kind of know what he means. It seems obvious. How could those who were born with everything on a plate ever have a sense of yearning? They've got no fucking passion and no desire to better things. Why would they? But those who have blankets instead of central heating, those who go to school with holes in their shoes, and those who think chips and beans is a treat, they have something. Fire. Yeah. And couldn't this be put to use, this fire? "Yeah, I do," I say and then take a mouthful of lager. I still can't take my eyes off him. I see myself in him: his eyes, his nose, his mouth, even the way he drinks from his glass. We're just two feet apart, sharing the same DNA, and he hasn't got the slightest idea. I almost feel sorry for him. I almost want to kick his fucking teeth in. It's as if I want to hug him, hold him, really hold him, and strangle the bastard till he's blue in the face. Once that is over with, maybe we can begin as father and son.

"You don't say much, do you?" he says as he walks round the bar.

"You seem to do enough talking for the both of us," I say. I feel confident, witty, and no longer like I haven't got a right to be here.

He laughs as he sits on the stool next to me. "People say I've got a bit of a gob on me. But I'm a barman. It's my job to enlighten the punters, right? Anyway, you must know what it's like to enlighten people," he says.

"What do you mean?"

"That piece you wrote. It's got a lot of people talking. I'm sure you'll get a mention at the meeting tonight. Oh, and that one line you wrote," he says, "the bit about how people who were born here and live here, you know like the English Muslims, celebrated 9/11 and played a part in the 7/7 bombings? It got me thinking."

I see myself in Jake's kitchen, my heart racing, jaw swinging, nose running, scribbling words in a furious rage. I can almost feel the passion I felt that night but can't for the life of me remember the words. "What's it got you thinking about?" I ask.

He takes a large gulp from his pint. "It got me thinking that even though someone may be born here or lives here, this doesn't necessarily make them English. Far from it. They come here to our ancestral land, place their feet on the soil that our forefathers dug and ploughed, travel on the tarmac roads that our forefathers strived to lay, walk on our concrete pavements, and live in the houses that our forefathers built, inch by inch. This land which has been built on English blood, sweat, tears and pride, and these immigrants, they can't feel this. They can't feel this union in their blood. It's out of control, totally out of fucking control I tell you," he says.

Just how surreal is this? My father is talking to me about family, ancestors, blood, forefathers, union, and a sense of belonging.

"And they just keep flocking in," he says. "You know what I'm talking about?"

I shrug my shoulders. "Kind of," I say.

"Fucking politicians, they'll never change," he says. "They're the real hooligans in this country, vandalising the economy, the health service, and the right to be English." A large vein in his neck springs into life, throbbing and punching against his neck. His eyes have changed for the third time to a wild and angry glare. His knuckles are white on his glass. "They have done fuck all about immigration and now the people are scared to be patriotic for fear of being labelled a racist. You can see the fear throughout the country. Good old traditional nativity plays have been banned at loads of schools so as not to offend Muslims. Do people say anything? No, they don't. And what about St George's day? It means nothing; sod all. And can you believe that some councils have banned the St George flag in case it offends? What is all that about? Well the D.O.R have the steel and guts to stand up to all this. And do you know when the final straw came?" he asks.

I simply shrug my shoulders. "I'm kind of new to the group."

"Well I'll tell you buddy. The final straw came when the brave soldiers of the Royal Anglian Regiment returned to Luton from duty in Basra. Many of them brave souls had lost friends serving their country, and of course a number of families had lost loved ones who served in the regiment. When they arrived back in Luton, they were greeted by an absolutely fucking disgusting display of Muslim extremists who called them 'child killers' and 'butchers' and mocked their dead comrades. The police took more action against the patriotic people of Luton who confronted these vile bastards than they did against the extremists, who spew their hate against this country and our soldiers while living off benefits. It's a fucking disgrace; just as the fucking government are. And you know what else takes the piss? The government claim that they have put funds into solving this problem of Islamic hatred, but most of this money has actually gone to fund these preachers of hate. Apparently, they are entitled to these funds as long as they don't use violence."

I had no idea of any of this. Maybe I've been too wrapped up in my own problems to see the bigger picture. Mainly concerning this very man I'm talking to. He takes a large mouthful of beer and runs his hand through his hair as though he's trying to cool down.

"Anyway," he says suddenly, "I haven't introduced myself. I'm Kelvin."

My father offers me his hand. My father's hand, the hand that should have been around to raise me, the hand that should have been there more for my mother, the hand ... that is now there. "Reggie, as you know," I say.

As we link hands he looks at me intently and deeply. It's as though he somehow remembers me from somewhere before; a strange face that seems so familiar, a face that he can't put a name to. "So then, what does Reggie do with himself?"

"I work for an organisation raising funds for UK charities."

He places his hand on my shoulder making more contact with me in the last five minutes than in the whole of my life. Looking me in the eye he says, "I take my hat off to you buddy, you must feel proud to do a job that helps your country."

A shiver runs down my spine and I begin to feel that lump in my throat: the masculinity alarm bell. A lump which tells you, you are about to cry so you better man the fuck up. I swallow hard and tense. "Yeah," I say. I have a momentary flashback of my conversation with the Costsless guy. "I guess I am quite proud."

"Good on ya. Is that what got you interested in the D.O.R?" he asks.

"One of my mates told me about it."

"Oh yeah? Who is it? I might know him."

"His name is Jake. He's from Gravesend and he's quite a stocky fella with dark hair and a wonky nose."

He squints and thinks for a moment. Then it hits me that if he does know Jake then I'll be in danger of my father finding out exactly who I am.

"Doesn't ring any bells. But there are so many members around this way. Are you from Gravesend too?"

"Yeah, born and bred I'm afraid," I say.

He swirls his beer around. Once more his eyes have that sorrowful look. "I was born in Gravesend," he says as if hypnotised by the whirlpool of lager. "Wasn't a very good place for me."

"Why?" I ask.

"That town's a plague. It brings out the worst in you. It's everywhere. It's in the streets, in the Thames, in the people you meet and the people you love."

I'm beginning to feel like I'm in Cluedo. Does he mean my mother? Was it Lilly in the living room with the glass ashtray? Or was it Kelvin at the top of the hill with the Ford Escort? "Are you talking about women?" I ask.

"Yeah, partly. Dangerous they are. They brainwash you. They make you do things that you'd never even dream of doing and things you didn't think you were capable of doing." He swirls the lager around one more time before necking most of it in one gulp. "Ah, fuck it. Women will be the death of me one day."

I laugh. "Yeah, well they are hard work," I say.

"Tell me about it. You got yourself one? A woman like?" he says.

"No. Well, kind of. Not really. Oh, fuck knows what's going on at the moment."

"What seems to be the problem?"

"She never stirs the sugar in my tea. The top half tastes like shit and when you get to the bottom it's far too sweet. When she makes breakfast she's too impatient. When I make breakfast I always wait for her to get washed and changed so that she can sit down and eat it. But she just can't wait. The number of times I had to sit in the bath eating an egg sarnie," I say.

He has a funny laugh. It almost sounds like a kid pretending to make a machine gun noise. "That's unforgivable," he says followed by a "g-h-h-h-h, g-h-h-h-h, g-h-h-h-h."

And I really do miss her. Right now. I've got to go and find her. At that moment a man in a fluorescent jacket and gloves walks through the door. "Delivery, mate," the man says.

My father tells him he will meet him around the back. "Gotta go, Reggie. Been nice chatting with you. Make yourself at home, if not, I guess I'll be seeing you at the meeting."

"Yeah. I had better be getting off. Thanks for the pint," I say.

We shake hands.

The sun has decided to make an appearance. I could just be some ordinary bloke who has been to see his ordinary father. We had a chat, a laugh, and a pint and now I'm going home. Just like an ordinary father and son. That's what ordinary people do. Nice. I hang on to the thought of being ordinary for as long as possible while I take a seat on a bench in the town centre and light a cigarette.

A passer-by throws the drab end of some chips wrapped in greasy paper to the ground. The chips scatter across the pavement and a dozen pigeons swoop in. These ones definitely got the raw deal in the pigeon world. Nothing like the beautiful plump wood pigeons you see in the countryside, with their immaculate grey feathers and symmetrical flashes of white along their wings and their necks. Elegant birds those ones. Nice, clean, alert eyes and a strong yellow beak, living on a diet of berries, vegetables, and grain. But these poor fuckers? They look like walking bruises. Those beady, crusty, bloodshot eyes peering over a cracked-black-rotten fingernail of a beak. Maybe all pigeons started out the same, looking as beautiful as the ones in the woods. Maybe they were divided, and some moved to the country and some enjoyed the buzz of town life. Maybe it was town life that fucked these pigeons up. Town life altered and disfigured these pigeons and made them ugly.

I watch as they flock around the chips, pecking and nudging each other out of the way. One pigeon, not as big as the others, is trying to find a gap in the crowd so he can have lunch too. But with each attempt he gets knocked back. He tries to do this a few times and flaps his wings in frustration. And then finally, with a bit of a run up, he bulldozes his way through the other pigeons and returns with a golden chip. He flies off with it to the top of a phone box where he begins to eat his chip in peace. I close my eyes, inhale some smoke, and then breathe it back out slowly and peacefully. I feel almost like a new person. Content, assertive, strong; I've finally made contact with my father. Julie would be impressed. She needs to know.

Feeling on a bit of a roll, I get off the bus at Valley Drive and walk towards Julie's sister's house. Valley Drive is famous for the fried chicken shop, the dentists, and the massive pub with boarded-up windows which doesn't operate anymore. I bounce up the hill full of confidence.

"What do you want?" Julie's sister says to me as she opens the door.

"I'm not going to argue with you Carol. Is she in?"

Carol looks over her shoulder while standing firm in the doorway. Her broad shoulders and her mop of Mick-Hucknall-style-hair block my view. "Don't upset her," she says without even turning her head before waddling back into the house.

Julie appears at the door looking flustered and putting some boots on. I catch a whiff of her perfume and it creates a riot in my stomach. She looks at me briefly. "Pete, I'm in a bit of a rush."

"Look, I came here to apologise. I forgot it was this time of year when your brother died. I should have been there for you," I say.

She stops tying up the laces and sighs heavily. "Well there are things that we both should have done more of," she says. "I'm sorry at how I acted with the situation with your father. I was just angry and upset."

I want to grab her, hold her, and take her home. "You were right though, I shouldn't have messed about and wasted my time ... and yours. But I finally did it, Ju. I went down there today and spoke to him."

Her eyes light up and she removes her hands from the boot. "You did?" she says. "And what did he say? What did you say, more importantly?"

My heart starts to thud. Fuck, I didn't think this far. There I was on my high horse thinking that she'd be impressed. How can I tell her that he still doesn't know who I am?

"Well ... he seems a nice bloke. We had a chat and he came up with some interesting things. I think he's quite intelligent you know. Maybe you'd get on with him."

Carol appears behind Julie and casts another glance at me, screwing her eyes as though hoping to cast a spell on me. "I'm going to start the car," she says to Julie.

"Broom broken down?" I say under my breath.

Julie gives me a cheeky grin and tells me to stop it and then says, "Pete, that's great. I want to hear all about it."

"You do? You want to come home with me?"

"No. I'm going to be really late for a seminar if I don't hurry up," she says.

Carol revs the engine as though she's about to start a Formula One race.

Julie finishes putting her boots on, closes the door behind her and walks out to me. "Is that a bruise on your face? What have you been up to?" she says as she gets closer to me.

"Oh, it's nothing really. I'll explain when we talk," I say.

"Well, I've got to go to Waterstones in Bluewater tomorrow to pick up a book that I've ordered. Why don't we meet for a coffee and a chat down there? I know you're not that keen on the place, but it will be nicer than meeting in Gravesend won't it?"

And she's right. I can't fucking stand Bluewater but if there's a chance to sort things out with her and get her back then I'm there. "Ok," I say.

"Cool," she says as she gets into the car. "See you tomorrow."

As the car pulls away, Carol looks at me as though she's got a mouthful of battery acid. I make the sign of the crucifix and aim it towards her.

I feel chuffed. Everything seems to be falling into place nicely. Except for my father not knowing who I really am.

Exhausted by my productive day, I decide that a little lie-down is in order. My father and our possible new friendship race through my mind and my eyes become heavier and heavier ... My father is next to me. I can't see him, but I feel him next to me. We swoop over the Thames and wake the dead souls that lie unsettled on the bottom. We join together and fly over the town centre towards the memorial plaque at St Paul's. There we are joined by the souls of the soldiers who fought for this country. Now we are a force, a fucking reckoning. We fill the sky like fighter planes on D-Day. It is dark, not because daylight has ceased. No, it's dark with disease, destruction, desperation. Diseased residents walk with no destination through the plague town. Black shadows crawl up buildings and houses, scuttle along the cracked pavements and slither through doorways. At once we look to one another in the air and join together. We form, link up, connect, integrate, and BANG. Nothing but a bright light, pure fucking illumination, and like a cannonball we hurl, we sweep through the town like a tsunami. And then there's nothing for a second. A void. But then there is heat: a distant sun on the horizon. It doesn't burn or scald. It is peaceful; a comfortable warmth. And then the town appears beneath us, the shape of a pea. It starts to grow; trees, buildings, and people. There is no more darkness when it is restored to its full size. Trees are green, the Thames is blue, and the people are smiling. I see my father. We feel sublime, exalted, cleansed.

I feel like a ninety-year-old as I stumble out of bed and rest my elbows on the windowsill. The sun that was out earlier is gone. There's nothing now: no clouds, no rain, no birds; just a featureless mass of nothing. Where do I go in moments like these? I don't know, but I like these moments. I feel relaxed. The thing is with moments like this, you can't just decide you are going to have one.

Two young kids are racing each other through the Asda carpark. One is wearing an Arsenal football shirt, the other in a Chelsea shirt. What is the point of seeing my father again when he thinks that I'm called Reggie? I wonder what he would do if he found out who I really was? The kids run towards their mother who is gesturing them to get in the car. Maybe I would ruin everything if I told him who I really am. Would it be ok just to carry on getting to know him as Reggie? What a stupid, cowardly idea. I'm going to tell him tonight who I really am. But then I'll look a right prick. He might tell the D.O.R and then it might get back to Jake, and he'll tell me I've got cherry pips for balls. If the kid in the Arsenal shirt wins then I'm going to tell my father who I am tonight. Who cares if he thinks I'm an idiot. The kid in the Chelsea shirt edges ahead. But would Jake and Sid and Tony never want to see me again? Arsenal shirt catches up and they seem dead even with only a few feet to go. Arsenal: tell him, Chelsea: not yet. But maybe I should just go with the flow and pretend to be Reggie just a little longer. Arsenal comes on strong and pulls slightly away. Wouldn't do much harm would it? No fuck it ... I'm definitely telling him tonight. The Arsenal kid trips and falls at the last moment and the Chelsea kid jumps into the car and punches the air in celebration. The Arsenal kid is in tears. His mum comes over to console him and attend to his bleeding kneecap. Fuck it, I'm going to go over to Jake's before the meeting and make sure nobody calls me Pete tonight. Tonight, I'm going to be Reggie.

CHAPTER TEN

Sidney opens the door still wearing just his boxer shorts. He then immediately resumes his position inches away from the television. Scattered around him are empty crisp packets, a half-full litre bottle of Coke, a packet of Jaffa Cakes, an ashtray full to the brim, some screwed-up tissues, and a Freeman's catalogue open at the lingerie section. A trail of crumbs runs from his goatee through his chest hair and ends in a small pile in his belly button. His boxer shorts are smeared with chocolate. At least I hope it's chocolate.

"Busy day?" I say as I take a seat on the sofa.

"Yeah. Been to the kitchen a couple of times and had to get up to change the DVD," he says.

"What you been watching?"

"Done the Star Wars trilogy again. Never get bored of them. Was brought up on those films," he says.

"You've watched all three of them today?" I ask.

"Yeah, and I was thinking about sticking one of the new ones on, but they fucked them up a little bit, didn't they?"

"I don't know mate, I haven't really got around to watching the new ones," I say.

"Big fucking disappointment," he says. "You just can't tamper with something so great. I mean, they bring in all these new two-bob characters that are shit. Pointless they are. They just ruin the whole thing. And that poxy Jar-Jar Binks is a disgrace to the Jedi. Such a bumbling, big-nosed, stupid-voiced, waste of space. You've got C3PO and R2D2 for the comedy side of things and you don't need this stupid alien running around trying to be funny. Should have left it exactly how it was."

"Right," I say.

He looks at me and laughs. "Sorry mate, you have no idea what I'm talking about, do you?"

"No. But when I watch them I'll be sure to tell you what I think."

Sid picks up a Jaffa Cake and starts to eat round the edge of it without touching the orange piece in the middle. "It's a real religion now, you know that?" he says with a mouthful of chocolate. "I've looked into it a bit. Started in 2001 when shitloads of people wrote that they were of the Jedi religion on the national census. It's massive in New Zealand. Apparently, there are more Jedis than Jehovah's Witnesses over there. They've got churches and chapels," he says.

I start to laugh. "Some people," I say. "It's only a film. It's not even real."

Sid looks serious for a moment. "But don't some people think that Jesus ain't real? And that the Bible has just been made up? There's more proof of Jedi because we have seen it in our lifetime."

Maybe he has a point. I mean, people worship something and someone that they've never even seen. All that they have as proof is a little book that was written thousands of years ago. It seems pretty crazy, really. But I guess it gives people something to believe in. So what if nowadays, someone like Sid watches Star Wars, and some element of that film gives him hope, makes him feel good and makes his life seem better? Isn't it the same thing? I start to think of all the wars religion has caused and all the blood that has been shed, blokes that have been decapitated, and bodies that have been burned. A shiver runs down my spine. Sidney starts waving his hands around in the air making lightsabre sounds.

"Wouldn't it be cool to be a proper Jedi and be able to and kick the shit out of people with a lightsabre and fly spaceships?" he says. The brief bit of sense he momentarily possessed takes a severe nose dive.

Jake walks in and looks as though he's got the raging hump.

"You alright mate?" I ask him.

"No not really. I've got the fucking bollock-ache to be honest with you," he says. He puts his hands on either side of his head as though he's stopping it from falling off. Then he clears his throat and goes to say something but then he switches his gaze to Sidney, who has now sucked off all the chocolate from the Jaffa Cake and is playing with the orange centre. "Tell me you haven't been sitting there since this morning," he says.

Sidney quickly swallows the remains of the Jaffa Cake. "Well, yeah I have. I've had fuck all else to do, have I?"

"Fuck all else?" Jake says. "How about getting off that skinny little arse of yours and finding somewhere to live."

"I haven't got the money for that yet though Jake. You know this. Plus, I'm not getting enough hours."

"Well go and sign on or something. You're sitting in front of my TV, using up all my electric, eating all my Jaffa Cakes and drinking all my Coke. Oh, and sniffing my coke too. And what the fuck is that?" he says pointing to the open catalogue.

Jake walks over to where Sidney has been nested for the day. Sid quickly tries to turn the pages over, but Jake puts his foot on it before he can do so. "You sick fuck. I've been looking for this. I'm supposed to order something for my mum," Jake says picking up the catalogue and hitting him over the head with it.

"Ouch," Sidney says rubbing his head. "Well you've got the iPad in your room and your door is always locked."

"And why do you think that is? Because if it's not my shaver, it's my iPad; if it's not my iPad, it's my deodorant. It's always something with you. You're a little ponce."

"But Jake. I was watching Return of the Jedi and you know as well as me how fit Princess Leia looks when she's in that little gold suit. Gives me the right horn. You can even see a little bit of her left bum cheek if you pause it at the right moment."

A smile looks as though it's trying to break its way through Jake's concrete features. "Go and get yourself cleaned up, fuckhead. We've got the meeting soon," he says.

Sidney sprints up the stairs and Jake sits down next to me on the sofa. Just as I'm about ask Jake what's wrong, there is a loud knock at the door. And then again, and then again. Jake looks on edge. "Who is it?" he calls out.

"JAKEY BOY, OPEN THE FUCKING DOOR," a deep voice replies.

"Vic? Is that you Vic?" Jake asks.

"DON'T MAKE ME RIP THIS FUCKING DOOR OFF. COURSE IT'S VIC. OPEN THE DOOR. PRICK. IT'S VIC. PRICK."

Jake opens the door and this lump of a man walks in wheezing and puffing. His face looks like it's got too much skin on it, as though it's made from play dough, and his bald head is covered with bumps, dents, scars, and creases. Tattoos are scattered over his forearms. He looks like an ASBO version of Jabba the Hutt.

"Fucking hell, my nuts feel like they've got frostbite," he says with his hands on his hips trying to catch his breath. "You forget Vic was coming or you just being a rude cunt?"

"Sorry Vic. I forgot you were coming over."

Vic stands upright and notices me for the first time. He blinks and screws his eyes in the manner of someone who's got bad eyesight. Jake sees this. "Vic, this is Pete," he says.

He walks over to me looking stern. I feel nervous looking back at him. He pokes his head close to mine and kind of sniffs; loudly. Is he smelling me? Without saying a word, he turns around and walks back to Jake. "Kitchen, Jake, now," he says.

The two of them disappear and I'm left on the sofa amongst Sid's wank rags and Jaffa Cakes.

It's not long before they reappear. Once again, Vic looks at me as though he wants to take my head off with his teeth. Then he switches his gaze to the catalogue on the floor.

"You sure you don't want a cuppa or anything Vic?" Jake asks.

"No. No. Vic doesn't want a cup of tea. He's got things to see and people to do," he says and licks his knuckles. He then walks over to the Jaffa Cakes and puts about four in his mouth. "What you doing? Apart from making me some money?"

Bits of Jaffa Cake fly through the air.

"We've got a meeting in a bit, down the legion," Jake replies.

"Boring, boring, fucking boring," he says and then looks at the catalogue again.

There's a moment's silence. An awkward one. The only sound being Vic eating the Jaffa Cakes. All of a sudden, he just picks the catalogue up, puts it under his arm and simply walks out of the front door.

"Bye Vic," Jake says as the door closes.

Jake then sits down on the sofa next to me. I don't even have to ask the question. "That was Vic. A bit odd, but someone you don't want to ever mess with. He's a good person to have on your side. Plus, he gives me what I need," Jake says and then lets out a big sigh.

"You ok mate? You seem a bit stressed," I say to him.

He pulls his hair as if he's trying to yank his own head off. "I'm proper stressed. I'm losing more and more business every day. All the fucking stoneheads are flocking to the Pakis and buying their stuff. I just can't get my head round it," he says.

"Is it that bad? Why don't you just lower the price of your stuff?" I say.

"It's not that easy Pete. Fuck knows who they are getting it off, but it must be at a cheaper price than what I'm getting it for. I'm gonna have to start cutting it up more."

"Cut it with what?" I say.

"I just bought a bit of the old Billy Whizz from Vic. You see, speed is cheap as fucking chips. So, you mix a bit of speed into the coke and it still gives people a buzz. Makes them think the coke is good because it sends the ticker racing and gives them shitloads of energy. I always put a little bit of it in but I'm gonna have to start drowning the coke with it now."

"Won't anyone know the difference?" I say.

"Only the old-school cokeheads will; the geezers in their fifties that still go raving and sprinkle the stuff on their cornflakes. But if I do it carefully, I'll be able to leave their stuff alone and just give the heavily-cut coke to the pissheads who drink so much that they don't care what shit they sniff up their hooters." Jake sighs. "It's got to be done Pete. Those Pakis are selling to most of Dickens Way,

Kings Farm, and they're even getting their mitts into Northfleet way. They're fucking everywhere, I tell ya."

He turns and looks towards me. "Anyway, I'll stop drumming on. How you been today? Looks like you could do with a dab of this," he says and pulls a bag of white powder out of his inside pocket.

"Is that the speed?"

"Want a taster?"

"Nah, I've done enough drugs in the last couple of days," I say.

"Suit yourself then, but if you want a little livener just give me a shout," he says and puts the bag back into his pocket.

"I will do. Thanks. Look Jake, there's something I want to talk to you about," I say. "I was just wondering if tonight at the meeting you could make sure that you don't call me Pete. And ask the other lads to do the same."

Jake looks at me puzzled, as if he's trying to work out a mathematical sum. "Well, that's a bit weird," he says. "Why's that?"

Once again, I'm tempted to tell him about the situation with my father. After all, he has partially opened up about some of the shit he dealt with when he was a kid.

But as I stare into his eyes something prevents me from doing so. "It's just, well, that thing I wrote was claimed to be written by Reggie and if people find out that my real name is Pete then they're going to think it's a bit strange. They'll either think I'm some kind of div or that I haven't got the bollocks to attach my own name to it."

Jake nods his head. "Yeah, I see what you mean. Good point, Reggie. I'll tell the lads. So anyway, are you looking forward to tonight? You're gonna go down a treat. You gonna be alright reading it in front of all those people?"

My stomach jumps. "What? I have to read it?" I say.

"Well no one is gonna force you. But more than likely the speaker will ask you to go on stage and read your masterpiece," he says.

"Fucking hell, I haven't even read it myself," I say.

"No probs. I've got a copy right here."

I open the newsletter with sweaty palms. There I see 'Reggie' in bold lettering. Below is his masterpiece. I read the words and my kneecaps tremble. My stomach is now in bits. "Maybe I will have a dab of that after all, Jake," I say.

The meeting is in a private hall adjoining the Royal British Legion Pub just off Echo Square. We pass through the pub to get to the hall and it seems as though we have stepped back in time. It is small, dimly lit, and has a lingering musky smell. The carpet is tatty and is faded brown, green, and gold. There are dark wooden tables and chairs with green seating. Old beermats are scattered around the tables along with little ramekins containing Mini Cheddars and chunks of cheese. A dusty grandfather clock which looks like it stopped working years ago stands in the corner. Old advertisements cover the walls. A navy man stands at the forefront of a warship flying the Union Jack and smiles as he holds out a tin of Colman's Mustard. A lion wearing a crown is selling Imperial Assorted Biscuits. Two gentlemen being served tea by an Indian man in a turban promote Patterson's Tea, and Queen Victoria herself is peddling Queen's Honey Soap, riding a white horse, and being saluted by numerous soldiers in red blazers, waving their swords in the air. A few of the elderly punters peer over their jugs of ale and nod at us. One man in particular wearing a blazer decorated with medals catches my eye. He stands with the help of his walking stick and raises his glass to us.

There is quite a mixture of people, mostly men but also a few women. The majority are middle-aged, but there are others at both ends of the scale. A couple of elderly people are being wheeled around. One wheelchair has a flag attached to it. There are also children and babies in pushchairs. The past, present, and future of our country united for one cause, all with the yearning and desire to live in a better, safer place. And in this place tonight there is no aggression, no conflict, no dirty looks, no eye-balling, and not one inch of animosity, which makes a big change around this way. The majority of people are wearing white t-shirts with 'D.O.R' printed in the colours of the Union Jack.

I look around for my father but can't see him. It's not long before the crowd is silenced by the sound of a microphone being turned on. The speaker holds the microphone in his hand and faces his audience. He is a guy possibly in his fifties. He has short grey hair shaved at the sides and cropped on top. Thick glasses magnify beady green eyes. His cheeks are red and scarred with lots of tiny holes where acne once resided. He is dressed in a grey suit and wears a blue tie with 'D.O.R' stitched into the middle of it. He introduces himself as Martin and thanks us all for joining him tonight. I shiver. The dab of speed I had on the way is starting to work.

"It is obvious that we are a multicultural country," he begins. "And while we are not a racist group, it is easy to see that the idea of England being a multicultural nation has served only to dilute our sovereignty and our national identity. Our society is being threatened, our language is being ruined, and our freedom is in tatters. This once great culture of ours, which developed over centuries of wars, struggles and trials, in which many English people laid down their lives, hangs in the balance. So, what are we going to do about it?"

There are a few cheers and shouts such as "fight for it", and "take our country back". The speaker acknowledges the audience and takes a sip from his drink, which looks like whiskey.

"That we will. What do the government expect when their immigration policies are so downright ridiculous? It allows people to come in who hate our country and then practice their hatred. The way I see it, the rise in patriotism has been incredible since the attacks in London. The dust has barely settled since these horrendous bombings and already the politically correct gang have begun to suggest that our patriotism offends others. We must do everything in our power to voice our opinions but is hard to do this when the government welcome so many foreigners into this country. Did you know that in North Korea if you cross the border illegally then you get twelve years hard labour? Did you know that if you cross the Iranian border illegally then you will be detained and tortured? If you cross the Saudi Arabian border you will be jailed? And the Afghan border, you will be shot? And what happens when someone crosses the British border illegally? Can anyone tell me?"

A few people bang the tables and begin to talk among themselves. "We give them a life," a middle-aged woman shouts out.

The speaker acknowledges her and nods. "Exactly my dear, we give them a life. They get a job, they get a driver's licence, they get a pension, and they get welfare. They get credit cards, subsidised rent, or a loan to buy a house. They get free education and healthcare. And then how do some of them give their thanks? They thank us by spewing hatred. It's our own fault. Our government's frailty has allowed our country to deteriorate. We gather here tonight ahead of our march through London. As you are well aware, we are protesting against Islamic hatred, so tonight I would like to talk to you a little bit about this," he says and slowly walks to the other end of the stage with his back straight, shoulders firm.

"We hope to open a few eyes. We hope to make Britain a better place and I believe that the first step in doing this must be to wipe out the doctrine of hate, intolerance, and murder which Muslim extremists are importing into our country. This plague has been ignored for too long and has been left to fester. Something must be done, and it must be done quickly. Our government are blind to the threat of militant Islam and we must make them see. We oppose the building of any more mosques until the problem of Islamism is dealt with. It is in these places that Muslim extremists promote their doctrine of hate. And I'll tell you something else. The majority of the management structure in the mosques has been educated by extremist ideology which demands the extermination of our society," he says and then pauses to witness the crowd's reaction.

"I hear your gasps, I hear your sighs, I feel your terror, and I feel your anger. Does anyone in this room know the Koran?" he asks.

Whispers travel through the room. No one answers the speaker directly. "I'm sure you have heard of it, but I'm sure that you do not know of its contents. Well let me tell you," he says and then has another sip of his drink. "The Koran is the religious book for Muslims: their Bible, so to speak. It gives Muslims their religious practices and priorities. The doctrine is simple: to imitate the conduct of the prophet Mohammed, who is believed to be the perfect Muslim, and to establish an Islamic society arranged by the rules contained in the Koran. But do you know what practices Muslims learn from their divine Mohammed? There is no freedom of expression and no right to question. There is only obedience to the commands of Allah and Mohammed. Nothing in this religion is compatible with human rights. They learn that threats, rape, pillage, trickery, and murder are all acceptable, and even more acceptable when applied towards the destruction of the kafir. What is a kafir, I hear you ask? Well the Koran suggests that anyone who is not a Muslim is a kafir, and a kafir is not equal to a Muslim. Kafirs are inferior, despicable, cursed by Allah, and are destined to burn in hell. Islam divides humanity into two blocks: Dar-ul-Islam, which is the house of peace, and Dar-ul-Harb, which is the house of war. Islam urges Muslims to wage war in the Dar-ul-Harb until the whole world is conquered and ruled according to Mohammed's law. Once they have control, all non-Muslims will be de-humanised and non-Muslim women will be taken as sex slaves. This religion breeds hatred. Islam works towards the destruction of every religion in order to install a universal Islamic civilization. Through a Muslim's eyes, every one of us in this room is a kafir."

He pauses once again amidst all the gasps and whispers. "Loving our country is not a crime, a craving for freedom is not criminal, but the need for a secure country and the elimination of those who threaten this is surely a must."

The majority of the audience, including myself, rise to their feet to give the speaker a standing ovation. The thunderous clapping makes my hairs stand on edge. It makes me want to roll up into a little ball, soak up all the patriotism in the room and bounce off the sound of the cheering and the clapping.

We sit back down and I neck the remaining beer in my glass. The crisp lager blends nicely with the speed and I get a little rush. There is no other place in the world I would rather be right now.

"Thank you, my faithful compatriots. You're very kind, very kind indeed. But I don't seek your praise, just your strength," the speaker says after the applause. "Tonight, I would like to mention someone and extend to him our warmest thanks. Those who have read the newsletter know that a new member has written a wonderful piece in support of our cause."

My heart starts to beat faster, and Jake gives me a little nudge while Tony winks at me.

"Is there a Reggie present among us tonight?" Martin, the speaker, calls out.

Every single person in the room starts to shuffle in their seats and looks around. The adrenaline takes over my body. I find myself half sitting down, half standing up, as if I'm hovering over a bush taking a crap in the woods. "He's right here guvnor," Tony shouts out.

Hundreds of eyes all turn to our table. "Well come on up here," the speaker says and starts to clap.

The audience follow suit as I make way to the stage, floating it seems, not feeling the solid ground under my feet. I'm now face-to-face with Martin. The holes in his face look as large as craters this close up. I smell whiskey on his breath as he shakes my hand. "Hello Reggie. Face your audience son," he says.

I look out into the crowd and instead of feeling nervous I feel strong, confident, and proud. "Go on Reggie," someone calls out. Instantly I recognise the voice. My father stands to the left of the stage, clapping and sticking his thumbs up.

"So, Reggie," the speaker says. "What made you join us?"

He holds the microphone close to my mouth. I don't even find myself searching for words. They just fly out. "I was sick and tired of looking around and seeing nothing I liked anymore," I say. "Everywhere I looked there was nothing but hatred and anger. This isn't what our country should be like. It's like a scrambled jigsaw puzzle. So, when I bumped into my old friend Jake, he told me about the D.O.R and I saw a way of putting the pieces back together."

The crowd start to applaud once again, and I see Jake looking pleased that I mentioned him. "Well you've come to the right place Reggie," the speaker says. But I'm not finished yet. I've got all these words bursting to get out of me. I take the microphone out of the speaker's hand.

"This is our country. This is our beloved England. We can't be sitting in the shadows. We are rulers. This was once a great empire. The Queen, even her little corgis, Buckingham Palace, Big Ben, Parliament, Shakespeare, Bobby Moore, the '66 World Cup team, Michael bloody Caine, even Jack the fucking Ripper. It's all history, great history, history like no other. Oasis, The Beatles, cups of tea, the list is endless. Fish and chips, the traditional English break ... "

Martin grabs the microphone back off me.

"Mind the language Reggie," he says patting me on the shoulder.

But the crowd seem to love me. Their laughter and applause is topping up the effects from the speed. I feel like ripping my shirt off and diving into the crowd like a rock star.

"Reggie, we can see that you're a real patriot. Now why don't you read us the piece from the newsletter," he says handing me back the microphone.

I clear my throat and stretch my arms out as serious and as focused as a pianist about to deliver the performance of his life. I take the newsletter, look at the crowd and then to the eyes of my father.

Is this the country we once knew?
Where our countrymen are so few?

No! This land we forget, which is so dear,
So dear, yet we are living in fear.

We live in fear of those with twisted dreams,
Yet our government ignore our heartache and screams.

And amongst us, English Muslims rejoiced at 7/7,
And people born here celebrated and praised 9/11.

In shadows people have their say,
Because they are scared that the race card will come out to play.

Speech is squashed, our heads remain in the sand,
But hear US now: we must take back our land!

Look around! Our traditions are dying!
Yet Muslim extremism is alive and rising!

So now is the time to draw the sword,
Let us show our patriotism like never before!

We will fight even when things get wild,
For we are fighting for England: man, woman, and child.

Instantly the crowd are back on their feet whistling, cheering, and clapping even louder than before. Someone starts to sing Rule Britannia, and then people join in one by one, so that the song is loud enough to be heard the other side of the Thames. The speaker shakes my hand and directs me off the stage. My father is the first to greet me as I enter the patriotic crowd. He pats me on the back as though he's a proud father congratulating his son for receiving a sports trophy. Then others flock around me clapping me, patting me, and shaking my hand. I am now that little ball bouncing off the pride in the room. I am the conductor of this thunderous noise and singing. I am an element of this united crowd of believers, of revolutionists and patriotic soldiers.

I reach my table and am swamped by Jake, Sid, and Tony. Jake pushes a pint of lager towards me and tells me he's proud of me. Feeling content and necessary to the cause, I sit back to listen to the remainder of the meeting and the plans for the march on Saturday. Jake passes me a bag of speed under the table. I wait until the crowd's stopped focusing on me and then I lick my finger and scoop up a generous helping to rub into my gums. The chemicals strike instantly, and my front teeth go numb. It leaves a sour taste in every corner of my mouth, so I wash it down with the lager.

CHAPTER ELEVEN

It's about two hours later and my father is standing at our table. "Brilliant Reggie, absolutely brilliant," he says. He sways, and his cheeks are flushed with alcohol. His smile is as wide as a letterbox as he shakes my hand.

"Thanks. Oh, these are my mates," I say. Casual. "And this is Kelvin."

My father offers to buy us all a drink. I have another dab of speed while my father orders.

"I never knew all that stuff about the Muslims and all that Koran shit," Sidney says.

"It's bloody frightening," Tony says.

"Too fucking right pal," Jake says.

My father joins us. He likes us. He flings his right arm in the air as if he's throwing a stick for a dog to chase after. "This uncontrolled immigration is ruining us. It's leading to a demand for more housing, traffic congestion, lower wages, higher unemployment rates, longer hospital waiting lists. The list is fucking endless."

I find myself listening intently. My leg is tapping, my jaw is swinging, I feel like there's something growing inside of me, becoming angrier and angrier and it just wants to be released. "What about all the street crime that's going on? That's got to be stopped too," I say.

My father looks at me. "And what would you do about that if you were in charge?" he says to me.

I think to myself for a moment. "Maybe I'd put more police on the streets, or maybe I'd be harsher with the younger ones who commit the crimes to make sure that they won't do it again," I say.

"Fair point," my father says. "But let's concentrate on wiping all the scum out first yeah?"

Sidney starts to laugh and then he playfully slaps me on the shoulder. "Yeah, one thing at a time Pete," he says.

My foot ceases tapping, and my cheeks start to burn. The room spins, and I focus on my father. He stops his pint mid-air, looks at Sid and then turns to gaze at me. "Pete?" he says.

No one says anything for what seems like a lifetime and then Jake's chunky arm comes from behind Sid and clouts him round the ear. "Who the fuck is Pete?" Jake says. "Fucking hell Sid, you've had too much to drink already you lightweight."

"You pisshead," Tony says to him. "You'll be calling me Belinda next."

My father remains as still as Nelson's Column, his eyes serious and puzzled. Sid rubs his head for a moment trying to work out what's going on and then his eyes light up when he realises that he's just dropped a clanger. "Oh fucking hell, I'm shit with names. Just to double check," he says as he points to each one of us. "You're Pete, you're Ken, you're Beryl, and you with the shiny bald head must be the lovely Belinda. Show us yer tits," he says.

Tony pulls his t-shirt over his head and juggles his man boobs about. At this point my father bursts out laughing. "You lot are bloody nuts," he says raising his glass. "To getting rid of the scum."

We toast with him. My hand shakes as I raise my glass and then I down the remaining beer in one swift gulp.

"Right," my father says also finishing his pint. "I'd better be going. See you at the demo. You lot are bloody nuts," he laughs. He reaches out and ruffles my hair as he leaves.

Tony gets us a pint and a shot of whiskey each. The alcohol starts doing its job and is complementing the speed. It seems as though everyone is buzzing. Tony is speaking about the need for a street army. He suggests that every city that is overpopulated by immigrants should have D.O.R 'officers' patrolling the streets keeping an eye on them. Jake demands that we march through every city in England so that people hear our message loud and clear, and then we can also continue to grow and strengthen in numbers. I'm sucking it all in, proud of what I'm a part of, proud that I played a major role in the meeting tonight, proud of the recognition I received, and pleased that my father seemed proud of me. I feel so much enthusiasm running through me, my legs won't remain still, and I want more. I get that feeling in my stomach again, it's fizzling, sizzling, roaring, it's rattling the iron bar. Fuck, so much energy. Jake hands out bits of speed wrapped in cigarette paper. This is accompanied by another shot of whiskey. "This is the English Bomber," he says. We put the speed bombs in our mouths and on the count of three we wash them down with the whiskey. The chemicals run riot into my blood stream. It feels like fucking kryptonite. We sing, we chant. There was one German bomber in the air. There was one German bomber in the air. There was one German bomber, one German bomber, one German bomber in the air.

On the way out, I shake hands and hug people as though they are relatives. The air is bitter, and the sky is illuminated with colourful fireworks. It's bonfire night. Every inch of my body is tingling. I feel as if I could steam-roll all of the crap in Britain and then double back just to make sure. Sid trips over the kerb. We all help him up. We are united. The four of us all on the same level, sharing the same beliefs and sharing the same energy. We get into Jake's car. He says speed makes him a better driver. I feel the energy running through us, floating around us, guarding us, driving us on. And the RAF from England shot it down, and the RAF from England shot it down, and the RAF from England, the RAF from England, the RAF from England shot it down. ENGLAND. Just think, four of us with this passion, multiplied by two-hundred, three-hundred more? I'm no good with numbers but imagine what a difference we can make. Where are we going? Fuck knows. Feels like we are in a rocket. Light speed. Street lights flicker like a strobe. Want to go faster. Put some music on Jake. What music? Bit of Drum & Bass? Yeah. Nice. Crank it up. Feel that bass. Something powerful about mates uniting in music. Strengthens us. Strengthens the bond. We are a fucking unit. Where we going? I got an idea. Do a right. Which right? The one opposite your left, you dozy bastard. I know my right. Next right. This right. That's it, park just here. Get that baseball bat out the boot. Why? Look. GRAVESEND MUSLIM CULTURAL CENTRE. I see. They want a war? Let them fucking have it. I'll do it. About time we made a statement. Wrap this scarf round your face and put this beanie hat on Pete. Cover your face. Smash it for the D.O.R. Smash it for your country, smash it for your family, for your countrymen. The bass is pulsating. Feel it everywhere from head to fucking toe. Give me the bat. The building smiles. It takes the piss. It is wrong. My heart is a giant mouth, a snarling, growling mouth with sharp fucking fangs craving some destruction, some demolition, some obliteration, and some vengeance. SMASH. Crack the sign. Break the symbol. SMASH. Ruin their identity. SMASH. Break them. Break them. Broken. Fucking broken. Useless little pieces. SMASH. Kick the door. Defenders of our nation. Our nation. Quick get back in. Never knew you had it in you. You're a legend Pete. A warrior. A true soldier. I AM THE BEAT OF THE DRUM.

Midnight closes in and the town looks worn out and lifeless. Burnt-out rockets lie dead in the street. We stop off for a drink at The Somerset Arms because it has a late licence. To judge by our faces, I'd say the speed is wearing off. We have been drawn here to try and regain the high, to put the comedown off for a couple more hours at least and hold onto the connection that has fused us together this evening. But this seems an ordeal. Speech has failed, and we appear to be deep in thought, worrying about our own problems and wondering what the fuck tomorrow will bring.

This dark and dingy pub doesn't help. It is full of sombre shiftworkers from the hospital, local factories, and the docks. Some of them are here to pass the time. Some of them are here in need. The ones in need are easy to see — they cling onto the bar like shipwreck survivors. They hang their heads muttering.

We walk towards a table in the corner, almost feeling the need to tip-toe. I still feel I've got so much energy inside of me, but I'm not capable of using it anymore. We sit around the table looking into our glasses, waiting for someone to say something. It might as well be an Alcoholics Anonymous meeting.

"Fuck this shit," Tony says to break the silence. He then necks the majority of his pint and stands up. "This is like a funeral. I don't need to be in a place like this when I'm coming down off the speed. I'm off. Catch you all later."

Sidney appears to be feeling the same, so he says goodbye and follows Tony out of the pub. Jake and I both nod at each other gloomily as though we both know the situation we are in and accept it. It brings us closer, makes the friendship stronger. I feel like I could tell him anything right now. I feel like I need to tell him.

"You know that bloke we were talking to tonight after the meeting?" I say to him.

He lifts his head slowly. "Kelvin?"

"Yeah," I say.

"Seems a top geezer. What about him?" he asks.

I take a deep breath and then exhale. "Well ... he's my father."

Jake rubs his eyes and looks at me. "What are you on about?"

"I know it sounds mad, but when I was a kid he was a rotten bastard. Well I think he was. I think he tried to kill me."

Jake puts his hand in the air and laughs which turns into a chesty cough. "You're off your rocker pal. Too much of the old Billy Whizz I reckon. Let's make a move," he says.

My head is a fruit machine that's just hit the jackpot. My heart feels like it's giving birth. Fuck, what if this is an OD situation? What if my heart can't take all this shit? Hang on in there Mr Heart. Don't fail on me now. There are too many things I want to do. You can do it. Be strong. I take a deep breath. Calm down. Everything's ok. Easy does it. Need to sleep. Get rid of the scum. I think of Julie.

I heard sobs coming from the bedroom. There was a copy of *The Gravesend Reporter* on the table. A picture of Julie's brother was on the front page and below it a picture of an evil bastard. The difference between the two was unreal. Julie's brother was smiling, a look of excitement in his eyes, as though he was looking forward to the rest of his life. Which he was. The other guy, Bremner, just looked evil. There was nothing in his eyes. Some of the copy was smudged by tears.

LOCAL FAMILY'S WORLD TURNED UPSIDE DOWN BY RE-OFFENDER

A local family from Parrock Street are mourning the death of their beloved son. Michael Turner, 17, was a bright, friendly young man who was looking forward to starting an NVQ in Sports Science at Gravesend College. But his dream of becoming a sports physiotherapist was cut short after he was brutally stabbed to death shortly after leaving a Halloween party.

On his way home, Michael and one of his friends, who remains unnamed, were approached by Tommy Bremner, 20. Bremner held the two at knifepoint with the intent of robbing the young men, though Michael only had twenty pounds and a pay-as-you-go mobile phone. A struggle ensued and Bremner proceeded to stab Michael twelve times directly to the chest. Michael's friend fled the scene and phoned police, but Michael was dead by the time paramedics arrived.

Tommy Bremner, from Kings Farm, Gravesend, was no stranger to local authorities. He was eager to live up to his family's notorious criminal name. With 23 separate convictions against the family, Tommy looked up to his father, uncle and two elder brothers who have each served time in jail.

At the age of just 16, Tommy Bremner stabbed a boy three times in the back after a row. Just a few hours later, Bremner, who was alleged to have a severe heroin and cocaine addiction, forced his way into a two-bedroom house in Suffolk Road. There he tied up a man and woman, put pillow-cases over their heads and threatened them with a hammer, demanding money. But the man managed to untie his binds and raise the alarm.

He was later arrested at his grandparent's house in Kings Farm. He received an eight-year sentence but was released after serving just three years and four months.

Bremner had only been out of prison for five months before the slaying of Michael Turner. Michael's mum Sandra said, "Michael didn't have a bad bone in his body. He was such a loveable boy. I am disgusted that his murderer was released from prison. If he was made to carry out his sentence, my boy would still be alive." As well as mum Sandra, Michael leaves behind father Ben and two sisters, Carol and Julie.

CHAPTER TWELVE

Bluewater is a miniature world guarded by chalky walls. They are scars of the countryside as it was before the diggers arrived and ripped the land apart. It was a land where I would ride my bike and climb the great trees. I used to like looking at the animals roaming around in this area. Rabbits, deer, squirrels, birds. I wonder whether the diggers heard their screams. It's not as if they gave them an eviction notice. They were the rightful residents of this land; they were placed here by nature. How many of them knew what was about to happen? How many knew that their homes, their freedom, and their land was about to be massacred? A modern day big-fucking-bang wiping out their history, their existence, and their identity. And for what? To create another world: a world of indulgence, narcissism, and excess. And somewhere in here is Julie.

Hollywood stars on posters wearing sparkling watches, super-good-looking models in suits, perfectly toned mannequins in tight jeans and tight shirts gripped around bulging biceps. Fancy foreign aftershaves and perfumes rammed up my nostrils, organic health bars stuffed down my throat. Perfect holidays: white beaches, blue skies, fruity fucking cocktails teasing me in shop windows. HD, widescreen, 48 bastard inches, Dolby surround sound TVs with Botox-induced, white-toothed, big-breasted celebrities being paraded in front of me, telling me what I should buy, what I should look like, and what I should be. The pretence that designer labels make ugly life pretty. "Be beautiful" this place says. Every person in this place wants to be beautiful. But they all look the same with their fake tans and arrogant swagger, and they all look down their noses at the likes of me. I wonder whether they realise that there are people out there.

Starbucks winds me up even more. More people pretending to be beautiful. It just seems a sham. Perhaps it makes them look more upper class if they drink in places like this. Perhaps they think that the poor people won't be able to understand all the fancy coffees on the menu. I know I can't. I mean what is all this grande skinny latte mocha chocca?

"Pete," Julie calls out to me as I'm trying to make arse-about-tit of the menu.

I walk over to her and her absence affects me more than I was expecting. She may as well stand on my chest holding a ton of bricks. I feel that bastard lump rising in my throat and try to blame my recent over-use of Class A drugs, my lack of sleep, and my lack of nutrients. But I think I genuinely miss her.

"How's it going?" I say not knowing what to do with my hands, whether to put them in my pockets, shake her hand, or hug her. She orders us a cup of tea and a cappuccino and slowly sits back in her chair as if she's trying to ease into this situation. I wonder what she's thinking. What is she expecting from this? What am I expecting from this? Closure? I hate that word. Closure is for losers: it's for people that give up. I wonder if she felt the way I did when she saw me walk in. Did it make her stomach go funny, did it bring back memories for her, did I make her toes curl, did it make her want to fuck me the way she used to fuck me when we first met? We look at each other and smile nervy child-like smiles. All I need now is for Take My Breath Away to come on the stereo and then we can lunge at each other across the table, pushing the cappuccino to the floor, tearing at each other's clothes before embarking on a rough, wild, tender, reconciling fuck.

"So," I say, "what have you been up to?"

She blows on her cappuccino to cool it and she looks sexy. "Just the usual. Uni is keeping me really busy."

Does she mean the work is keeping her busy or the professor? "Keeping on top of things?" I say and then realise that these words just gave me a horrific mental picture.

"The support of the lecturers is really helping."

This just gets worse. I need to know but I can't just ask. I don't want to come across as needy, desperate, and jealous. Maybe I should just ask. No: bad idea. Try to delve a little deeper first. Maybe she knows that I know. I can tell that she knows that I am thinking about this, and now she probably knows that I know that she knows, and she is now probably thinking of something to say to stop me thinking about it. But at the same time, I don't want her to think that I'm thinking about it. So now I'm thinking of something to say to make it look like I'm not thinking it, but I just can't stop thinking about it.

"Are you sleeping with him?" The words just fly out of my mouth.

"Bloody hell Pete, sleeping with who?"

"I'm sorry, it's none of my business."

"No come on Pete, let's be honest with each other. Sleeping with who?" she asks.

I feel my face redden and my balls shrivel as if they are trying to climb inside to hide. "Your professor. Jerome wasn't it?"

Julie pushes her cappuccino to one side creating a clear path on the table for us to make contact. She kind of moves her hands towards me but then suddenly pulls back. "Look, I want you to know there has been no one else. I just couldn't do that, and I hope you believe me. I've only been gone a couple of days."

I release a big sigh and my balls come out of hiding. But then thinking about my failed attempt at a one-night-stand, a pang of guilt hits me in the stomach. "I do believe you," I say.

She kind of blushes and shrugs as if being modest yet proud of her unblemished morals.

"I know I said this to you the other day, but I really do owe you an apology. I was so obsessed with finding my father that I totally forgot about Michael. I understand that this time of year must be really hard for you."

She stares into her cappuccino. "There is not a day that goes by where I don't think about Michael. But I've learned to live with it, however hard it may be. And I take comfort in knowing that I'm working towards preventing things like Michael's death occurring again."

"He'd be proud of you," I say.

"Thanks," she says. "I think he would be too. I think that if that Bremner boy would have been given the correct counselling and rehabilitation then Michael would still be alive today."

"He was released too early."

"He wasn't ready to function again in society. He was bound to reoffend," she says.

"Well it doesn't help that the prisons are overcrowded," I say.

Julie's eyes light up as though she's surprised that I'm adding some serious input to the conversation. "I agree," she says. "Psychologists can't do their jobs properly."

"You know what I'd do? I'd deport all the foreign criminals back to their own countries and put them in their own prisons. That way we wouldn't have the problem of overcrowded prisons and then criminals wouldn't be released early," I say.

"I don't think it would be as easy as that. A lot of them will probably have families over here and that would take away their right to see them," she says.

"Well deport them too," I say, feeling myself becoming quite heated. "Look, the government haven't dealt properly with the problem of immigration and now people like us are suffering."

She looks at me as though she's trying to remember my name. "Blimey, where did that come from?"

"I'd put a total stop to all immigration until this country sorts itself out. We are always looking to solve other people's problems when we've got a whole load of shit to deal with in our own back yard," I say.

Once again Julie's eyes light up, but not in an intrigued way. Instead she looks shocked. "You can't ban them all Pete," she says. "Some of them are skilled workers that are needed to fill certain jobs. I agree that there are some problems due to immigration but maybe it's best to put a slight cap on the amount coming in and then spend some money on training."

"Yeah, yeah, but we've heard all this shit before. Nothing ever gets done. It's just broken fucking promises," I say.

She stares at me without saying a word as though she's studying every inch of my face.

"I'm sorry, I didn't mean to swear or sound rude. I've just been thinking about a lot of things recently. I've been thinking differently," I say.

"You can say that again," she says. "You seem totally different. You sound different and you look different. Have you not been sleeping? Your eyes are heavy, you're frowning. There's a kind of aggressiveness lodged in your features, Pete."

Aggressiveness? What am I going to ... then it hits me. I'm bound to earn some brownie points with this one.

"Well, like I was saying, I was selfish before but now I'm thinking of others. And just as you are working towards solving certain problems in our country, I'm now doing the same," I say.

"What are you talking about?" she asks.

"You're aiming to help our country by making sure that criminals don't reoffend, and I'm now making sure that our country isn't being polluted by foreign hatred. We are both in this together if you think about it."

She remains silent for a moment and the sound of clinking saucers, background chatter, and the grinding of coffee beans fills my ears. Outside of the coffee shop, a blizzard of faces and shopping bags fly past the window. "And where exactly is this foreign hatred coming from?" she asks.

"First of all, we wipe out the hatred coming from Islamic extremists. Instead of recognising this problem our country is treading on eggshells."

"And may I ask who we are?" she says as she crosses her arms.

"Defenders of the Realm. But this is just the first step towards fixing our broken country. Soon we are going to stop all the bad things. And that means people like Bremner will be stopped. We will make sure that what happened to Michael won't happen to someone else."

"The D.O.R?" she says. "Have you lost your mind?"

I feel my back arch as though some defence mechanism has been activated. "What do you know about us?"

"'Us,' huh? I know more than enough. Just the other day some students on campus were campaigning against them. I looked into it," she says.

"So, some spotty little bastards who have their heads in books and Pot Noodles all day think they know what the fuck they are talking about?"

"Open your eyes Pete," she says. "Do you know that the D.O.R are linked with football hooligans up and down the country? It's also rumoured that violent Neo-Nazi groups have been attending the marches."

"Yeah, well, the Neo-Nazi thing is a load of crap. Maybe one or two of us had some trouble at football grounds in the past," I say thinking of Tony. "But people change, they've realised that football hooliganism is pointless violence and now they want to put their passion towards a good cause."

Julie breathes deeply and springs her arms out like an umbrella being opened. "I can't believe what I'm hearing. This isn't you, Pete. The D.O.R use these false political motives as an excuse to kick the crap out of people. They're just racists."

I sigh, trying to keep calm and trying to keep my composure. "How can we be racists when we encourage British Muslims to stand up to the radical Islam laws which have a total stranglehold over them? Yeah that's right. We believe that they should be able to safely demand reform of their religion. Surely even you can see that their ideals need adjusting to be more relevant to the needs of the modern world. They're taught to totally despise the western world. It seems to me that you're just another one playing the race card," I say.

"Don't be so ridiculous. It seems to me that as a country we fought the Nazis for good reason. We lost millions and spent millions in stopping them. And look at us now. Or should I say look at you. Taking on Nazi methods on the pretence of a terrorist threat. What was the point in wiping out hatred like that only to adopt their ideas?"

I feel my composure slowly deteriorating. "Fucking hell, Julie, that's a bit strong. Can't you see that it's for the good of our country? We need people to know the dangers they face. We need to ensure that the public know all aspects of Islam and are aware of the implications that could arise for non-Muslims. This is why the wheels have been set in motion for a campaign of public education."

"Jesus, Pete," she says as her cheeks flame. "Do you really think that a few violent marches against Muslims and mosques will make England better? Look at the state of our economy, look at the shambles of the NHS, look at the thousands of soldiers that are dying in the name of anti-terrorism, when really it's all about oil, money and power."

I know that I'm fighting a losing battle with her. It's an argument that she will win every time, and I don't really want to get drawn in any further as it won't be long before I start tripping on my words and fumbling around for valid arguments trying to remember everything that was said at the meeting. I decide to play it cool. "One step at a time," I say.

She doesn't decide to play it cool. She's in full warrior mode. "One step at a time? And you think that the D.O.R are going to fix our country with a bunch of fascist football hooligans?"

I try to remain calm. "As I said, people change. And I don't know what your problem is. You always used to tell me that I didn't fit in anywhere. And you were right. I've gone through life like a headless chicken and now I've found somewhere that I fit in, somewhere where I am accepted and respected. You just don't like it one bit."

She shakes her head as though there's a wasp flying round her face. "You're right. I don't like it at all that you are mixed up with these kinds of people. And what is all this business about people changing?"

"I just think that people can change. People should be allowed second chances in life," I say.

Once again, she squints and studies me. "Something's not right about this," she says. "Has this got something to do with your father?"

I laugh nervously and look around the room. How does she figure out this stuff? "Well, kind of," I say.

"And he has something to do with the D.O.R?"

"Yeah, he does. But I didn't know that until I had already joined them. Bit of a coincidence really don't you think?" I say.

"And how did he react when you told him that you were his son?"

I pick up my cup of tea and blow into it. I wish I was small enough to jump into it and swim to the bottom. "Well ... he doesn't exactly know yet."

The tone of Julie's voice becomes higher pitched. "What?" she says. "So, you're just running around with him playing at saving the world? This is madness."

"Trust me. I know what I'm doing. I've spoken to him a couple of times now and he seems like a nice bloke. It's like he's got his head in the right place. Speaks a lot of sense too," I say. Julie bows her head as though my statement isn't worth answering. "Besides, you should know all about giving people another chance. Aren't you working towards changing people?" I say.

"Yes, but it takes a lot of work," she sighs. "I hope that he has changed, for your sake, Pete. But his being part of the D.O.R tells me that he hasn't."

My fuse is reaching its end. "For fuck's sake Julie. Can't you just be happy and supportive? I'm working towards something great. And if, at the same time, I can build a new relationship with my father, then I will."

"Pete," she says clamping her hands together and closing her eyes for a moment. "I just want you to be careful. This is the same man who put you in a van at the top of a hill and let the handbrake off; just remember that."

The anger inside of me seeps out when she puts her arm across the table inviting my hand into hers. "This stupid group is not the answer," she says.

Her studying must be working because right now I want to curl up into a little ball, sit on her lap pouring my heart out while she strokes my head and talks soothingly to me. Psychology. "So, are you going to come home then?" I say to her trying to get her off the subject of the D.O.R.

She smiles and strokes my palm with her fingertips. "When I finish my degree, there is a chance that I may be placed in a job somewhere else."

"I'd move with you," I say.

"It's easy to say that now Pete," she says. "But let's not get too far ahead of ourselves."

But I already am. I'm picturing the two of us living far away, walking a couple of Labradors by a stream, and picking fresh vegetables from our garden for a Sunday roast; red wine and log fires, comfy jumpers and a wooden staircase, tender fucking in the warmth while the wind is howling outside.

"It'd be perfect," I say.

"Some things will have to change," she says. "We are going to have to be more honest with one another for a start. No more lies. I want to be included in everything. I'd also like you to make more of an effort with my university friends and support me more in what I want to do. And whatever the hell you have just got yourself into, wake up and get yourself out. I mean it."

I nod. "That's fine. I promise to be more honest and supportive."

"I also know that I have to change too though. Any thoughts on that?" she says. This may be a trick question. I may get into trouble listing her faults. "It's ok you can be honest with me," she says as though reading my mind.

"I'd like you to stir the tea properly when you make it because the sugar always sits on the bottom," I say.

"You sod," she says. But she's smiling.

"I think we should allow ourselves out. Have fun ... the way we used to. You know; just go out, get pissed, have a dance and have some dirty drunken sex."

For the first time in a long time she looks like my Julie again: the sexy, caring, fun loving, kind-hearted Julie. "You've got yourself a deal. Seriously though Pete, I don't want to hear any more D.O.R nonsense OK?"

She's going to stay with Carol just for a couple more nights so that they can spend a little more time together. This means she's going to try and convince Carol that I'm good for her.

CHAPTER THIRTEEN

I hear a knock at the door and almost shit myself — two blokes with their hoods up wearing Union Jack masks which cover their noses and mouths.

"Rule Britannia ... Britannia rule the waves ... Britons never never never shall be slaves." Jake and Sid singing on my doorstep. They walk in and Jake hands me a jumper and a mask. "What do you think pal?" he says giving me a twirl. "Got these made up for the march on Saturday."

The jumper is black with an embroidered red crucifix on a white background. NO SURRENDER around the top, DEFENDERS OF THE REALM underneath. A smaller version is stitched into the right arm and GRAVESEND DIVISION on the left.

"What's the mask all about?" I say.

Jake removes his mask and snorts through his nose like a pissed off silver back. "It's a fucking statement," he says. "It's alright for Muslims to wear their Burkhas and it's just fine for Indians to wear their turbans. So, we should be allowed to wear Union Jack masks. Plus, it protects our identities."

"Why would we want to protect our identities?" I ask.

"Fucking hell Pete, you know what fanatics are like. It's just a precaution. Try it on."

I look in the mirror. It feels kind of good. It feels nice to be a part of something, wearing a uniform. I take the jumper off and leave it on the side of the sofa.

"Fits you like a condom," he says. "Oh yeah speaking of condoms, guess what young Sidney here got up to last night?"

Sidney looks embarrassed and pulls his hood up. "Forget about it. Where's the TV controller?" he says to try and change the subject.

"You wet flannel. It's fucking funny," Jake says.

Sid looks around for the remote.

"Well I'm gonna tell him then," Jake says and then leans towards me. "Last night when we got in after the meeting, I was just dropping off to sleep when all of a sudden I heard Sidney shout out 'PETER CROUCH' from his room. Anyway, I was ... "

"All right. I'll tell him before you make it sound worse than it is," Sid interrupts. "Last night when we got in, after bashing up that mosque and having a drink in The Somerset Arms, I just couldn't sleep. That speed was fucking strong. Anyway, I'm lying in bed with my heart racing like a fucking Derby winner. And what I normally find to be the perfect cure for times like that is to have a wank. But that wasn't going to happen because the iPad is always in Jake's room. So, I tried to get the internet up on my phone to try and access some porn, but I didn't have any poxy credit. It was bad Pete, I was a desperate man in a desperate situation. I seriously thought that if I didn't shoot my load I was going to have a heart attack. So, then I remember I still have that prostitute's number on my phone."

"The one with the lazy eye?" I ask.

"Yeah. I gave her a bell and luckily she was still up. Don't think she remembered me but chicks like that will go anywhere for a bit of dough, no matter what time it is."

"She'll remember you now though," Jake says with a big grin.

"Tell him to fucking stop going on at me," he says. I pretend to zip Jake's mouth shut

"She turns up fifteen minutes later and looks just as wrecked as me: chewing her lips, gurning, and her head bopping around. Looked like she'd popped a couple of e's. So, we go up to my room, she throws her clothes off and instantly starts sucking me off. She smelt weird; a mixture of bubble bath and sweat. And what with her lazy eye an all it wasn't much of a turn on. But I was charged right up and couldn't really give a fuck. I just dimmed the lights a bit and thought of that TV bird who's a chef. Oh, what's her name?"

"I never can think of her name," Jake says.

"Well I was thinking about her with my eyes closed. So, this prozzie pops a condom on the end of my knob and starts riding me. The problem was, I haven't exactly been drowning in pussy lately and I thought I was gonna blow my load instantly. So, I mentally start to pick the best starting eleven for England. She's jumping up and down on me like her life depends on it and I'm working my way from the goal keeper through to the strikers. Then I'm concentrating so much on not blowing my load that I accidentally shout out 'Peter Crouch!' And she thinks that it's some kind of fetish of mine. So, she carries on riding me shouting out 'Crouchie, oh Crouchie.'"

"Apart from you even considering Peter Crouch in an England team, tell him the worst of it," Jake says.

Sid looks a bit sheepish. "After she jumped off me I realised the Johnny had split ... "

Jake interrupts: "And then the silly wanker doesn't even have enough money to pay her. So, Sid owes me fifty quid for a dose of the clap!"

Jake holds his stomach in laughter. He has this trait of finishing other people's stories so as to kind of get the credit for them.

"You better get yourself down the clinic," I say to Sid.

We sit down and chill for a while, flicking through the channels. Sid dangles a piece of string over Dolly. She just looks at him with an expression that says, "grow up." I start to think back over last night's events. I can't help but feel slightly childish and Julie's words spring to mind. *No more D.O.R nonsense.*

"Do you think what we did last night was right?" I say to Jake.

He looks at me puzzled. "Why's that pal?"

"Well I just can't help but think it was pointless. I mean it's not going to change anything by doing little things like that, is it."

Jake stretches out and takes a deep breath. "Not feeling chicken?"

"No, of course not mate. I just think we could be doing other things, that's all."

"Look Pete," he says and pats me on the back. "What we did last night was like a little bruise. We need to spread some bruises, before making the real blow. Do you think that they would bat an eyelid if they demolished one our churches?"

"This is a real cause, isn't it mate?" I say struggling to think of Jake ever mentioning going to a church. I can't exactly see him with a side parting singing hymns. "I mean it's not just an excuse to kick the fuck out of people is it?"

Jake looks genuinely offended. "What's got into you?"

"Oh, I was talking to Julie earlier and she reckons that the D.O.R are just a bunch of racists who use political motives as an excuse."

He puts his hand to his heart as if he's just been shot with an arrow. "This is exactly what I was telling you about. It's so easy to play the race card. Jesus Pete, you don't doubt the cause do ya?"

"Er. No. I don't."

"What was you doing seeing her anyway? I thought she left you?" he says.

"She moved out. But I was thinking today how nice it would be to get out of here one day. Maybe start a family and all that."

Jake looks out the window slightly confused. "She's a trainee shrink ain't she?" he says. "No disrespect pal, but you have to be careful of those people."

"How do you know?"

"Had to see one of them a few years back, didn't I?"

"What happened?"

He swallows hard and looking out over the river he starts to talk as if he's addressing the waves instead of someone in this room. "Well it was either that or I would have had to do a stint in jail. It was a fucked-up period. My family were out of control, feuding amongst them and some of my poxy brothers kept stealing from my mum's handbag. My mum was living on antidepressants and vodka. Everywhere I looked people I knew just kept getting beaten senseless. It becomes a way of life you know? I guess I just took my frustrations out. A few petty burglaries here and there, a few fights, and I got caught in possession of some smoke. They were gonna throw the book at me, but they decided that what I really needed was this therapy bollocks. After a few meetings I wished they had put me behind bars. Fucking awful."

"How come, mate?" I ask.

"It only made things more confusing for me. Clouded things even more. Didn't clarify a fucking thing. It gave me the creeps. Sometimes you just need to be told what you are instead of trying to make you something you're not. Life makes you work these things out. You don't need some stiff in a suit trying to find out what makes you tick. And if you accept their theories and all the shit they tell you, then you're fucked; proper fucked. You turn into a vegetable; a dependent vegetable, you're attached to behaviour they tell you are. You're controlled, you're a clone."

Jake sits next to me again. "You want to just jack all this in do you? Just forget about all the problems in this country? Be easy that; just to walk way in ignorance," he says.

"Nah, I didn't mean now, mate," I say.

He starts to chew one of his fingernails. "Don't tell me you want to be one of them." He has a weird look in his eye.

"I still believe in the D.O.R, mate. I'm just saying that I like the idea of all that stuff with Julie in the future."

Jake's eyes are now wide open. "But there won't be no future if people keep leaving someone else to deal with the problems. Don't you want to make a change, live your life to the full; live it with passion, determination? Don't you wanna engrave PETE JARVIS on history itself? Be the fucking saviour of this nation?"

I don't know what to say.

"Anyway, I've got to shoot over to Big Tone's and give him some of this D.O.R clobber. Fancy coming along? We'll get a bit of grub and then go down the boozer to watch the England game. England games are always good for business. There's nothing better than a few lagers and a bit of gear while watching the game, it gets them right in the mood."

We drop Sidney home because he's got an early start in the bakery tomorrow. Before we drive off Jake shouts out the window to him. "See ya later Crouchie."

Is that guilt that I feel? Am I betraying Julie? Maybe she'll warm to the idea. Maybe it's just another problem I can deal with later...

The clouds look low enough to reach out and touch as we make our way to the sports bar. Roads covered in puddles and potholes make the journey a bumpy one. The rain is falling at an annoying speed which confuses the windscreen wipers. We pass a kebab house on the left and some council houses. Bricks, bricks, bricks.

"Perfect weather for football this. Hope it's pissing down in London too. Makes the pitch all wet and slippy. Perfect for crunching slide tackles," Tony says putting his hands on his head. "Ahh, I fucking love watching England in a boozer."

"Only because a boozer is the only place you can watch football — you're banned from most of the stadiums," Jake says.

The atmosphere is electric.

Most of the people acknowledge Tony and Jake as we mingle our way through the crowded pub. Jake becomes increasingly frustrated when nobody buys any gear from him. They all say they haven't got enough money. Tone says it may be true because people aren't exactly loaded nowadays, but Jake isn't having any of it. He thinks something isn't right.

England are one-nil down at half-time as aggravated punters make their way to the bar. Jake is tapped on the shoulder by a bloke wearing a yellow cardigan over a grey polo shirt buttoned up to the top. His jeans are those skin-tight ones that come down just above the ankles. He wears some slip-on beige shoes with no socks and he's got ginger-coloured hair with a side parting. Everything about him says "Essex boy." There's probably a Citroën Saxo with a big spoiler and alloys sitting in the car park.

"Awright Jake, owz it goin guvnor?" he says in a strong cockney accent which seems like it's for show.

The bloke showers Jake in affection, putting his hand on his shoulder. Jake jumps back slightly. "Fucking hell Eddie you look like some kind of banana split," he says.

The bloke, Eddie, starts to laugh loudly, stupidly, and falsely. "Ha ha, you always like to av a bubble. Ain't seen you in donkey's," he says putting his arm on Jake's shoulder again. "Ere, you remember that time those geezers kicked off with us in McDonald's?"

Jake who seemed a bit annoyed at the first sight of Eddie now seems to warm to him. Perhaps it's because he's got a story that will boost Jake's ego. Jake makes sure that both Tony and I are listening.

"Yeah, kind of, what happened again?" he says blatantly already knowing.

"Well," Eddie continues looking at me and Tony. "Jake had just given me a gram of the old rocket fuel and I was about to go to the bog to get some up me hooter. But as I was on the apple and pears these two chavvies knocked me off my fucking feet. Must av been skagheads or something clucking for a fix. Anyway, they start putting their hands in me pockets trying to rob me and then I see Jake come from nowhere and land a fuckin peach of a right to one of these idiots. He goes fuckin flying. The other geezer shits himself and then Jake grabs him by the throat and says ... "

"I'm gonna make you look like the fucking mug that you are," Jake says interrupting Eddie to finish the story. "I didn't even hit him, I spat in my Big Mac, put it on the floor and told him to eat it like a dog."

"You should've seen the look on his Chevy Chase," Eddie says. "The fucking sight of it. One geezer with a bloody nose sprawled out on the steps in McDonald's while his mate is trying to eat a burger off the floor without using his hands. We fuckin showed them skaggy bastards."

"What do you mean we? You were still picking yourself up off the floor. The only reason I did that was because I didn't want them idiots stealing my coke from you. It would have given you an excuse not to pay. You shit yourself really you ginger tart," Jake says.

Once again Eddie starts to laugh embarrassingly. "You're mustard you are mate. Always having a bubble. That's why I fucking like you," he says to Jake.

What Eddie really means is that he fears him. He doesn't particularly like him, but he's shit-scared of him. Plus, he provides Eddie's coke.

"Listen Eddie," Jake says. "What's up with all these boys in here tonight? Not one of them has had any gear off me; they say they're all broke. You'll have some won't ya pal?"

"Er, yeah course I will. Can I pay you at the weekend though? It's just I picked up a gram last night," Eddie says. He then instantly looks as though he regrets saying this.

Jake screws his face up and fierces his eyes. He leans closer to Eddie tugging on his yellow cardigan. "And who did you get that off?"

Eddie's face turns as red as his hair. "Look mate, I've always been loyal to you. I'm still buying from you mate; I think you're a diamond," he says, the cockney accent disappearing.

"Pull your tongue out of my arse and answer my question, you brown-nosing ginger twat," Jake says, grabbing his cardigan with both hands much to Tony's amusement.

"I got it off one of those Indian blokes. But it ain't just me mate. All of these boys in here are waiting for 'em to arrive. Should be here any moment."

Jake looks as though he's ready to bite Eddie's Adam's apple out of his throat. "Fuck's sake," he says. "What's the deal with everyone getting their gear from these Pakis now? Am I missing something? Is it some kind of sick fucking joke? Some kind of let's-buy-our-drugs-off-some-cunt-who-ain't-even-English joke? A fucking protest to piss Jake off? I mean tell me Eddie-o cos I'm all fucking ears."

"It's just pretty good stuff, and more importantly it's cheap," Eddie says.

"It's probably cut to fuck," Jake says.

Eddie looks as though he is going to open his mouth to say something but this time he refrains. Jake looks round the pub for a moment.

"So, they've got the balls to turn up here on my patch to sell to my customers, have they?" Eddie doesn't say anything to that. "Listen Eddie, seeing how you think I'm so much of a diamond — oh, and the fact that I rescued you in McDonald's — I want you to never buy from them again. And I want you to tell everyone else not to. Tell 'em that the gear is really bad and is cut with some really nasty shit. You got that?"

"Crystal fucking clear. You're my main man Jake," Eddie says fitting back into his cockney-Essex-boy skin.

We leave Eddie looking quietly confident that he's escaped a kicking and make our way through the pub to a position just by the back door. It gives us a perfect view of the entrance and Jake keeps his eye on it while Tony and I watch the game from a distance. It's not long before two Indian guys walk in. Both of them are dressed in designer gear. The tallest one looks like an Asian Elvis impersonator. His black hair is slicked back with a wavy quiff. He has a light blue shirt tucked into some black jeans with a black belt that has a chunky gold buckle. Gold keeper rings cover his fingers and a gold chain hangs down his un-buttoned shirt. He walks confidently, with an air that he knows something no one else does. His companion is shorter and stockier with a fully-grown beard and a blue turban on his head. He too wears a lot of gold. A long grey overcoat hangs over a white shirt which is tucked into some black trousers. He shuffles fast to keep up with the long strides of Elvis.

Jake watches them as they make their way through the crowd pulling wraps of coke out of their pockets and putting money back into them.

"Fucking liberty, ain't it Tone?" Jake says.

"Sure is," Tony replies.

"It's about time I met these business rivals of mine I think."

"Some of them bastards are a bit tasty in a fight," Tony says.

"How do you know?" Jake asks.

"You can see just by looking at them; it's in their blood. Years of being colonised and all that shit; had to fight for themselves. Plus, I've seen one of them bite a chunk out of a geezer's ear outside The King's Head."

Jake smiles and licks his lips as though there is a giant steak floating in front of him. "Good," he says.

The game finishes. England have lost one-nil, but the punters remain in high spirits. Probably something to do with the amount of coke that has been sniffed. We exit the pub sharply and Jake insists on sitting in the car park until the Indian guys appear. They leave in a crowd, laughing and joking with the others, which seems to piss Jake off even more. They say their goodbyes and climb into a black Range Rover with blacked-out windows and large alloy wheels, a gold star and half-moon on a sticker at the top of the windscreen. Jake starts the engine. "Think they're fucking gangsters driving around in that," Jake says sounding more jealous than pissed off. "How the fuck did they afford that?"

"By stealing all your customers," Tony says and Jake just grunts.

"What you gonna do Jake?" I ask.

"I dunno. Ain't thought that far yet," he says with his gaze on the Range Rover.

The Range Rover moves out and when it comes close Jake pulls out directly in front of it. "Stay in the car Pete," he says as he opens his door and springs out of his seat. I feel a bit left out yet relieved as I watch through the rear window. The two Indian guys get out.

"What the fuck do you think you're doing? You almost went straight into me. You fucking blind?" Jake says to them and I see that he has already created a confrontation.

"Leave it out, you pulled out on me," Elvis says.

"You getting fucking mouthy?" Jake says.

The guy in the turban steps forward. "What you gonna do about it if we are?"

"Oh, look it's the fucking Turbanator," Tony says. "How about I open you up and spill your Paki guts out all over this car-park."

The guy in the turban goes for Tony but Elvis holds him back. "Wait a minute, I know what this is about. I thought I recognised you," Elvis says to Jake.

"Good, well then you know that I'm going to burst your fucking mouth open," Jake says.

I can't believe it when Elvis laughs. "You're just what I expected. No wonder you're losing business. You're a typical loudmouth who thinks he can throw his weight around to get what he wants. Well I'll tell you now: I ain't one to be pushed around," he says.

"I tell you what," Jake says edging closer to him with clenched fists. "How about you fuck off home back to where you came from and then I might only hurt you a little bit."

Once again Elvis laughs. "This *is* my home, you dickhead. I was born and raised here. I'm as English as you are."

Jake points towards the Islamic symbol on the car. "No, you're fucking not. If you were English, you wouldn't go around parading that piece of shit on your car."

Jake looks like he's struck a chord as Elvis now walks towards him. No laughter this time. "You better watch your mouth," he says.

Tony and the guy with the turban are nose-to-nose as if waiting for a bell to signal them to fight. A line of traffic has formed as the encounter has blocked the exit. Drivers hit their car horns in frustration.

"You turn my fucking stomach you know that. You Muslim scumbags," Jake says as though he's waiting for and wanting Elvis to throw the first punch.

"You ignorant fucking fool. You know nothing."

"I know that there are too fucking many of you," Jake says.

"Maybe that's a good reason not for you to fuck with me then," Elvis replies.

Jake shrugs his shoulders. "I'm telling ya to stop dealing to my customers or I'm gonna cripple ya."

People have got out their cars and are shouting at us to get out the way. Car horns are blaring.

Elvis looks to the ground, sighs, and then takes his jacket off. "OK. Cripple me then."

As if this was the bell Tony had been waiting for he lunges towards the guy in the turban and gives him a swift headbutt to the nose sending him flying back. A crowd has now gathered to watch the spectacle. I shout out of the window just as Jake puts his fists up. Acknowledging me he seems to realise that this isn't the time or place, tells Tony and then they both jump back in the car. Jake pulls out of the car park as quick as a rabbit at a greyhound track.

"Bollocks," he says as he hits the steering wheel. "I really wanted to land one on that wanker."

"If you get collared for fighting again they'll lock you up," says Tony.

"The Turbanator," Jake says laughing. "I liked that. But in all seriousness, something's got to be done about these wankers."

"What you got in mind," Tony asks.

"I think I'll go and see Vic tomorrow."

When I get in I see Dolly sitting under the tap in the kitchen hoping to catch some loose drops of water. I top her bowl up with fresh water. This makes me feel good about myself; like a good parent. So, I treat myself to smoking a cigarette in the front room. The smoke rises to the ceiling performing double somersaults and back flips on the way.

Julie's on my mind. Is there a way to have both her and the D.O.R in my life? When I'm with Jake and the lads I feel ... what? Alive? Part of something? Dangerous? Julie would say that's the wrong word to use and maybe she would be right. But when I'm with her I feel ... secure ... safe.

I sleep pretty much the whole way through and have a weird dream in which Jake and I are conjoined like Siamese Twins. We are in a fight, but it is always my half of our body that gets beaten. Our opponent is my father and in the corner of the ring my mum is trying to throw a white towel in, but it keeps bouncing off the ropes.

CHAPTER FOURTEEN

We are off to see Vic. Vic. We find a place to park at the end of Shamrock Road. Someone has scribbled a C in place of the R on the street sign making it look like ShamCock. A children's playground is full of unshaven, scruffy drunkards sitting on the roundabout drinking shitty cider and probably talking about how crap life is; or how easy it is. A silver Mercedes with a personalised number plate VIC 09 is parked just outside this council house, putting the clapped-out, rusty Ford Fiestas to shame. Next door a guy sits on his garden wall, wearing green slippers and a nicotine-stained dressing gown. He peers over the top of the Daily Sport with a rolled-up cigarette attached to his lips, acknowledges us with a slight nod of the head and raises his paper again. We walk through the front gate, which is hanging by one hinge. We avoid the rusty washing machine that has been dumped in a flower bed and kick the numerous armless and legless dolls that are spread out on the grass. The door opens before we knock. A powerful odour of cigarette smoke and baby wipes rolls out of the house.

The first thing I see is a massive belly with VICTOR tattooed in a semi-circle round a belly button. A picture of a gun sits under the V and a dollar sign under the R. He stands in the doorway wearing just boxer shorts and a chunky gold chain around his neck, munching away on a sandwich, not saying a word. Egg yolk dribbles down his chin and onto his hand which is covered in gold rings and unrecognisable tattoos.

"Alright Vic?" Jake asks.

He just looks at the three of us, eating his sarnie. Then he diverts his gaze to next door where the bloke in the dressing gown is sitting. "Oi, Nobby," he shouts out. "You look like a fucking scarecrow sitting there; you're giving me the creeps. Fuck off inside you cunt."

The man drags himself from the wall, mumbles something and disappears inside. Victor then looks back to us. "Where you been?" he says finishing off his sarnie and licking the yolk from his fingers.

"Business has been bad Vic. It's those Pakis," Jake says.

"Alright, alright, don't go shouting your mouth off to the whole of fucking Gravesend. Get inside," he says.

The living room looks like some kind of X-rated Argos. There are stacked boxes everywhere of knocked-off goods. Calvin Klein boxer shorts, Adidas jumpers, plasma TVs, DVDs, microwaves and even Pampers nappies. There is one corner of the room totally dedicated to porn as well. Hundreds of magazines and films;

something for everyone: lesbians, schoolgirls, nurses, pissing, squirting, Asian, mature, bondage, threesomes, foursomes, orgies, big tits, small tits, hairy pussies, shaven pussies, bukkake ... what the fuck's that?

We take a seat on the tatty sofa in front of a coffee table scattered with cans of CS gas and knuckle dusters. The wall to the side of me is covered in cracks like huge varicose veins. The sound of crying babies comes from upstairs and Vic shouts up to "keep the fucking racket down". A heavily pregnant woman comes down the stairs smoking away on a cigarette. I get the feeling that the foetus has already got his name down for HM Prison Wormwood Scrubs, just as a foetus of a rich bastard is university-bound and destined for a career in medicine. Poor little fucker. Weird that I think: how foetuses have already got their future planned for them before they have even entered the world.

Vic plonks himself down in between Jake and Sid. Sid slowly edges away and then sits on the arm rest.

"So," Vic says. "I know this skinny ugly bastard here," he says as he leans across and ruffles Sidney's hair. "But him," he says pointing to me. "I don't know him. Who's yer chum Jakey boy?"

"That's Pete, you saw him round mine the other day, remember?" Jake replies.

"Oh right. Pete? Of course it's Pete. Stupid fucking Vic, stupid fucking Vic," he says slapping his own head. "How did I not know it was Pete. Pete, Pete, Pete. Plain old Pete. Everyone knows Pete. Vic knows Pete, doesn't he? No, Vic doesn't remember Pete from the other day."

Vic turns to Jake and pokes his head towards him with wide eyes and an open mouth revealing some pretty dirty gums. Jake pulls a face that I've never seen before. He looks nervous. "No Vic. Stupid me," he says laughing nervously. "He's a good friend of mine. I've known him since he was this tall," Jake says lowering his hand to indicate a small person.

"What were you, a fucking hobbit?" he says laughing.

I guess the three of us realise that we need to laugh also ... so we do.

Vic nods and seems to congratulate himself. Then he suddenly stops and raises his finger to me. "I'm Victor," he says pointing to his tattoo. "But you probably know that anyway. Most people do. So here we all are, sitting in Vic's house. Vic's nice cosy house. And you — I guess I know why you are here?" Vic says slapping Jake's knee. "You be wanting some of Vic's special stuff, right?"

Jake looks on edge; somehow smaller. "Well actually Vic, that's what I've come to talk to you about," he says.

Vic puts his hand out in front of his own face and stares at it as if it's an enemy. "So Jakey not be wanting any of Vic's special stuff then?" he says speaking to his hand.

"Well not at the moment Vic, I'm having trouble shifting it. I've even got some of that speed you gave me the other day," Jake says.

Still looking at his hand Vic says, "Trouble shifting it he says. What's wrong with Vic's stuff? Is Vic's stuff shit? Shit Vic, shit Vic, shit Vic. Is that what it is?"

Jake looks to me and Sid who are doing everything to not try and stare at this lunatic talking to his hand speaking about himself in the third person. "Of course it's not Vic. It's just that some other dealers seem to be taking all my business," he says.

Vic stretches his fingers out as though he's mimicking a bird with a beak. "So, Vic's stuff is good? It's just the other stuff is better?" he says still not taking his eye from his hand.

"No way Vic, it's just cheaper," Jake says.

In one swift swoop Vic pretends to take a bite out of this imaginary bird and then kind of growls. "I see. Vic sees. Vic sees everything remember. Vic understands that Jake wants Vic to lower his prices too. Is that it? Is this some kind of sick fucking conspiracy against Vic? Does Jake make up this shit about other dealers with cheaper gear cos he wants cheaper prices himself? What is this, pick on Vic day? Let's-all-take-the-fucking-piss-out-of-Vic-day? Let's-all-pull-Vic's-pants-down-and-shaft-Vic-up-the-arse-day? Cos that would be funny wouldn't it?" he says and then directly looks at all three of us. "Is that what you want to do today? All fuck Vic up the arse?"

What I would describe as an awkward silence descends. I mean what the fuck can you say to this? We all shake our heads and mutter "no."

"So, what's wrong with Vic's arse then? Is it an ugly arse? Is it a fat arse? Are you all saying that Vic is fat?" he says.

I find myself digging my finger nails into my thumb. As if that is going to solve anything. I guess the others have done the same too because the tension in this room is fucking suffocating.

"Come on you useless cunts. Is Vic fat?" he asks again. "You: You answer me." I hear him say.

Its times like these I wish I could just crawl back up into the womb where I came from. Legs shaking, I lift my head slowly, praying that he's not pointing to me. I'm fucking relieved when I see him pointing towards Sidney.

"W-w-who me? Oh, no, Vic. No fucking way mate. You ain't ... "

"And my arse; what's that like?" Vic says standing up and bending over in front of Sid. He then pulls his boxer shorts down.

With a big fat arse in his face, Sidney glances over to me with fear in his eyes. He then turns back to Victor's arse and then looks to be studying it as though his life depends on it.

"It's ... er ... great Vic. Nothing wrong with it. Not fat in the slightest bit. Fucking great in fact mate. Great arse to have Vic. Wish I had one like that," Sid says.

Vic stands up straight pulling his boxers up. "So, you do want to fuck me in the arse then?"

Sid's mouth opens, and his chin almost drops down to his lap. He turns pale and looks like a man who is minutes away from death. The big box of pampers stacked next to him seems ironic right now.

Laughter then booms off the walls. "You fucking poof!" Vic says holding his stomach. "Only joking you cunt. Want an arse like mine? Ha you fucking fairy."

We all look at one another not knowing whether to laugh or fucking cry. Laughing seems the better option; so we do ... until Vic stops laughing. He then pokes his head into Jake's face. "So, you're not mugging Vic off then?" he says.

"Of course not pal. I would never mug you off. I'm telling you the truth," Jake replies.

Vic closes his eyes for a second and then sighs. "Good," he says sitting back down. "Then we can all have a nice time now. Drink, anyone? SYLVIA!" He shouts upstairs. "Go and get some tins for me and the boys here."

The pregnant woman floats down the stairs and into the kitchen leaving just a trail of cigarette smoke behind her.

"So, you were telling me about some Pakis?" Vic says to Jake.

"Yeah they're fucking ruining me."

"And you're letting them do it?" Vic asks.

"Well I don't know what I can do."

The pregnant woman comes in with a can of lager for each of us. "Everywhere they are, them Pakis," he says snatching a beer from Sylvia. "Wasn't always like this. No, used to be a few of 'em scattered about the town. Just a few corner shops and stuff like that. But now? Now they've fucking multiplied by the millions; got their mitts into every pie. Garages, construction businesses, supermarkets, and now they're stepping on my toes. And Vic doesn't like this," he says taking a mouthful of lager.

"What do we do then Vic?"

"We let the cunts know that we ain't gonna just roll over. We'll hit 'em hard: wallets and ribs. I want both of them broken. In fact, I want every one of them piss-taking wankers to never walk again and I want to take every fucking single penny off them. We need a plan. Maybe we need a fall guy — some silly fucker to help us," Vic says while looking into space, fantasizing about a bloodbath.

"And how are we gonna do that? What's the plan?" Jake asks.

Vic looks at Jake as if he's pissed off that he's just interrupted his vision of broken ribs. "You sound like old bill."

Jake laughs but I can tell that Vic has just caused himself a major dose of paranoia. He jumps up and goes to look out the window. He closes the blinds and starts to pace up and down the living room. We sit in silence again and the paranoia burning out of him makes the place as steamy as a sauna. "Fucking hell Vic, you know I'm not the police," Jake replies, drips of sweat rolling down his forehead.

Vic looks at Jake, the whites in his eyes standing out like light bulbs next to his red face. "Stand up. All of you stand the fuck up," he says putting his fists in the air. "Now take your shirts off. I wanna make sure you ain't got no fucking wires on you."

He approaches us one by one making sure he's satisfied that we're not plotting against him. I begin to wonder what I've let myself into. I don't want any part of this ... nothing to do with people like this.

Once he's certain that we aren't the police he sits back down. "Ok lads, my fault. You know how it is with the old bill and my family. We're like a fucking monopoly set; the cunts ain't happy till they've claimed the lot of us. They've got my eldest Brian locked up and they've got young Doogie too," Vic says.

For some reason I start to think of Julie's brother and how it is people like Vic that breeds criminals.

"You get to see them much Vic?" Jake asks.

"Nah, not really," Vic says taking another mouthful of lager. "Brian's been in and out all his life; he knows what he's doing, how to handle it. And Doogie? Well he's just starting out. So, this will be good for him, it will make him more of a man."

"What did they do?" Sidney asks Vic.

"Brian got collared knocking off that post office down in Southfleet and Doogie the mad fucker decided to stab some cunt he was trying to rob," he says laughing.

Some cunt? Probably some innocent kid just like Julie's brother who had his whole life to look forward to.

"Doogie's a silly fucker," he continues. "Still maybe he'll be a bit more cautious next time he pulls something like that. You always learn from your mistakes. Prison will teach him that. And when he gets out he'll have to be on his toes cos he's gonna have some others to show the ropes to," Vic says pointing to the sound of the screaming children coming from upstairs. "Got a whole army of them in the making."

I start to feel sick; sick that he talks about crimes as though they are Boy Scout awards. The more you do, the more fucking badges you get. A surge of anger flows through me. I look at this fat, nutty bastard already committing his kids to a future of crime, sitting on his fat arse without a care in the world. I want to hurt the bastard, I want to hurt him real bad. I want him to know that it's people like him that messed up Julie's life. It's his fault that he produced a nasty evil bastard. It's his fault that he brought a specimen of fucking evil into this world; a specimen of evil like the Bremner bastard that killed my Julie's brother. And he's going to keep doing it; he's going to keep producing these nasty fuckers until he hasn't got one last drop of spunk left in his balls.

Vic's phone starts ringing with the Eye of the Tiger tune. Vic stands up to answer it and points to the door. On the way out I hear him saying, "you better be up here with as much money as you've got, otherwise I'm gonna cut your Jacobs off, you little prick. You don't wanna piss Vic off now, do ya boy?"

CHAPTER FIFTEEN

Silence fills the car. I'm too busy thinking about the Bremner bastard and how I feel as though I've just mixed with his type. I feel as though I have betrayed Julie. Jake perhaps feels a little like his macho pride has been dented in front of his friends and I guess Sidney is still traumatised at having a fat hairy arse in his face and almost getting a kicking because of it. Eventually we park in the nearest car park to Ella's café, but food is the last thing on my mind.

As we walk down Queen's Street, the smell of cannabis instantly hits us. "Smells like someone's got a good bit of leaf on the go," Sid says.

The smell becomes stronger as we continue down the street. Dodgy looking shops reserved for side streets like this look diseased with faded signs and crumbling brick work. Bored shop owners stand outside smoking cigarettes, others sit behind empty tills doing crosswords just to pass time. A butcher's displaying a window full of flesh just seems a waste of an animal. If you're going to get hacked to death, then at least die for a reason.

The cannabis is now strong enough to get high from and then I see why. Two young lads appear from behind the pawnbrokers. As they turn our way I instantly recognise one of them. I freeze for a moment before dropping my head and quickly walking to the other side of the street. Noticing this, Jake follows me.

"What the fuck's up with you?" he says.

"Nothing," I say. "Just keep walking."

He puts his hand on my shoulder to stop me. I quickly glance round and see the Smurf Shady kid looking over as if trying to put a name to a face. Perhaps he's too stoned to remember. Sid now joins us on the other side of the road and asks what's up. I turn to continue walking and then I hear it.

"Oi! I'm still gonna gut you bitch," Smurf Shady shouts out.

I pretend to ignore it and walk on, but Jake stops me with both hands now. Smurf Shady starts to laugh. "Yeah you better run you chickenshit," he says.

Jake tenses up, looks over at him and then to me. "Is he talking to you?" he asks me.

For a second, I think of telling Jake that it must be some kind of mistake, but his eyes look like they could do some damage and I find it hard to lie.

"I guess so," I say.

"Who is the scrawny little wanker?" Jake asks turning his gaze over to the other side of the road.

"He was the one who I had the trouble with the other day."

"The ones who gave you a pasting?"

"Yeah, but it's all forgotten now mate."

"Like fuck it's forgotten. Grow a pair of balls," he says and crosses the road pulling me with him.

As we approach, the two of them start to laugh and continue to smoke the spliff. "Oh yeah," Smurf Shady says passing it to his mate. "You not tough enough to fight yer own fucking battles?"

Jake approaches him putting his hands in their air as if he's retreating. "No not all pal, we ain't here for trouble, just want to have a chat." Smurf Shady looks confused. Jake puts his hands on his shoulders in what seems to be friendly gesture. "Why can't we just all get on?" Jake says, before swinging his arm from Shady's shoulder and hitting him square in the jaw with his elbow. Shady falls to the ground and Jake puts his foot into his stomach to stop him from getting up. Shady's friend turns and sprints down the road.

"Not so fucking tough now?" Jake says as Shady tries to wrestle Jake's foot which is keeping him pinned to the concrete. A dribble of blood runs down Shady's chin, but the little wanker is determined to fight his way through this. I see the blood and something funny comes over me. I grit my teeth, clench my fists, and think of Bremner. The sight of Shady struggling is like a piece of art. And I want a piece of it.

"Come on Pete, hit the little shit," Jake says.

I walk up to him. He is slouched with his back to the wall. He is my prey, my enemy, my fucking nemesis. I focus on his head bobbing from side to side in frustration. It looks so inviting, so delicate, so fucking vulnerable right now. This is my head to do what I want with it: A football to kick, a potato to mash, a fucking pumpkin to cut. He spits a mouthful of blood at me and it hits me on the shoe. Jake removes his foot, drags Shady off the ground, and holds both arms behind his back so he can't move. "Go on, fucking hit him," Jake shouts.

Without even thinking of aim or technique I just swing my right arm and hit him. I don't see where it lands but it feels good. Feels like I'm alive. Shady laughs and spits more blood at me. This just adds fuel to the fire. So, I hit him again ... and then again ... and then again ... and now I'm swinging my fists in his face in a fury as fast as a propeller. Jake drops him, and he falls to the floor. He is no longer laughing. He is just a piece of useless meat, a pathetic, helpless mound of bloody flesh: blood coming from his mouth, nose, and a gash above his eye. I see the fear in his eyes. I feel no pity. I want to tear him apart. I want to hear his bones break. So, I kick him in the ribs ... and then again ... and then again ... I hear Jake laughing; a dirty laugh as though he's getting turned on watching this. I continue kicking him, loving this power, this control. I hear a woman's voice shouting but can't make out what she's saying. Her babbling is like a strange soundtrack, like a nursery rhyme being played in a horror movie. Eventually I stop my foot from swinging into his ribs when I hear the words "you animal".

It's an elderly woman standing in the doorway of the Salvation Army shop. I look back at the mess on the floor and he smiles at me revealing blood stained teeth. It's almost as if he's enjoyed getting battered.

"I'm going to call the police," the woman says.

"Shut yer fucking gob," Jake shouts to her.

I look at the smiling mess again, look to my knuckles, look at the blood on my shoes and on my clothes and the reality of the situation kicks in. Look what I've done.

Next thing I know I'm just running. Don't know where. Just running. I hear Jake and Sid shouting after me, but I don't turn back. I continue running, past the car park, past the promenade, until I'm out of breath.

Shaking, restless. I'm craving something. I need something to take my mind off things, something where I can just mess myself up and deal with the consequences later. I need a drink. I need some fags. My bank account and pockets are empty. I can't believe that the money Jake lent me has gone already. And what have I got to show for it? Dark rings under my eyes, a sore nose, and some cuts and bruises. Remembering that the Asian guy from the shop said he would like to repay a favour I make my way there, feeling desperate.

At first, he looks pleased to see me as I walk through the door. But then his face seems to drop.

"Come for your reward, have you?" he says barely looking at me. "Have you been fighting?"

"Not the most terrific day I ever had," I say. "I don't want to be cheeky. I just remembered what you said and being a bit short on cash I thought I'd take you up on it. But if it's a problem then don't worry," I say.

He looks at me again with disapproving eyes. "I'm a man of my word," he says. "So, take what you want within reason. A pack of beers or a bottle of something. Maybe a packet of plasters?"

Struggling to understand the change in his attitude from our last meeting, I half-heartedly scour the shelves looking for something to take. But this doesn't seem right. How can I take something from him when he looks like he really doesn't want me to? "Look, Hasan — it is Hasan, right? Have I done something to offend you?"

A younger Asian man, well-built with a shaved head pops his head around from the back of the shop. "Everything alright here Dad?" he asks followed by a menacing glare at me. Hasan sighs, tells him that everything is fine and then walks round from the counter with a box containing bottles of wine. The other man disappears again out the back.

"You know Pete, it is not easy for a Muslim to live in this country," he says as he starts to stock the shelves with the bottles of wine.

And then it hits me. I'm wearing my fucking D.O.R jumper. No wonder he looks pissed off. "Oh shit, look I'm sorry about this jumper. It's not really me, well I thought it was but now I'm not too sure."

He turns and looks at me deeply as though he's trying to solve a puzzle. "Since the terrorist attacks in America and London, my life hasn't been easy. People give me the most disgusting looks. Do you know how that feels? I've been robbed on many, many occasions, and even beaten. I can't even sit on public transport without people looking worried, threatened, or angry. I tell you that it isn't fair. And it isn't going to stop. You just don't get to hear the other side of the story."

Hasan's hands tremble slightly. The wine in the bottle he is holding splashes against the glass. He looks at my jumper again. "So, you're a member of the Defenders of the Realm then?" he asks calmly yet with a touch of disgust. "I've heard some horrible, horrible things about that group."

I think back to the D.O.R meeting the other night for a moment. "Look, please don't take offence when I ask you this, but don't you think it is wrong, say the 7/7 bombings for example, that young men born and bred in Britain with all the same rights and freedoms that British citizens have, could decide to blow themselves up on a bus? Isn't it true that the Koran promotes this kind of violence?"

"I've lived here for nearly fifty years, I own three shops in this area, and I have three children and eight grandchildren, all born in this country. By most measures, I'm a successful man. None of us, *none of us*, have any desire to blow ourselves up. You can't equate us with those animals, any more than I can equate the actions of the D.O.R with the Church of England.

Hasan puts the final bottle of wine onto the shelf and then starts to dismantle the empty cardboard box. "The problem, as with anything, is interpretation Pete. I bet you heard about the Koran through the D.O.R?"

I hang my head. "Yeah."

"Look Pete, I'm a mere shopkeeper from Pakistan who has come over here to make a better life for my family. I just want to be able to do just that," he says.

"But are you happy doing this? I mean you say that you have been robbed ... "

"It never used to be this bad," he says with an unconvincing laugh. "I never thought I'd see the day when I would feel afraid to enter my own place of prayer. Do you know that just the other day our own local mosque was vandalised? Right here in Gravesend?"

Guilt hits me like a ten-ton lorry. I start to panic that he can see this guilt, but then a part of me thinks that I want him to know that it was me. I deserve to be punished for what I did. "I'm sorry," I say quietly. "It shouldn't have happened, it was evil." He looks me in the eyes for a moment and remains silent. I struggle to maintain eye contact and it feels as though he knows the part I played in vandalising his mosque.

"Evil," he seems to say to himself. "Do you know what I always think of when I hear that word? I think of one of the survivors in the 7/7 bombings. This lady who was sitting just metres away from the bomber thought she had already suffered the worst ordeal in her life. Three years before, she was raped and almost killed in her own home. So, if anyone knows of evil, it is her. And when I read an article about her, her words on evil just seemed to stick with me. She said 'I am asked about evil. I think the bombers were not born evil; it is because they fell into a trap of hate and despair and alienation.'"

I feel myself welling up. Hasan seems to notice this and places a hand on my shoulder. "Pete. This jumper doesn't fit," he says pointing to my chest. "How many members of the D.O.R would have stuck up for me on that bus, how many of them would have foiled a robbery in my shop? How many of them would be talking to me now as you are?"

I leave Hasan's shop with just a packet of cigarettes, no longer wanting nor needing a drink. A clear head is all I require now ... and some comforting.

I pick Dolly up and hold her to my chest, but she obviously doesn't like the attention and starts wriggling to get out of my arms. She jumps to the floor and then takes refuge under the kitchen table. I find myself still shaking and look at the dried blood on my hands and clothes, so I go to the bathroom and turn the shower on. My reflection in the mirror scares the shit out of me. It's a stranger: a bloodied, angry-looking stranger with gaunt cheekbones and deep dark rings round the eyes. Even the pot belly has gone; ribs stick out like piano keys. Who the fuck is this? Everything that seemed so clear just a few days ago has turned to murky water. The reflection starts to distort as the heat from shower steams up the mirror.

I turn the heat on the shower to almost full blast. It's blistering hot, scorching, stinging. It's like I'm being scrubbed hard by a million scouring pads. But it's what I want. I need to get rid of this blood and dirt and get rid of this stranger; wash him away down the plughole. When I get out, I'm bright pink, wrinkled and tingling as though I've taken off a layer of skin. I sit on the toilet for a moment or so trying to get my head together. I call Julie at Carol's.

"Hello?"

"Carol?"

"Oh, it's you."

"Hasn't anyone landed a house on you yet or thrown a bucket of water over you?"

"Julie ... it's prat-head."

There is some mumbling and crackling down the line before Julie speaks.

"I miss you so much," I tell her.

"Are you ok? You sound a little flustered," she replies.

"I don't want to talk about it now; I'll tell you everything tomorrow. Right now, I just want to feel normal. Talk to me Ju," I say as I lie down on the bed.

There is a pause for a moment or two. "Ok, would you rather be a hero with the weight of the world on your shoulders, or live out the rest of your days in peace and quiet and be content?" she says.

"I'd rather live out the rest of my days with you even if you do make a pretty awful cup of tea."

And so we talk like that, as though we were kids again, for the next hour or so. When I hang up, I'm determined to get things back on track and that starts tomorrow.

During the night I have a fucked-up dream. Jake and Sid and I are dressed in some really weird clothes; robes or something. We are each carrying pots with labels: Gold, Frankincense and Myrrh. But on closer inspection, Jake's pot actually contains loads of coke and Sid's pot is full of Jaffa Cakes. I try to get the lid off mine to see if there really is gold in it, but the lid is jammed. The next thing I know we are in a stable peering over a cot. A blanket covers what's inside, and Jake removes it.

"Fuck me, that's not him," Jake says.

I look down and see Hasan's face on a baby's body. My father comes storming through the stable wearing a crown and followed by soldiers. He gets down from his horse and looks into the cot. "That's him. This is the one we are looking for. Take him away and kill him," he says signalling to his soldiers.

Then my mother appears from nowhere, screaming and pleading with my father not to hurt the baby.

"Kill the little bastard," Jake says.

"Wait a minute," I say. "You're a fucking wise man. You're supposed to stick up for him."

"Bollocks," he says. "He ain't one of us."

CHAPTER SIXTEEN

Apart from being a bit freaked out by my dream, I wake up feeling fresh. The first I've felt this way in a long time. I look in the mirror. My face looks more alive, features pointing north instead of south and as though the creases have been ironed out. I bounce into the kitchen feeling like someone in a Special K advert.

Today I'm going to sort everything out with my father. No more messing about. It's the new Pete. The new strong and determined Pete. The real Pete. But I decide that a trip to Granddad's will be first on the agenda. I might even be able to borrow some money off him for breakfast. Dolly's pacing around her bowl like a fly trying to get out of a window. I tell her just to hold on a little longer. She arches her back in a way that says, "No food, no love."

"You look like shit son," Granddad says as soon as I see him.

Christ, I must look bad if he's acknowledged this straight away. Still, I guess it's better than having to sugar-coat him first. "Been a bit under the weather lately," I reply.

"You look like you've been living off a keg of bloody beer. It's no good for ya. No wonder you're having troubles with Julie," he says.

"What do you mean by that Gramps?" I ask, failing to see his point.

"It affects ya in more ways than one son. Messes with your mind and your body. Things don't function properly," he says pointing to his groin.

"Jesus Gramps, I'm alright in that department."

"Well maybe you are at the moment son, but it will soon catch up on you. Take me for example; I'm nearer the grave than the womb, but I still wake up every morning as hard as cast iron. No bloody difference between myself and a spotty teenager, I tell you that for nothing."

"Gramps, I don't reall ... " I try to interrupt but he's going off on one of his rants.

"You see it makes me bloody laugh. People moan about all the immigrants, rant on about economic disasters and how we are gonna be an ethnic minority soon enough, but the real bloody reason the population has decreased is because youngsters like you are getting too pissed to get it up."

"Look Gramps, I didn't come here to talk to you about erections," I say.

He looks at me through a frown and lowered eyebrows then snorts through his nose. "Brought me over any smokes?" he asks.

"No not today, sorry Gramps."

"Oh well," he says getting up and going over to his drawers where he pulls out quite a large pouch of Golden Virginia. "Grab my coat son."

We walk out of his accommodation and Granddad walks with a kind of celebrity swagger. This becomes even more apparent when a nearby young, blonde care provider gives him a smile. He returns the smile with a wink. "Told ya son," he says.

Granddad rolls his cigarette in a matter of seconds as soon as we sit down on a bench in the communal gardens. I light a cigarette also. The sky's fighting off the rain and just in front of us a few pigeons are fighting over stale bread. Granddad seems mesmerised by the ugly little birds as he inhales the first few drags. "So then," he says turning to face me. "What gives me the honour of seeing you again? You know something I don't? I'm not dying, am I?"

"I just need to talk to someone that talks sense."

Granddad puffs his chest out and gives himself a nod of approval. "Yeah, well you've come to the right place son," he says. "What's on your mind?"

"Well, like I was saying before," I begin. "You know, I see what happened to Julie's brother, what happened to Nan, and even lately I see beatings and robbery and bullying, and it makes me want to change things. Make things better you know? Well anyway, I felt I was on the right path. I made friends with a load of people I thought felt the same as me. But now I'm starting to see differently."

He looks at me all serious. "What do you mean, 'what happened to Nan'?"

"Well I remember her being scared to leave the flat, and you said that was because of the state of this town."

Granddad takes in a deep breath, closes his eyes for a second and then re-opens them sharply as if he's just unlocked something inside of him which has been closed for long time. "I used to blame the town son. I used to blame everything I could; anything just to make me feel better. And you know what?" he says putting his hand on my shoulder. "Of course, the town didn't help. But it was age. It takes the life out of you, takes the energy, takes your blinking marbles," he says pointing to his head, voice shaky and hand trembling. "It's bloody scary, this getting old business. You try to forget about it, but it lets you know every bloody day. So that was what really got her in the end, god rest her soul," he says looking to the sky.

I feel that bastard lump start creeping up in my throat and feel shocked as I've never seen Gramps like this before. "Don't you worry Gramps, you've had a good life, and everyone loves you," I say putting my hand on his shoulder.

His jaw and mouth start to quiver slightly and once more he looks to the sky before removing my hand; as though it's a gesture that is too hard to handle. "Bloody hell son, you're starting to sound like one of those pooftas. And you're talking like it's my bloody funeral."

He stands up for a moment and appears to be shaking out all of the emotional distress in him. Then he lets out a loud, exaggerated, perhaps false cough and then takes a long deep drag on his roll up.

"Anyway, what about these friends you're trying to change things with?" he says, smoke creeping out of his mouth.

I tell him everything. I tell him about my problems with my mum and Bruce, I tell him about the D.O.R and how my father is a part of it. I tell him about how I've been pretending to be Reggie and I tell him about the demonstration and even the vandalising of the Muslim centre. All the time Granddad listens intently and rolls another cigarette. When I finish he sits back down next to me.

"Your heart's in the right place son. It always has been. If you think things need to be changed round here, then you bloody well tell them what needs to be changed. And you are one stupid sod for getting involved in that mosque business. You don't need to bash a load of buildings up just to pull together. Look at those Indians and the temple they built just off Wellington Street. That shows how a group can really pull together to achieve something they want. Not only did they raise the money themselves, but they bloody-well built it as well. Their community were even volunteering to help with the construction. That shows bloody unity if you ask me."

"You're spot on there Gramps, it says a lot about them. I'm not sure how my mates would react if I used that as an example though," I say.

"Well if they're sensible and real friends then they're gonna listen to you. Get it off your chest; let them know how you really feel. The same thing goes with that father of yours. Tell him who you really are. Only then are you going to find out who he really is. And as for your mum; talk to her the way that you talk to me, cos I bet that's what she wants more than anything."

The pigeons have now formed an orderly circle around the bread so that each of them can peck at a piece. "You see pigeons," Granddad says, "they're not as bad and as ugly as most people think."

It seems as though I'm not the only one feeling productive today, as a few of the shops have started putting up Christmas decorations in the windows. The Debenhams window looks great with a floor of fake snow and frosted windows, but on the other side of the road the picture framing shop has the usual spooky looking Santa ringing a bell. It's been there every year for as long as I can remember, and I swear it ages. The beard has become knotted and filthy with dust, the face has become as cracked as an old brick wall, and the arm ringing his bell has become slower and slower. Still, you've got to admire tradition. Trafalgar Square has its Christmas tree brought over from Norway and Gravesend has the famous Arthritis Santa in Fast Frame.

After a manky old sausage roll and a coffee I ring my father to arrange to meet him tonight. He gives me his address. Something I've never had in my entire life, I think. He tells me to come over around eight. For the next few hours I have to build my courage. Tonight is the night.

Pacing up and down, throwing punches in the air, one, two, three, four ... and a half press-ups. Press-ups? What the fuck am I doing? It's not as though I'm preparing for a fight. Or am I? I try some self-motivation in front of the mirror but once again I find myself drifting into some display of masculinity by flexing my bicep muscles. It doesn't work. My arm looks like a worm that's choked on a new potato.

Kelvin, I'm Pete Jarvis. Yep that's right. Pete Jarvis. Pistol Pete to some around this way. Go ahead Pops: Make my day. Hi Kelvin. This face yeah? You recognise this face? You should do. No? Well I'll give you a clue: A hill, a handbrake, and a van. Hi Kelvin, there is something I need to talk to you about. It's not going to be easy to hear. Let's take a seat, yeah? Hi Kelvin, there's no easy way to put this so I'm just going to come straight out with it. Dad! Dad! Daddy! It's me. Hi Kelvin, I'm your son. You tried to kill me. Why? Kelvin, put the kettle on Dad. What? You didn't know? Yeah, I forgive you; let's just get on with it now. Hi Kelvin, look ... What's that you say? Oh, you know already? Yeah sure, of course I'll call you Dad from now on.

Dolly strolls in and looks at me as though I'm pathetic for talking to myself in the mirror. Did you know your father? Shut it then. You've had an easy ride.

Next, I'm searching through the CD collection. A bit of music always does the trick. Although I can't remember the last time I bought a CD. It's hard finding a suitable album. Robbie Williams?

Would rather rub a cheese grater against my ears. James Blunt? I want to make it out of the flat without slitting my wrists. Steps? Fucking Steps? Chipmunks repeatedly being kicked in the gonads. Drum & Bass? Not after the other night. The Cranberries? Ah the Cranberries. Zombie ... So powerful.

I crank the volume up, lie on the sofa and close my eyes. I picture his face, how I remember him as a child and also as I see it now.

It's now or never ... It's time to find the real him ... time to reveal the true me.

Who is he? Who is he really? What is his life now? What was his life then?

I freeze, arm extended, finger tickling the doorbell. Have I thought this through? Every time we've met it has been on neutral ground. Once I go in here, I step into his world; a world of which I have no idea. This is where he lives, sleeps, shits, dreams. Does he dream of me? Does he still picture me as a young kid? Does he dream of my mother? Surely, he can't forget those days. Maybe he wakes up sweating, gasping for air and longing for those that he lost. Maybe I'm on the verge of turning this dream into a reality. I hear the doorbell go without realising that I've pressed it.

A light appears through the translucent glass and I see a distorted figure moving slowly towards the door. It feels a lifetime until the figure opens the door on a latch. "Who is it?" a female voice asks cautiously without showing her face.

"It's Reggie. Kelvin told me to come over at eight," I reply.

There's no reply for a moment. Then the door opens wide. I see the back of a woman walking away leaving me to let myself in. "He's not back yet. He won't be long, but who knows."

I hesitate before following her through, feeling unwelcome and uncomfortable but I've come this far now, and I'm determined to not just turn around and jack it all in. When I reach the living room a strong smell of cigarettes, dampness and burnt food hits me. The carpets are balding, the coffee table chipped. The curtains are filthy and look as though they haven't been drawn open in a long time. There are no pictures, no framed family photos, no nothing. The walls are bare except for shredded pieces of floral wallpaper clinging on. There's a dusty television on a stool in the corner and a small moth-bitten sofa covered in cigarette burns. I get a strange feeling in my stomach, an eerie one; somehow it feels like I've been here before. The woman, who I now see for the first time, is frightening. She looks like she's never seen daylight. She's dressed in a light blue dressing gown covered in brown stains. Pale, bony, stubbled legs stick out at the bottom. She faces me, shakes her legs, and taps the floor. Her brown greasy hair purposely hides her drawn skeletal face. Her cheekbones and jaw stick out of her tight white skin, and small masses of dark sagging flesh hang under her eyes. I can't work out if they are bruises or wrinkles.

"Are you ... Kelvin's partner?" I say, trying to make conversation. What do you say to a ruined woman who answers your father's door?

"I guess so," she says so robotically that I don't even see her lips move. The woman is frozen, she's confused, unable to smile or frown. Now I can see that there was a pretty lady in there; perhaps once. She looks not so much old as incomplete, like an unfinished jigsaw puzzle.

A quiet murmur comes from next room. The woman's heard it too because she's now looking round. "Mummy?" A child's voice.

"It's ok love, your daddy's not home yet, you carry on playing," the woman calls out.

At that moment a small boy, still wobbly on his feet, comes around the corner holding some action figures. His frightened eyes flicker from side to side as he looks around the room as if to confirm that what his mother said was true. Time seems to stop as he sits down on the floor and starts to play with his toys, delicately, quietly, like he's scared to make too much noise. The woman lights a cigarette and bites at her stumpy fingernails. My eyes dart back to the boy on the floor when he says, "I'll be getting some new toys." Memories come flooding in.

"Is this Kelvin's ... Kelvin's son?" I ask the woman.

She just nods and rolls her eyes.

"Who are you?" the little boy asks me.

"I'm Pe..Reggie. I'm a friend of your dad's," I manage.

The small head looks up at me timidly. "Oh," he says. "So, do you work for Santa too?"

A wave of nausea travels through me and I feel like I'm caught in some kind of twilight zone. It's as if Santa has seen my worst dreams and is now presenting them to me on a fucking plate. I dig my fingernails into the shitty sofa. "No. I don't work for Santa," I reply.

"My daddy does. He doesn't like me to play. He and Santa get really angry. But sometimes he buys me toys," he says carefully picking up one of his figures. Memories of my own childhood seem to hit me like a train collision. My head throbs.

"Don't keep pestering him love," the woman says, tendrils of smoke creeping out of her nose and mouth. "He didn't come around here to be bothered by you."

At that moment I want to tell her that I'm not a mate of my father, her man, his father. I want to tell her that it's not too late to get out. I want to pick the little boy up, hand him to her, and tell her to leave. But I can't. I'm unable to speak, unable to find the right words. My plan to reveal myself tonight has disintegrated. I no longer want to reveal myself. I want to save myself, even if I can't save this woman and the little boy.

I take one last look at the boy sitting on the floor. I want to pick him up, give him a hug and tell him to be strong. But I just jump up and head for the door without even saying a word. All I know is that I need to get out of this place. I need to clear the debris of past memories. I need to get back to the present and I need Julie.

The air has that Christmas smell to it. Maybe it's because there's not too many cars on the road so the air is fresh and crisp. I've never been able to put my finger on the exact odour, but it only smells like this when Christmas is around the corner. It's a still night too. No sharp winds slicing through. The Thames is quiet. No boats on this stretch of river and the waves are snoozing, idly drifting away from Gravesend towards Tilbury docks.

I keep glimpsing my shadow in between the lampposts. It freaks me out a little bit, the way this black figure mimics my arms swinging, legs striding; except it's not me. It doesn't have my brain or heart. It's just like some kind of demonic fucking clone or something.

And once again I've forgotten the fucking cat food. I start to panic that this means that I'll be a bad parent. I also panic that Julie's coming around. This isn't Bluewater or Carol's. This is my ... our home, where we've shared intimate moments, physical and emotional. I start rushing around trying to hoover, dust, wash up and change my clothes all at the same time. When I'm done I text Julie to ask her to get cat food.

CHAPTER SEVENTEEN

It's not long before I hear the door open. I forgot she still has a key. The fact that she doesn't knock gives me hope. My spirits are raised even more when she walks in with all the confidence of a model on a catwalk. Her hair shines, a beautiful chestnut colour like something you'd find on a bottle of Timotei shampoo. Her cheeks are rosy — just a touch of makeup. She may have even have had a sun bed because she's got a beautiful tint to her skin. Dressed in tight jeans and a short-cut top, showing her belly and hip bones, she's casual but sexy.

The fucking cat darts by me and gets to her first. Julie crouches and picks her up and the cat acts like she's won the lottery. Her eyes light up even more when Julie empties a can of rabbit fillets into her bowl.

It feels sort of like a first date as we sit on the sofa. It's awkward to start with, and I can tell I'm not in the clear just yet. I open up to her about everything, the fight with Smurf Shady, my vandalising the mosque, the drugs, the little boy around at my father's earlier ...

She then proceeds to give me an absolute scolding for the next half an hour, with the words "immature", "dick-head", "brainless", "thug", and "idiot", frequently occurring.

I have no comeback. It's deserved.

"Now, shall I tell you what worries me the most?" she continues. "Your new friends. This demo. Are they going to let you walk away so easily?"

I think about it for a moment or so. "I know that Jake is a decent bloke. He's just been handed a crap set of cards. He's a good friend ... I think, and I know that he wants a better life. He's just going about it the wrong way ... I think he could change."

"Or maybe he's too bitter to change. Maybe he's had this face for so long now that he doesn't want to remove it," she says.

"Well that could be the case. To be honest I just hope he doesn't turn up tomorrow to pick me up for this demonstration. I don't think he will after I ran away from the fight yesterday."

"What if he does though?" she asks.

"Then I'll try and persuade him not to go either."

"And if you can't?"

I pause for a moment. "Then that's the end of it."

"I really hope so Pete, for your sake and for ours. I love you, but you're easily led. You need to be your own person Pete. I mean it when I say this — any more idiotic behaviour or any more of this

D.O.R business and I'm straight out of the door again. We've got too much history to just throw away, so deal with it."

"I know, Julie," I say. "I've been a real dickhead, and I'm not making excuses, but I've just felt ... lost. You're the only part of my life which makes sense and I'm going to fight fucking hard to keep it that way. You're right, we've got a long history together and I want us to have a future too."

She looks at me in an approving, proud way. It's a face that I haven't seen in a long time ... and it feels good.

"What gets me most is I've got a little brother out there that I won't ever be able to see." I instantly regret saying this. She had a brother that she will never see again either. Just as I go to say something stupidly apologetic she reaches over and grips my hand.

"Never say never, Pete, who knows what the future may hold," she says looking me deep in the eyes.

Maybe she's right. Maybe one day my brother and I will meet for a pint and share experiences of our mutual sperm donor, Kelvin the Great of Gravesend.

I risk putting my arm around her and she doesn't object. The conversation seems to have ceased and the silence is welcoming, comforting. We flick through the channels until we come across About a Boy. Fuck.

Julie's eyes light up and she looks over at me like a kid wanting sweets before dinner.

"Do we have to?" I ask.

"Why do you hate Hugh Grant so much?"

"Because he is a knob and he plays the same role in every film. The stereotypical English bloke hard on luck. It isn't real. Look at him," I say pointing to the TV screen. "The fucking floppy hair, the puppy dog eyes, the quivering lip, the posh voice. Jesus, he's a walking wet fart."

This makes her laugh slightly. "He's lovely," she gushes. "And he plays the lead in a fairy-tale romance really well."

"Exactly — that's what it is, a fairy-tale romance. It's bollocks. Love doesn't happen like it does in the movies. It's not all floppy hair. And besides, your man got caught with his pants round his ankles with some prostitute. Remember that? And he was with Liz Hurley at the time. If that doesn't put you off him, I don't know what would," I say.

"Just watch the film, Scrooge," Julie says. "It isn't about puppies."

"You're crying," Julie says as the film finishes.

"No I'm not, you are," I say as I try to wipe a tear away without her seeing. The bastard lump in my throat has been up and down like Hugh's prostitute's knickers.

"Come here," she says as she pulls me into her. "What's wrong?"

Her motherly touch wells me up even more. "That Hugh Grant is a fucking prick. Can I have another tissue?"

She reaches into her bag. I fill the tissue up with a big blow of my nose while she strokes my head. "I think I've got an allergy or something. It's probably because it's dusty in here, or maybe Dolly has been rolling in something that's got up my nose. Or it might even be my hay fever starting early."

Julie laughs and hands me another tissue. "Pete, you're not allergic to anything."

"He's still a wet fart"

"Is it because of your mum?" she asks, and then I start to well up again.

Blubbing and wheezing, I try to get a grip. "It's just an emotional time right now," I say. "I felt sorry for the mum in the movie. I mean she had to deal with a lot. I guess it made me think of my mum. And why can't I have a relationship with Bruce like the one that fuckface and the little kid have."

Julie hugs me tighter.

"I miss her."

"I think you do. I also think that while you've been searching for your father all this time, what you really needed was to reconnect with your mum," she says.

I wipe my eyes and give my nose a final blow. "Never, ever watching a Hugh Grant movie again," I say. "The guy is a... "

"Let's go to bed," she says.

Just lying in bed with Julie and feeling her warm skin is enough. Having her here feels like a torch in all the gloom.

CHAPTER EIGHTEEN

Dawn is breaking when I wake up and the sky is clear. I stretch out and realise that Julie isn't next to me. I'm relieved when she comes in holding a mug of tea, wearing just her knickers and one of my t-shirts. Could this get any better? It makes me feel secure seeing her in my clothing. It's like she's mine to keep ... for good. She sits down on the side of my bed and passes me the mug. "Morning," she says and kisses me on the cheek.

I take a sip of the tea and the sour taste of it not being stirred properly almost makes me heave. But I don't care. An unstirred tea from Julie is better than no tea. Putting the cup of tea aside, I pull her to me and start to gently run my fingers up her thighs. I feel little goose bumps surface.

We lie together until the sun makes an appearance. I see the small fair hairs on her arms in the sunlight as she puts them over her eyes.

"I've got to go to the university," she says.

"Ok, you're coming back here, right?" I ask.

She gets out of bed and starts putting her clothes on. "Of course. Oh, and I do hope that you're not going to go to the demo because if you do I won't be coming back."

"I won't be going," I say leaning over and checking my phone. "Besides, he would have called by now."

"Good," she says as she walks to the door.

I get out of bed pulling my boxer shorts on, following her. Dolly comes running towards her and Julie picks her up. When we get to the front door we hug. "Promise me something?" I say.

"What's that?" she asks.

"That you'll be here when I get back?"

She looks at me briefly and then hugs me tighter. "I love you," she says.

I'm left standing at the door in my boxer shorts and the fucking cat runs after Julie down the stairs. I try to call her ... Julie says to leave the door open so that Dolly can get back in.

When I'm getting out of the shower the bedroom door flies open and here's Jake, all in black in his D.O.R outfit, swigging from a can of beer. Behind him are Tony and Sid and a couple of other guys I've never seen before.

"Morning pal," he says. "You left the door open. We let ourselves in."

Fucking cat. Wrapping the towel round my waist and feeling pretty intimidated I walk past him to the wardrobe. "Jake," I say quietly, "I'm not coming."

"Don't be stupid now, Reggie. Put some clothes on," he says.

"It's Pete, not Reggie. And I don't want any more part of this," I say putting on a white t-shirt. "Just look at what I did yesterday. I've had enough of the coke and the violence and the D.O.R. And you should've had enough of it too."

He screws his eyes, bites his tongue, and walks towards me so the others can't hear him. "You're fucking Reggie if I say so. The whole of the D.O.R know you as Reggie." He nods back to where Sid, Tony and the other members are. "Do you really want me to tell them who you really are, and also that you think that what we're doing is shit?"

"Why are you doing this?" I say.

A big smile appears on his face and he comes even closer: it's like looking into the jaws of a great white. "Look, Reg, you're going to change your mind once you get involved in the demonstration. You're going to have a blinder. You're just not thinking right at the moment. Now be a pal, put some clothes on, and get some of this down your neck," he says passing me his open can of Carling.

Tony walks into the room, nods at me and hands me another D.O.R jumper. "I suggest you put this on matey. I heard it's going to snow today. Or tomorrow. Now come on, we're going to miss the fucking train."

I stand motionless, Jake in front of me, Tony to the left of me. Both edge closer to me so that the fabric of our clothes is touching. "Put the fucking thing on," Tony whispers in my ear aggressively.

Jake nods, winks at me. "Don't let this get ugly. Your missus won't be pleased to see blood all over those clean bed sheets, would she now?"

Sid gives me a nervous smile as we leave the house. The air is bitter and still with that pre-snow feel. The clouds loom like icebergs. We go down the stairs and I feel cowardly and bullied. The worst feeling for any man; rots the heart, shatters the pride.

The last time I was on a train it was to go to work. It seems a lifetime ago. I almost miss the quiet, monotonous atmosphere of the office. It's a far cry from what I'm in the middle of now. This whole carriage is full of D.O.R members all dressed in their black uniforms, some draped in St George's flags, some waving England football scarves and flags, some hoisting D.O.R banners. One of the men standing in the aisle holds a placard with a Muslim woman crying with blood running down her face. The writing on it says, 'Sharia Law Oppresses Women'. I wonder if he really gives a fuck about this. Just for show, I think.

The aggression and excitement are reaching a high. A chant bursts through the carriage. "We have joy, we have fun, we'll have Muslims on the run." People stomp their feet and bang the windows like tribal drums before a sacrifice. Cigarettes are smoked, and beer cans are thrown around.

Tony's phone rings and he shouts to the guys around him to be quiet for a moment. He hangs up with a great big smile across his face. "It's kicking off already, and the demo hasn't even begun. This could be tasty," he says and then repeats himself in a louder voice. "YOU HEAR THAT LADS? IT'S KICKING OFF ALREADY!" This is greeted by a loud chorus of cheers and applauds. It cranks them up even more as they down their lager and grapple with each other. Men are roaring and grabbing hold of each other's heads to psyche themselves up, the way that gladiators might have done before they ran into the Colosseum. Another chant breaks out: "D-D-D.O.R, D-D-D.O.R, D-D-D.O.R."

I sit motionless and silent on a seat in the corner, lowering my head each time the train pulls into a station. Some commuters refrain from getting onto the train after seeing the state of this carriage. Jake notices my lack of enthusiasm and hands me another lager. I'm not even halfway through the one he gave me earlier. He taps the can with his finger, gesturing me to drink up. He's serious.

"How fucking great is this?" Jake says, looking to see I've finished the first can.

I shake my head. "I just don't understand why I need to be here," I say. "Why don't you just let me off?"

"Ha!" he roars. "Do you really want to be seen getting off in front of all these people? You'd be battered before you even put a foot out the door."

I look around and realise he's right. How could I explain getting off the train to these guys?

He puts his arm round me. It looks playful, but it feels angry and I'm afraid. "Look, stop being a pussy. Give it a chance. Drink your beer and enjoy yourself pal. I'm glad you're here," he says before whacking me on the back pretty hard and standing up. "Look everyone, I got Reggie here with me," he announces. "Reggie wrote that fucking amazing piece in the newsletter. What was it Reggie? Oh yeah … 'Look around! Our traditions are dying! Yet Muslim extremism is alive and rising! So now is the time to draw the sword. Let us show our patriotism like never before!'"

The carriage roars even more so. "REGGIE, REGGIE, REGGIE."

Tony leans forward and gives me a sarcastic wink. Sid doesn't even make eye contact. He's just lapping up as much as he can of the free coke being passed round. Tony puts a little pile of it on a bank card and lifts it towards me. When I turn my head to ignore him he lets out a booming laugh. I get up and make my way to the toilet. Jake clocks me all the way. I'm patted on the back, hugged, and even kissed by the other members. As I close the door, I hear someone spouting another line from the piece in the newsletter: "We will fight even when things get wild. For we are fighting for England: man, woman and child."

My fucking nerves are all over the place and my legs can barely stay still. Anxious about what's going to come off, and also frightened at the possibility of seeing my father, I try to take some deep breaths. But the smell in this cubicle makes it hard. There is piss all over the place: on the toilet seat, up the walls and over the floor. There's piss in the sink and in the ceiling light, and dripping out of the empty towel holder. There's shit in the pan, bogeys on the walls and mirror, graffiti over the sink, and dried puke in the corner. I try to balance myself in the centre of the cubicle, careful not to tread in or put my hands in anything filthy. Can I really piss into a toilet four feet away?

I get the feeling that no matter where I am today, I'm going to be surrounded by bad things.

I re-enter the ruckus just as the train pulls into Victoria. Jake's waiting for me outside the bog. The members are eager to get off, all pushing and shoving to get near the door. Waiting on the platform are more D.O.R members from Rochester and Chatham. They applaud as we depart the train and then we all join as one. One guy points out a train departing for Glasgow on the next platform and a chorus of "ENG-ER-LAND, ENG-ER-LAND, ENG-ER-LAND," starts up. Some members start showing the wanker sign to passengers on the train.

An ocean of black, white, and red, we sweep through the turnstiles and into the concourse of the station. There we are greeted by numerous police officers dressed in riot gear. My heart is still banging away and even my jaw is swinging now. What the fuck's going on? I down the remainder of my lager just to settle my nerves and I'm immediately handed another by someone I don't know. This guy then shouts, "Piggy piggy piggy, oink, oink, oink," towards the police, which is acknowledged with a loud cheer from the other members.

The lager is making this situation even more surreal than what it is. I keep drinking it. I suck it down fast. Another. I hear Sid ask Tony why we're just waiting in the middle of the station and Tony says we're waiting for more soldiers. Then the tannoy announces a train from Manchester. More applause and cheering, and Tony raises his hands above his head and starts another favourite: "Rule Britannia, Britannia rule the waves, Britons never, never, never ... " His companions join in and then another wave of members surge towards us.

"We've got all the top firms with us today," Tony yells in my ear. "We've got the Red Army from Manchester, we've got the Bolton Wanderer Cuckoo Boys, Luton's Men in Gear, we've even got some of Chelsea's Headhunters in the mix. Fucking brilliant."

I hear Julie's voice in my head telling me about the football hooligans associated with this group. I look around and see these men who would normally be kicking and punching each other on match days carrying hammers, knuckledusters, cans of CS gas; one guy even has a bottle of bleach. They are united today. It's not about clubs today; it's about nationalities. No fuck that, who am I kidding? It's not even about that. It's not about politics either; it's about beating the shit out of someone. What a thrill. It doesn't matter who that person is. It doesn't matter if they're black, white, Muslim, Catholic, or support Tottenham.

I get lost for a moment and then I see Sid standing by himself, so I make my way over to him. "Are you looking at this Sid? Have you seen all the weapons floating about?"

He gives me a hostile, frightened look. "Yeah, what of it?" he asks.

Before I can answer, Jake is at my side again rubbing my head roughly. "Up for it are we boys? COME ON!" I put my hand to my stomach in a bid to stop it jumping around. "Oh, look who it is," Jake says, grabbing my head and turning it in the direction of my father.

"Reggie!" my father shouts out. "Where did you get to last night? My missus said you were there one minute and gone the next."

I turn my back. I hear Jake say, "Ignore him Kelvin. It's his time of the month."

The crowd oozes out of the station, then comes to a halt. I hear a police officer telling a member to take off his D.O.R mask. The member says, "Oh so it's OK for them to wear burkas in public, but we're not allowed to cover our faces. Whose side are you fucking on?" The police officer tells him to do as he's told. But the guy shakes his head at him in disgust and continues forward.

A bright winter sun hits my eyes and my heart pounds in my ribcage. Jake doesn't leave my side as we walk up to Trafalgar Square. I'm staring at the cracks in the pavement unable to lift my head. Riot police hold hundreds of people back protesting against this march. This spurs the D.O.R on even more; give a wild animal a scent of blood and it goes crazy. My head spins as different voices, chanting and slurs blend together into an awful song ...

Muslim bombers, off our streets, Muslim bombers off our streets.

Fucking racist bastards.

My ENGLISH pride I will not hide, My ENGLISH race I will not disgrace, My ENGLISH blood flows hot and true, My ENGLISH people I will stand by you, through thick and thin till the day we die, Our ENGLISH pride stands so high.

English? Call yourself English? You should be ashamed.

I lift my head and glance at some of the faces in the crowd being held back. A whole mixture of people: white, black, Chinese, Muslim women in burkas and young mums with pushchairs, their faces registering anger ... anger, yes, but disgust, contempt, and pity. I look at the tide of men I'm rolling with into the heart of London and their faces show something quite different: a different kind of anger, a deep hatred, an unstoppable yearning for inevitable mayhem and violence.

I'm England till I die, I'm England till I die, I know I am, I said I am, I'm England till I die.

Nazi scum out of London, Nazi scum out of London.

Stop the mosques, stop the mosques, stop the mosques.

Jake puts his arm round me and pulls my head into his. A dribble of saliva runs down his chin, his eyes bloodshot and wild. "Enjoying this?" he says. I pull away from him, but he just laughs and tugs me closer to him. We reach Nelson's Column, the man himself guarded by four lions. He towers above everyone; a true British man, who defended this country from a real threat. He looks ready for war, as though he's about to unleash his lions. I find it hard to look him in the eye.

Bloody racists. You give England a bad name.

D-D-D.O.R, D-D-D.O.R, D-D-D.OR.

The crowd being held back are becoming agitated. It seems ironic that the police are controlling them while the D.O.R are free to move as they wish.

Gonna make you bleed, gonna make you bleed, gonna spill some raghead guts.

Ignorant, blind, a bloody disgrace.

It's fucking patriotism ... true patriotism.

But what is patriotism? What is true patriotism? A love for your country? A deep devotion which means that you'd put your life on the line to defend it? Or is it an excuse to release frustration by kicking a fellow citizen's head open?

In the middle of Trafalgar Square, in the capital of England, two groups of 'patriots'. England. What's in a name?

A glass bottle is hurled into the wave of D.O.R. A war cry erupts. Gaps start to appear in the fluorescent wall of riot police. The two sides mix into a blur of fists, screams, and roars. Mayhem ...

This is it boys ... Let's fucking have 'em ...

A drifter caught in heavy seas.

Jake collides with a protestor and wrestles him to the ground, kicking him and stamping on him. The protestor on the floor, a young Muslim lad, looks up horrified as though this moment could be his last. I run to Jake and pull him backwards, both of us tumbling into the mass of bodies in violent motion.

"Fuck off Pete."

The Muslim kid scarpers.

"Don't do this. It's not you."

"You don't fucking know me," he screams.

"This doesn't make sense, Jake. Let's get out of here. Leave with me."

His eyes are glazed with hatred, fear, destruction; the scar just above them pulsates, brought to life like a burning Swastika. Breathing heavy, body tensed, he works out what I'm trying to say. He steams towards me, pushes me in the chest and stops. "This is the only thing for me."

"No, it's not ... let's g..." I don't even see the punch. The sky spins and stomping feet are by my head. The taste of blood in my mouth; everything is carnage. I try to get to my feet and focus, as though I've been swept under by the undertow at Margate and am just resurfacing. Dizzy. I manage to pull myself to my feet and see the arse of Jake steaming back into the violence.

Throbbing, feeling trapped, I stumble through the crowd looking for gaps to escape, and then there is he is ...

"REGGIE! REGGIE! REGGIE!"

It's him ... Kelvin fucking Jarvis. Blood splattered over him. He's drunk. Purple in the face. His stupid tracksuit bottoms are hanging off him ... but there's a terrifying look in his eyes ... one that he's comfortable with ... a look that has embedded itself in him ... one that will never be removed. It's crazy. It's pathetic.

"COME ON REGGIE! LET'S SHOW 'EM!"

What's in a name?

A thousand fucking volts run through me. I've never wanted to hurt someone as much as I do right now. He stares, waiting for me, inviting me to enter his world. A shard of glass from a broken bottle. It's blood-stained. It's in my hand. I approach him.

"It's not Reggie. That's not my name. You know my name. You always have done, just as I've always known yours."

"What the fuck you on about?" His red eyes drift to the broken glass in my hand.

Broken ... broken ...

"What are you gonna do to your new family? Fuck them up like your old one? Try and kill your kid the way you tried to kill your first born?"

He freezes. My words seem to have extinguished him.

"I know all about you, Kelvin Jarvis. I know because I share the same name as you. But unlike you ... I'm proud of who I am."

Without making a sound, I see his lips mouth the word "Pete...?"

He doesn't deserve to have my name in his mouth. He doesn't have the right. My name in his fucking mouth? Gripping the glass tighter, piercing my own skin, I approach, feeling the heat steaming from him. I can smell the sweat of his flat, his pub breath.

Now he speaks. "Pete? I ... tried to make contact. I did. They wouldn't let me. I promise," he says putting his hands in the air and looking down.

"I want to know why you did what you did."

"It was just a big fucking mistake, Pete ... but they ... blew it up out of proportion. It was drugs ... " His eyes dart from side to side as though he's looking for something. A script maybe. "It wasn't a good time ... that whore of a mother of yours ... "

He suddenly stops mid-sentence and knocks me off my feet, scrambling for a broken bottle he's spotted. Before he can pick it up I kick it out of his reach.

I raise my shard of glass and he sinks down and covers his face with his hands. "You're a coward," I yell. "You pick on the weak? You're weak. Thank fuck I'm nothing like you."

He takes his hand away from his deflated football of a fucking face. He's done for. He simply nods at me and spits. "Well go on then, you bastard. That's what you are." He laughs, a sinister, strangely careless laugh. "Take your revenge, bastard."

"I pity you." I throw the bottle away. I turn my back, tear off my D.O.R jumper, throw it in the air and run and keep running till Victoria, till the mayhem, till all my fellow citizens are behind me.

CHAPTER NINETEEN

I burn my mouth with strong coffee and immediately order another one. Victoria is a nicer place on a weekend. It's more relaxed, no suits or briefcases whizzing around. But hell, I think, those people are just trying to make a living. They struggle through the shit just like everyone else. And at least it's an honest living. They don't hurt anyone. Except themselves. Today there are children and parents with happy faces excited about the places they are travelling to. You'd never know the D.O.R and Kelvin Jarvis had passed through here this morning, leaving a trail of invisible infected slime. I take a seat outside Burger King and hold a tissue to my nose to stop the bleeding. It's throbbing like fuck.

Seeing these happy families makes me think of the film last night. It's funny how a film can affect you. It couldn't have been easy for the mum in that film. But at least she got her act together in the end. And you could tell that she never stopped loving her son.

I stand up and check the departure board, trying to work out what train station is closest to Istead Rise. Meopham ... Meopham ... I see it. Platform Six. Two minutes.

I look at my phone and there are countless missed calls from Julie. I call her to explain and then tell her where I'm going.

My mum peers through the curtain and opens the door hesitantly. She looks upset, possibly still wounded from the last time we met. We stand looking at each other for a moment or so without saying a word. I feel myself start to well up and my mum's face starts to melt. A tear rolls down her cheek and all the tension, pain, and anger fades away. I see my mum for the first time in a long time. It feels as though I've seen things through her eyes and she has seen things through mine. We embrace. It feels ... fixed.

We walk into the house arm in arm, and it's hard to tell who is supporting who. I glance around the house and my mum puts my mind at ease. "He's out for the evening love," she says before going into the kitchen. "What happened to your face, Pete? Have you been fighting?"

"Do you remember when Dad came around with the police that time?" I say sipping at my tea.

She looks nervous and terrified as though it's something she's afraid to talk about. "Of course I do love," she says quietly.

"Do you remember what you said to me after he left?"

She looks to the floor in a guilty way.

"You said, 'we don't need him and ... '"

My mother puts her hand out to signal me to stop, " ... and that as long as we had each other we didn't need anyone else," she says and seems to choke on her words before her eyes fill with tears again. "Pete I'm sorry. I didn't live up to my words, did I? I tried love, honestly, I did. Perhaps when you got older I got selfish. It's just that ... he ... made my life hell. He's made your life hell. I just wanted to get away from all of that. It sounds so selfish now, Pete, but I needed to wipe away everything to do with him. Otherwise I would've ended up in a loony bin or something. And the truth is ... as you got older you scared me. Sounds pathetic I know, but you were the one thing that still connected me to him. I was so afraid of you turning into him, every time I saw you I remembered the bad times. I just wish that we'd spoken about this earlier."

"Well we are speaking about it now mum, and it's not too late."

She puts both her hands on my face, interrogating it like a blind person reading braille. "You're nothing like him."

"No," I say and then I begin to tell her everything that I've had to do with my father in the past few days. I tell her about Trafalgar Square and his face and the broken glass, and I tell her that I guarantee I'll never see him again.

"God I'm proud of you and the way you've turned out. I can't take any credit for it."

"Mum you were always there for me when I was a kid. You had a right to get on with your own life after I reached a certain age. And look around," I say pointing to the house, "things have worked out pretty good."

"What? Even Bruce?" she says with quizzing eyes.

"Well I still think he's a prat. That won't change," I say.

"Look love," she says putting her hand on mine. "Bruce is good for me. Really good. He makes me feel young and he respects me. He is kind to me and would never lay a finger on me. He gives me security."

"What's his problem with me then?" I ask.

"Maybe because you've got a problem with him."

Maybe she's right. Maybe I never gave Bruce a chance. Maybe I just hated anything that looked like a father.

"Bruce can't have any children," mum adds. "I won't go into detail. It's just the way it is. It must be hard for him to see me with a child, knowing he'll never be able to have that bond. And you never made it easy for him. When you were angry you used to say to him, 'Why don't you get your own kids from somewhere?' It was a sensitive subject for him."

"Yeah, I guess it would have been," I say, feeling a pang of guilt.
"But you are right about one thing," she says.
"What's that?" I ask.
"He is a prat. Sometimes."

We laugh together for the first time in God knows how long. And we continue to laugh and talk and share memories and details about the parts of each other's lives we've missed out on. I text Julie to tell her where I am and that I may be here for the rest of the night. Daylight creeps in and the conversation is still flowing.

"I like this time of day," mum says. "It's nice being up before everyone else. It's so peaceful, undisturbed, and clean. No people or engines. It used to antagonise me though, Pete. It used to signal the end of the night and cue the start of reality. The drugs would be wearing off and the hangover would start. As soon as the birds started to sing it was game over. God it was awful," she says. "I used to blame everyone and anyone for my fuckups. But everyone had someone to blame back then."

"But you had a right to blame someone mum," I say.

"Blame is never right, Pete. Some people I knew back then even blamed Mrs Thatcher. 'Maggie Thatcher made me a scaghead,'" she laughs. "Can you imagine? No, I should've been stronger. Your granddad got up at this time of day too. He'd go crazy seeing me just getting in when he was off to work. I always used to think he was an unhappy man who scanned the world constantly for something to disapprove of. But all he was doing was looking out for me. He never blamed anyone for anything. 'The Iron Lady doesn't scare me ... people will always need bread,' she says, mimicking Granddad's voice. 'But the bloody state of it girl! The eighties were a lingering hangover from the sixties ... then the drugs changed for the worse and the people got worse ... it's gone from tripping out and peace man, to flipping out and BLOODY CHAOS!'"

"That's a pretty good impression," I say laughing.

My mum's laughter quickly fades. "I only wish you had a dad like I did. It took him a while, but he made me see sense. If it wasn't for him I'd probably still be slouched over a bottle of god knows what."

It hits me — I feel stupid. I am fucking stupid. I've been searching for a father when the real one, the one who raised me and never let me down, was in front of me the whole time. "I do mum. I do have a dad like you. He's my dad too," I say.

I watch my mum fall asleep; she looks content and peaceful, a ray of sunlight on her forehead. It brings to light the creases and wrinkles and scars. But now the scars are healing. I grab a blanket and pull it over her. I'm exhausted. We ploughed through a minefield tonight and come out unscathed. We've come out as friends.

On the way home, I speak to Julie again — I've never looked forward to getting home and getting into bed so much. Normality has never seemed more appealing. In a weird way I'm even excited about returning to work tomorrow. I think about how I'm going to make more of an effort; more of an effort at work, more of an effort with Julie and more of an effort with my mum ... maybe even with Bruce.

As I reach my block of flats a voice calls my name, which hits me like a Taser. Jake's getting out of his car and jogging towards me. He's wearing the same clothes as yesterday. There's dried blood on his D.O.R jumper and on his knuckles, a couple of bumps on his forehead and a bruise on his cheek. I get the feeling that he hasn't been home yet. Tony and Sid peer out the windows of his car.

I prepare myself for a beating, thinking that I have no other option than to try and put up a fight. But when he gets to me he is smiling, and his arms are relaxed by his side. He wipes his nose and I can see that he may still be buzzing after an all-night coke session.

"How's it going pal?" he says as if nothing has happened.

Anger. Frustration. Betrayed. Let down. Fucking everything springs to mind. "How's it going?" I say. "Well apart from you hitting me in the face and apart from being involved in that fucking mess yesterday ... not too bad I guess. How do you think it's fucking going?"

I surprise myself saying this to him and I flinch, expecting another whack. But he looks disappointed rather than angry. He pulls a pack of cigarettes out of his pocket and offers me one. I shake my head. "I thought it would come to this. I didn't want it to though," he says as he lights one up.

"Come to what?" I ask.

He inhales deeply, holding the smoke in his lungs and closing his eyes before he lets it trickle out of his nostrils. "You really let me down Pete. You know that?"

"And how the fuck did I let you down?"

"We were mates, we had something in common. I was there for you when you was down, wasn't I? I was the one who fucking picked you up after losing your bird, being suspended and getting a kicking wasn't I?" he says, aggression starting to creep into his voice.

I take a short step back. "Mates don't punch each other," I say.

"I gave you money, I gave you coke, I introduced you to people, I got you friends. And how do you repay me? By acting a fucking fairy and turning your back on me."

"I didn't turn my back on you. I turned my back on the D.O.R."

Jake finishes his cigarette in one heavy drag and then flicks it into the road. He looks at me in disgust with the effects of the coke becoming more and more apparent: his jaw is twitching and he's chewing the inside of his mouth. "So, you got my money?" he says, ignoring what I just said.

I remain silent.

A menacing smile creeps into his face as though he's got me hook, line and sinker. "I tell you what," he says. "If you've got my money, then you can just climb those stairs and get back to your stupid, boring, easy life with your headfuck of a girlfriend. Oh, she is in by the way. She turned the lights out about two in the morning and then got up to walk to the shops this morning about nine."

"You fucking touch her and I swear ... "

"Don't swear Pete, it's rude. And besides, we both know you're a pussy."

"Look, I'll get your money as soon as I've been paid. Just leave us alone and I promise I'll drop the money to you as soon as possible," I plead.

But Jake is just whistling now, not listening to a word I'm saying. "You're not understanding me," he says sarcastically. "That wasn't an option. I said that the only way that you are walking up those stairs is if you give me my money NOW."

"I haven't got it now," I snap back.

"Oh," he says putting his hand to his mouth. Then he pulls his phone out his pocket and presses the buttons. "Take a look at this," he says shoving the phone in front of my face.

My stomach turns. It's a shaky video of some guy breaking windows. The person looks like a thug you'd see on Crime Watch. The guy cackles and roars and looks deranged. Evil. Pure fucking evil. A dodgy Queen song is playing in the background and the people behind the camera are all egging Pete Jarvis on. Except it is Reggie, not Pete.

When the video finishes he places the phone back in his pocket. "Great song that, don't you think?" he laughs.

I feel like throwing up on the spot.

"Anyway, the way I see it is that you've got two options. Wanna hear the first one?"

I just stand with my head hung.

"Well I'm gonna tell you anyway. Either you get in that car and come with me, or this video will end up at Gravesend police station and in the local papers. And I'm sure you wouldn't want that, would you? Not only would you have to go to court and get banged up for a couple of months, or a hefty fine and some community service, but your name would be dirt. Everyone would know you as a racist. And I'm sure your big-titted brain-bird wouldn't approve either."

A possible escape hits me. Maybe I can play him at his own game. "Oh yeah?" I try to say confidently. "Well I'm sure the police would like to know how you make your money."

He laughs and slaps me on the arm. "Don't you think I thought of that, you silly wanker? It's in a place where no one will find it."

My head lowers again. He's got hardcore evidence of me and I've got jack shit to fire back.

"Now, I think that getting in the car is your best option," he says lighting another cigarette. "But of course, you are welcome to go for the second one."

"Which is?" I ask.

Jake pulls a knuckleduster out of his pocket. "I make mincemeat out of your face right now."

"So, I suppose what you originally said about force feeding me Sid's pubes isn't an option anymore?" I say feeling defeated already.

He laughs in between taking a puff on a cigarette, causing him to cough intensely. "I like your sense of humour Pete. A fucking shame all this."

"Why do you want me to get in the car?" I ask.

Now he sighs, waves to the car and Tony gets out of the passenger seat, he too wearing the D.O.R jumper. "I'm getting bored now. Just get in the car," Jake says clamping my elbow with his hand.

I consider making a dash for it, but then I think of Julie. And it wouldn't have worked because Tony's hand is now clamped to my other arm. I look at him and he smiles. "Nothing personal matey," he says.

They lead me towards the car and open the back door for me. I climb in and Sid stares out of the window without acknowledging me. He taps his foot and looks paranoid. His arms are folded, and he looks as shrivelled and small as a chipolata. Is he ignoring me out of guilt? Coke?

"Where are we going?" I ask as Jake pulls away.

"Vic's house," Tony answers bluntly. He starts chopping up lines on a CD case.

CHAPTER TWENTY

I get marched into Vic's house like some kind of prisoner. Vic is again wearing just boxer shorts and an untied dressing gown. He swigs on a can of Strongbow in between munching a chocolate bar. He greets me by ruffling my hair and tugging on my cheek. "Peter Piper picked a peck of pickled peppers," he says and then looks to the others for laughter, which he receives. "Pete, Pete, Pete. Missed your buddy Vic, did ya? Vic missed you," he says this time slapping me hard on the cheek.

I don't respond. He shoves me into the living room. He hangs back, saying something to Jake and Tony. There's someone sitting in the living room. He looks shaken and is holding a bloody tissue to his nose. Massive side burns — it's Percy, the bloke Jake had a run-in with at the King's Head. He looks at me awkwardly, tilting his head.

"Shit, you ok mate? What's going on?" I ask him.

"Don't give me none of that, you're one of them," he says in a muffled voice while pinching his nose.

"I'm really not, Percy. I haven't got a clue what's going on."

Percy looks me over. "Fuck, all I know is that I got a phone call from Jake saying that he wanted me to try out some super new coke. He said he wanted me back as a customer and to meet me here cos he wanted to give me a free sample. As soon as I knock on the door that big nutter out there punches me in the nose and drags me in here," he says almost in tears.

Whispers and laughter come from the doorway. I get the feeling that I'm in some serious shit. Any tiredness has disappeared. Fear is fuelling me. The sound of babies screaming upstairs, the greasy and musky smell of the house, and the sight of Percy's busted nose make me want to puke.

They march into the living room. "Take a seat," Tony says and pushes me into a chair.

"Cosy, cosy, cosy. Ain't this nice and cosy," Vic says rubbing his hands together.

He walks up to Percy, inspecting him the way an animal sniffs another to see if it is edible. He then does the same to me, sticking his face in mine, the smell of sweat and cider burning my nose hairs. "You know what Vic thinks?" he says. "Vic thinks that you two are the wettest pair of cunts he's ever seen. My kids' shitty nappies have more bollocks than you."

I try and work that one out but realise it's not worth it. Plus, I've got more things to worry about right now. "What the fuck's going on here?" I say.

Vic lets out an exaggerated gasp, "Did you hear someone say something then?" he says looking to Jake, Sid, and Tony. "Cos I swear I heard something. Thing is, I don't remember Vic saying that anyone could say anything." Then he turns to me and grabs my mouth forcing my lips together. "Zip zip zip it. Zippity doo dah, zippity ay, my oh my what a fucking wonderful day," he sings and then lets go of my mouth before giving me another slap round the face. "You know why it's a wonderful fucking day?" he asks.

I shake my head, look at Percy. His head is twisted back on the sofa and a stream of bright red blood runs down from his nose, down his chin and his neck and finishes at the collar on his shirt. He looks like a corpse.

"It's a wonderful fucking day because today is the day that Vic reclaims his throne. Today we put those Pakis out of business. And by we, I mean you two as well," he says pointing to me and Percy.

"Look Vic, I don't want ... "

"ZIP ZIP FUCKING ZIP IT," he shouts. A vein the size of a baby's arm appears in the side of his face. "It's too late," he continues. "You're already part of the plan. And what a fucking plan it is. Wanna hear it? Wanna hear it? Wanna hear it?" he says poking me in the chest each time.

There is no point in responding so I remain silent, looking at this fat, tattooed stinking nutter, wondering if he ever wears clothes.

"You remember last time you were here I said that we needed some mug as a fall guy? Well guess what? You're that mug. A crappy, stained mug. You've got mug written all over ya. Might as well drink tea out of ya, ya mug. Mug, mug, mug. Nothing but a mug," he says and then mimics drinking from one.

He bursts out in laughter and once again turns to the others looking for appreciation. All three of them laugh but it's nervous. They look twitchy and wired. I try to make eye contact with Jake, but he turns away. Sid does the same. I remember Sid watching Star Wars and think of the scene where Luke Skywalker confronts Darth Vader, believing that there is still good in him. He was right. Eventually. Maybe I've got some time left.

"But you're not the only mug," Vic says, pointing at Percy. "Muggy-side-burns-cunty-bollocks over there is all chummy with the Injuns. He buys all his shit from them now. Fucking disgusting," he says, spitting on Percy. "So, because he's got their trust he's going to call the dirty Pakis and say that he's got a mate who wants to buy a kilo of their coke. That's where you come in," he says and flicks me on the forehead. "The beauty of it is you're not a face around this town. You're a nobody. They won't suspect a thing. So, Percy the pussy will arrange a pick-up in town and you two will go along. But you won't be the only ones going, see? Not only are we gonna pocket every last granule of that coke, which will be worth about twenty grand, we are gonna hammer the cunts so hard that they'll be eating through straws and won't be able to walk, let alone be able to deal on my turf anymore. It's a game of Cowboys and Injuns."

Vic jumps on the sofa, patting his mouth and making a noise like a Red Indian. Then he plays cowboy and holds his hand like a gun. He fires it point blank in my face and then blows away the imaginary smoke. Now he jumps back into Red Indian. He pretends to die dramatically and falls to the floor.

Tony starts to clap as Vic gets to his feet and bows as though he's being awarded an Oscar.

"Right," Vic says walking towards Percy. "Get your pussy phone out and ring the filthy fuckers. And make it convincing."

Even though he's trembling, Percy does a pretty good job on the phone and arranges the pick-up for 8.30 at a scrap yard in the industrial area near the promenade.

"It's perfect," Vic says. "We just get there a bit early and tuck ourselves away. Anyway, we've got some time to kill, boys. Sid, go get some tins in. Jake, you chop up a few lines."

Everyone obeys instantly. Tony goes out with Sid and Vic goes upstairs. It's only me, Jake, and Percy. Once again, I consider making a run for it but decide that could only make things worse. If Jake has any guilt for stitching me up he's hiding it well.

"Why you doing this to me?" I ask him.

"Fuck off," he says simply as he chops the coke.

Instead of feeling anger towards him, I only pity him. I watch this man, this alpha fucking macho male, hunched over a pile of white powder. "You make me laugh, you know that," I say to him.

He raises his eyebrow slightly and pauses chopping. "And why do I make you laugh Pete?"

"You seemed so passionate about making things better. You drummed on and on about how the D.O.R would make a difference and how fucking great it would be for people like us. But you knew it wouldn't amount to shit. Didn't you? I reckon that it's something for you to use as an excuse; some kind of shield for you to hide behind. To make you feel better for being a fuckup. You say how bad society is, but you're one of the worst things about it."

"Yeah," he says. "Well done Sherlock, but what's society ever done for me?"

"Bollocks, Jake. What has it ever done for anyone? Most of us are fuckups in one way or another. It's just how you deal with it."

Jake puts the card down on the table and looks at me as if he's going to rip my head off. His mouth opens as though he's going to choke. Then he shakes his head and then returns to chopping up the coke.

The rest of the day becomes a crap movie on fast forward. Jake, Sid, Tony and Vic sniff coke and drink beer. Babies and toddlers crawl in and out of the room. Vic's woman, Sylvia, shuffles around, lazily picking the children up and bringing more cans of lager.

Daylight begins to fade, and the living room lights are turned on. It's cold. My fingers and toes have become numb. The dread and anticipation of what is to come hangs in the air. The four of them look like they've got rabies: wild, bloodshot eyes, twitching arms and legs, white gunk in the corners of their mouths, where food has been recently replaced for booze and coke. Percy's been living on his own blood all day.

"It's time now," Vic says checking his watch. "LET'S FUCKING HAVE IT."

The sky is oil-black when we leave the house. I feel a drop of rain hit me but when I look closely it's snow. They bundle me and Percy into the back of a white Transit van. Jake and Sid get in the back with us while Tony and Vic ride up front. Jake is rummaging through a sports bag.

"You really think this is going to work?" I say to Jake.

"Why wouldn't it?" he asks.

"Well there are only four of you. You don't even know how many of them will be there."

He starts to laugh. "Well they won't have these," he says and opens the bag where I see four wooden baseball bats. The wood looks splintered, flaky, and worn out, possibly from wrecking too many faces. "And besides they won't be expecting a fucking thing. Now shut your mouth."

"There's no hope for you, is there?" I say to him.

"There never has been," he replies.

When we pull up, Vic opens the back doors of the van and climbs in. "Now, we all know what we've got to do, right?" he says to me and Percy. "If either of you try anything funny at all, I'm going to kill every one of your family and then you. This I fucking promise you. Vic don't fuck about."

Percy and I walk towards the scrap yard. The van moves down the road, out of sight. There are no street lights and only a faint white sheet of snow illuminates the pavement. The snow is beginning to fall heavier. Warehouses and rusty wire fences surround us like a stage set.

The gate to the yard is open and we walk straight in where we are greeted by two men. Percy shakes hands with them and they only nod at me. I recognise one of them as the man wearing the turban from the football match the other night. I lower my head for a second but then I realise that it really doesn't matter if he recognises me or not.

We walk towards the end of the yard passing skips, two JCBs, wood pallets and a mess of tires. There's a pile of cars neatly stacked like a morgue for dead motors. There are three vans and a Range Rover parked in the yard. I begin to panic. There are going to be loads of them waiting for me.

In front of us are small units with a large one on top with stairs leading up to it. The two men lead us up them and I'm surprised to see only two others sitting in this room behind a desk. A light bulb dangles from the ceiling and sways from a draft. This is like an intense bad movie, I think. One of the men behind the desk is the Elvis-impersonator-look-alike, from the England game at the pub. He stands up and shakes our hands. Everything about this seems so wrong; so obvious. It feels as though all eyes are on me. I glance over at Percy. He looks as nervous as I feel.

"So," Elvis says to me. "A kilo is a lot of coke to be wanting. What are you planning on doing with it?"

I fumble around in my head for a reasonable answer. I almost have to ask him to repeat the question. Percy stares at me. "I ... I just want to sniff a bit and make a little money," I say. I could kick myself for giving such a stupid response.

A big smile forms on his face and he approaches me with a box of cigarettes. "You want one?" he asks.

Paranoia kicks in and I look around the room nervously — is this is some kind of trick? I fumble one out of the pack and he holds a lighter in front of me. The room is now silent and all I can hear is the cigarette burning and the crashing waves from the Thames.

Elvis takes a seat back behind the desk and puts his feet up. This is all too weird. It's as though we are all waiting for something to happen.

"I haven't seen you around before," Elvis says to me.

"I don't really go out much round this way," I say. "I work in ... town."

He doesn't take his eyes off of me. "Where's the cash then?"

Fuck. I drain the whole of my cigarette and am just about to tell him what's going on when heavy footsteps start to stampede up the metal stairs outside. I look at Elvis. He doesn't flinch or move a muscle.

Jake, Sid, Tony, and Vic all crash in with their baseball bats. "Right you stinking cunts," Vic shouts. "Give me all the coke you have NOW," and then hits the desk with the bat.

All Elvis does is laugh. Another stampede is coming up the stairway. At least ten Indian guys flood through the door, each carrying a baseball bat. The bats are aluminium, look strong, and are made up of different colours. Totally surrounded and outnumbered, Jake, Tony and Vic take a step back and raise their weapons. Sid's face turns sickly pale and he looks unable to move.

"Is this the best you could come up with?" Elvis says.

Not taking his eyes off the men with the multi coloured bats, Vic shrugs and glances down at his inferior wooden bat. "Who the fuck do you think you are? You know who you are fucking with?"

Elvis laughs again. Then he takes his feet off the desk and sits up straight. "I'll think you'll find it is you who are fucking with me. You were the one who arranged all this. How stupid do you think I am? You use this Percy, this thick junkie, as bait? As if Percy is going to have any friends who could afford to buy a kilo. I knew something was fishy when he called me up. I could hear the poor fucker shaking. I also happen to know that Jake here is pissed off with him because he's buying from me. It wasn't hard to put two and two together. And as soon as these two monkeys came fumbling through the door," he says pointing to me and Percy, "I knew your game."

I look around for a way out and try edging to the back of the unit. The wall feels rough and damp, but it helps me keep my balance. I place my palms on it behind my back to stop my head from spinning. There is no way out. There is hardly room to move. The whole scenario looks like one of those sick David Attenborough shows where the predators circle their prey before the kill. I'm trying to go unnoticed in the corner but one of the Indian guys keeps looking at me. His hands are gripped tightly round a red bat and I'm getting the feeling that he's picked me out as his special gazelle.

Percy steps forward. "They made me do it. I swear. Honestly, I'm nothing to do with it. Please just let me go," he pleads, almost in tears.

"Shut your fucking mouth Percy," Jake says. Then he points his bat at Elvis. "Too fucking right I'm pissed off. You're stealing my customers."

Then Tony chips in. "How the fuck would you like it if we came to your country and started fucking up your business."

"This is my fucking country," he snaps back.

The fuse of this whole scene is burning too quickly.

"No, no, fucking no. It's not your fucking country. Cunts, cunts, cunts," Vic says with a beetroot red face, spit flying out of his mouth. "I ain't having this. No fucking way. COME ON YOU WANKERS, LET'S SEE WHAT YOU'RE MADE OF!"

Vic steams into the crowd of Indian guys swinging his bat. Jake and Tony join him. Sid remains rooted to the spot shaking. I put my hands over my eyes and hear metal connecting with bones.

Darkness. Screams. Pakis this. Wankers that. Stomping. Crunching. Screams. I chance a look. A blur. Swinging bats. Kicking. Punching. Gashes. Bumps. Blood. Darkness. This isn't how I want it to end. Killed, in an industrial estate in Gravesend? No way. Just as I had everything back on track ... Some teeth splatter against my face.

I take my hands away from my eyes and fall to the floor. Jake, Sid, Tony, and Vic have disappeared in the mass as though they have been swallowed up by an earthquake. The Indian guys now move away, and I see the four of them wriggling on the floor like squished insects struggling in their last few moments. Jake tries to catch my attention by raising his arm, but it looks twisted out of its socket. His right eye is totally closed up and only a slit of pupil can be seen through the other one. He tries to crawl towards me but receives a vicious kick to the side of his head. His nose is clotted with blood and his mouth is wide open. Only a couple of teeth remain in his bleeding gums. "Pete," he calls out. "Help. Please. Please Jarvis. Jarvis." His words are cut short by yet another kick. He's out cold.

Percy runs over to where I am. He keeps saying that we are both innocent as he crouches down like me and hides his head in his hands.

"What we gonna do about these two?" one of the Indian guys says.

I open my eyes and I see floating lines and dark spots from where I've had them closed so tight. I try to focus on Elvis as I await his judgement. However, he says nothing and instead looks over his shoulder. "What do you think boss?" Elvis says.

From the shadows, a man I somehow recognise appears. He approaches and stares down at the two of us.

The rest of them surround us with blood-stained bats. "Percy," he says, "can leave. I believe him when he says he had nothing to do with this. Who knows — maybe Percy's done us a favour by leading those arseholes to us. They won't be bothering us again. Thank you, Percy."

This raises a few laughs from the group. I wonder how badly beaten they are. I manage a quick look but have to turn away quickly. Not only is it a disturbing sight but it could soon be me in that mess.

"Look, I'm nothing to do with those. I was made to do it too, just like Percy. Isn't that right mate?" I ask him.

Percy's frozen, the stupid fuck. The boss, whose face is familiar, looks at the ceiling, stroking his stubble.

"Fuck it, let's give him a pasting," one of them says walking towards me, the light reflecting off his red aluminium bat.

He raises his bat in the air and I close my eyes. I think of my mother, Julie and Gramps and every other good thing in my life.

"Wait a minute," the boss says.

"You're Pete Jarvis. Is that right?" he says to me.

"Y-y-yeah. Why?" I ask.

"I've seen you before in my dad's shop," he says.

When I focus on the man, I recognise him as the person who was keeping his eye on me from the back of the shop when I was talking to Hasan. "Y-y-you're the boss?" I mutter.

"My father speaks highly of you," he says and then turns around to address the other gang members. "It turns out he's done my father a couple of favours. He even stopped him from getting robbed."

"So fucking what? He's still connected with these racist bastards. I say we smash him," the man standing over me with the bat says.

"Wind your neck in boy," the boss says to the guy holding the bat inches from my face. "Last time I checked, I'm the one who makes the decisions round here."

"Sorry boss," he says as he slowly lowers the bat.

"I heard him chatting with my dad," Hasan's son continues. "My dad thinks he's a genuine bloke and I trust my father's opinion more than anyone's."

"What I want to know is," Elvis says stepping forward. "Why, if this is true, is he mates with these small-minded idiots?"

For a moment I consider telling him everything; everything about how I got involved in this mess. "I was in debt to them just as Percy was and they took advantage of me," is all I say.

The silence is deafening as Hasan's son contemplates what I said. "If I find out otherwise," he says scarily slowly, "and if I ever see you with them again, then I'm going to take it as a ... personal ... insult. Now get out, both of you," he says pointing to the door.

Percy is up instantly and sprints out. I stand on my feet and almost lose my balance; my legs are so weak. I slowly walk past the group. The guy with the bat still wants to break my face. I come to a standstill in front of Hasan's son and notice a pistol tucked into his belt. I give him a sincere nod. He does the same, more slightly.

I'm still shaking as I reach the door. I turn to have a final look at what's left of Vic and the gang. There's a lot of blood. A lot.

The snow is falling heavily. I can see Percy's crazy, running footsteps. Out here everything is white.

As I near the end of the industrial estate I hear four gunshots.

CHAPTER TWENTY-ONE

I walk through the industrial estate hazily. I'm in a dream with the sound of crunching bones ringing in my ears. I put my hand to my ribs. It could have been my bones shattered. I feel short of breath. Everyone in that dark dingy room had something in common. We all have bones. They break in the same way, shatter in the same way. They turn, bend, and rotate in the same way. We're all made of the same stuff. We all have the same colour blood. I saw that all right. Bloodshed, spurted, clotted. That is the real us. What is skin? A costume.

What makes us different? The head, the small power switch inside the skull? The sounds, words, promises, rejections, lies that you hear: these things make you who you are.

The snow illuminates everything. There's something beautiful about untouched snow. Everything looks so innocent. No one's been here before. Not Jake, not Vic. The path ahead is mine. I could be any place in the world that's cold: Alaska, Antarctica. I could be on a Christmas card. I walk but with no final destination.

I soon find myself staring up at the statue of Pocahontas. Her name is just visible through the snow. She was kidnapped, but still she fell in love with an Englishman. Must have been tough though ... being brought to England.

She looks magnificent with the snow falling on her, as simple and pure as one of those paperweights that you shake. She balances on one foot with the grace of a ballerina. Her arms are stretched out by her side with her palms facing front like Christ. Like she's forgiving Gravesend.

I reach the Tavern Fort by the pier. I feel like I'm in a foreign country. The Thames is just a black mass; snowflakes disappear as they hit the dark waves. Big artillery guns which I always took for granted point towards the river. The rust, scratches, and graffiti on them are hidden by the snow. Such big beasts, capable of vast destruction, now ornaments. I run my hand down the barrel of one and a shiver runs down my spine. It feels overwhelming touching something that was once so dangerous. I see a sign and scoop snow off of it, so I can read it. It dates back to when it was built in the 1780s. Its purpose was to be used as a defence against the threat of a French naval invasion. Then it was re-armed in the first and second world wars. I wonder if there was someone like me in any one of those periods, standing as I am now, thinking the same kind of things but wearing different clothes. Did he see the reflection of fire and chaos on the surface of the Thames? Could he see an end to all the destruction?

I near the desolate bandstand. It's eerie yet wonderful. If this was a movie I'd be seeing the ghostly figures of the performers and musicians that have played here. White dresses, powdered faces, slick side partings, bow-ties, pianos, violins, and accordions. Now the bandstand's a shelter for druggies to jack up or for alcoholics to piss the night away on cheap spirits. But the snow has brought it back to life. For me. I close my eyes. I'm playing the piano. A scantily clad Julie dances, candlelight projecting her shadow onto the wall. A wind sweeps through a tall window and makes her hair dance like wildfire. Dressed in a thin white gown, she approaches me. She takes my head in her hands. No words are needed: our bodies whisper together.

Shrill voices meet my ears as I leave the promenade and head back to the high street. The gates have been closed so that no vehicles can enter the high street. Kids and adults alike are playing in the road, building snowmen, and throwing snowballs. There is not one sad or miserable face in sight. It's amazing how something as simple as snow can bring a town together. I walk through the high street enjoying the feel of the snow crunching and prop myself against a lamppost just by the entrance of The King's Head. The glow of the lamp mixes with the whiteness of the falling snow creating gold coloured snowflakes. In the pub I hear someone put Louis Armstrong's A Wonderful World on the juke box.

I want Julie to share this with me tonight, whatever this is that I'm feeling. I want her to see everything through my eyes: see the things that I'm seeing. I pull my phone out.

"Pete? Jesus, are you ok? Where have you been? I hope you haven't been with those lot ..."

"I'm fine honestly," I interrupt. "It's all over Julie, I promise. But it's a long story. Listen, are you indoors?"

"Yeah, why?"

"Put on a coat and meet me at the promenade. Do you know where the bandstand is?"

"Why do you want to go there?"

"Trust me, just meet me there. Please."

"Ok, give me twenty minutes."

I continue to watch the residents of Gravesend forming together without a care in the world. A young kid falls flat on his face in the snow. His mother runs over, picks him up and gives him a cuddle. His mum scoops up a pile of snow and rubs it in her own face and he smiles and runs off to play again.

I make my way back through the high street. I get hit with a snowball on the back of the head and laugh as I empty the snow from my collar. It's impossible to see who it was as everyone is wrapped in woolly hats and scarfs and everyone is throwing snowballs. I don't care who it was.

The bandstand looks like some kind of house for angels. The snow is still untouched, and the white trees stand tall guarding this sacred little area. This area which is just going to be mine and Julie's, our secret paradise. I take a seat on one of the steps not caring that I'll get wet. It's perfect. So simple. So stunning.

For the first time in a long time, the future looks clearer. Life doesn't seem too bad after all and I know who I want to spend my life with.

I hear her footsteps walking towards me as I'm looking up at the ceiling. There's a robin perched on one of the arches. The footsteps come closer. The bird looks at me and turns his head to the side. "Julie, quick, look at this."

I feel a sharp pain in my stomach and then it feels wet.

"Told you I was gonna gut ya."

He runs off, ruining the untouched snow. I feel the blood trickling down into my trousers and into my shoes. I become lightheaded and suddenly fantastically cold. I try to reach the railing of the bandstand, but my legs give way.

I look to the bird and he flies off into the night. I hear footsteps coming towards me. I hear Julie calling my name. I hear the waves of the Thames. The banks of the river slip away. I see my blood seep into the dazzling snow. I can't feel anything.

CHRIS BENNETT

Chris Bennett was born in Gravesend and studied creative writing at the University of Kent.

Gravesend is his debut novel.

CREDITS

Cover design — Steve Foster

Author photograph — Mike Fendt

pleasantpublishing.co.uk